# UNTIL

### *the*

# LAST*of* ME

## TAKE THEM TO THE STARS, BOOK 2

Sylvain Neuvel has a PhD in Linguistics from the University of
Chicago. He is an amateur robotics enthusiast and lifelong fan
of all things science fiction. He is the author of two critically-
acclaimed series: the Themis Files novels, *Sleeping Giants*,
*Waking Gods* and *Only Human*, and the Take Them To the Stars
trilogy, including *A History of What Comes Next*, and *Until the
Last of Me*. He lives in Montreal.

# UNTIL
## *the*
# LAST
## *of*
# ME

TAKE THEM TO THE STARS, BOOK 2

# SYLVAIN
# NEUVEL

MICHAEL  JOSEPH

MICHAEL JOSEPH

UK | USA | Canada | Ireland | Australia
India | New Zealand | South Africa

Michael Joseph is part of the Penguin Random House group of companies
whose addresses can be found at global.penguinrandomhouse.com

First published in the United States of America by Tom Doherty Associates 2022
First published in Great Britain by Michael Joseph 2022
001

Copyright © Sylvain Neuvel, 2022

The moral right of the author has been asserted

Printed and bound in Great Britain by Clays Ltd, Elcograf S.p.A.

The authorized representative in the EEA is Penguin Random House Ireland,
Morrison Chambers, 32 Nassau Street, Dublin D02 YH68

A CIP catalogue record for this book is available from the British Library

HARDBACK ISBN: 978–0–241–44514–3
TRADE PAPERBACK ISBN: 978–0–241–44515–0

www.greenpenguin.co.uk

MIX
Paper from
responsible sources
FSC® C018179

Penguin Random House is committed to a
sustainable future for our business, our readers
and our planet. This book is made from Forest
Stewardship Council® certified paper.

Please note that all chapter titles are song titles from the years in which the story takes place. You can listen to each song as you read or enjoy the playlist on its own. You'll find the playlist on Apple Music by searching for "Take Them to the Stars" or at tinyurl.com/TakeThemToTheStars2. Spotify users will find it at tinyurl.com/neuvel2. You can also re-create the playlist yourself using the song list at the end of this book.

Billions of years from now our sun, then a distended red giant star, will have reduced Earth to a charred cinder. But the Voyager record will still be largely intact, in some other remote region of the Milky Way galaxy, preserving a murmur of an ancient civilization that once flourished—perhaps before moving on to greater deeds and other worlds—on the distant planet Earth.

—CARL SAGAN, *MURMURS OF EARTH*

# ACT I

# 1

*Helter Skelter*

**1968**

I watched him die, twice. I stuck a tiki torch inside his skull. Mother blew him up with a fucking missile. And yet there's more of him, always more of him.

Just another daybreak on Mallorca. Bluish light. Air thick as water. I cut through the morning mist to catch the first batch of *ensaimadas* out of the oven. I got there early; so said the red *cerrado* sign on the door. I walked the hilltop, watched the dark sea vent its anger before the sun calmed it down and painted it blue. I took in the town's quaintness before hordes of strangers defaced its narrow cobbled streets.

He looked right at me.

The baker unlocked her door, scolded the dog when she barged out. She waved at me through the window—I'm a part of her routine as much as she's a part of mine. I petted Blanca for a minute, wiped the hair off my hands, and followed her back in. Soothing heat, more smells than I could distinguish. "*Dos ensaimadas para llevar!*" she said. "*Cuatro, por favor.*" I was starving. I paid, rolled the paper bag, and smiled my goodbyes.

I ran into the Tracker just outside the door. Literally. Our bodies collided, like two old friends chest-bumping after a game. But he didn't step back, or move, or budge. It was like I'd hit a concrete wall. I looked up from chest to face, and there the devil was staring me down.

Slick warmth running down my legs. Mother's death flashing

before my eyes. I dropped the paper bag. The smell of fat and sugar mixed in with the stench of piss.

He raised his hand to my shoulder and nudged me to the side.

—*Disculpe.*

He didn't fucking know me. We killed him twice, Mother and I, but he's never seen us. Not this one. I watched him step into the bakery. I stood there, deer in headlights. I remember thinking about his accent. British, with a hint of something else. Eastern Europe, somewhere. I was stuck in some kind of trance until I heard the sound of children running up the street.

Running.

Run.

I grabbed the paper bag from the ground and dashed home. I made it in four minutes flat; we were out of there in ten. Lola didn't ask why. She grabbed her best seashell and waited for me by the door. Lots of memories in that house. All of Lola's. Crawling on the kitchen floor. First steps, first words. I looked around, tried to remember as much as I could before I poured gasoline all over it. Lola spoke only four words as she watched her world burn in the rearview mirror: "Don't leave a trace."

But I didn't. I fucking didn't. I was a ghost. Different name, different life. No loose ends. Lola and I laid low. We didn't stand out; I made sure of that. Stick bugs on a branch. Plain. Ordinary. Vanilla. I've made mistakes before, but not this time. I couldn't have found us.

Lola and I ate cold *ensaimadas* on the boat to Valencia. Lola didn't cry—or speak, for that matter. She just looked at me from time to time to gauge how scared she should be—she can read me like a picture book. My daughter is unyielding, stubborn as hell, but she's smart enough to realize her best option now is blind, unqualified trust. We hitchhiked from the port down to

Alicante. One more boat to catch. I screamed at them to wait for us as they unmoored the ferry to Algiers.

Here we are now, casting off into the unknown. The light from Spain is getting dimmer and dimmer. What life we had is fading with it. Thirteen hours until we hit shore and begin a new one. This is . . . limbo, the in-between. We're still high on adrenaline. None of this has sunk in yet. We were . . . a family. Now we're fugitives, refugees, castaways. The wind is strong on the main deck, but we'll spend the night up here. I keep staring at the sea, waiting for him to spring out like a shark. Stupid, I know. Regardless, confined spaces just aren't on the menu right now.

—Mom, can we look at the stars?

—Yes, honey. Let's get ourselves something to drink.

Every night, Lola and I watch the sky together, sharing a Coca-Cola. Tonight will be no different, not if I can help it. I brought her into the world. I made her prey. The least I can do is let her have these moments. Sorting through loose change. The tumble of the bottle in the coin machine. Pop. Fizz. This is our time. Our five minutes before I put the weight of a hundred lives on her tiny shoulders.

—Show me Venus.

—Venus is . . . over there, Lola. And that smaller dot above it is Jupiter.

She's six years old and living on borrowed time. It's horrible, but that's not what I find tragic. I think, somehow, she knows.

—Show me . . . Saturn.

—I can't. It's on the other side of the sun.

She knows how this story ends, how they all end. I die. She dies. If we're lucky, her child is born first and the Hundred and Two goes through the motions all over again. We're the hare at a greyhound race. We can't win; the best we can do is not lose.

It's not much, but it's all I have to give. That and a Coca-Cola from the vending machine.

—When can we see all the planets, Mom?

Funny. This is what she wants. Eight dots in the night sky. How I wish I could give her that. She just watched her whole world burn. All her drawings, Roger the stuffed bear. Captain Action. She owns one set of clothes and a fucking seashell, but she wants to see the planets. Yet another thing I have to take away from her.

—I don't know, honey. Probably never.

# 2

## Can't Find My Way Home

### 1969

What are we? The eternal question.

We're . . . the same. My daughter will look exactly like me when she's my age. Same sun, different day. I am what my mother was. We're . . . copies, I guess. There's no word for it. We're like that fish from some river in Texas. All females. They pass on all of their genes to their daughters, every time. We're like a plant cutting that turns into an identical plant. A twig.

Philoponus of Alexandria wrote about it in the sixth century. "If someone cuts a twig from a walnut tree in Athens and plants it in Patras, two or three years later it will bear nuts that are the same in every aspect, in size and taste and color and every other character, with the ones from the walnut tree in Athens." *Klon*, in ancient Greek. Good walnut wisdom, but it doesn't answer the important question. Is it the same tree? I wish I could spend a day in my daughter's mind and see if we're more than each other. Am I . . . me?

We are different. From everyone else, that is. We're stronger, better than most when it comes to math and science. We're . . . fierce—that's a diplomatic way to put it—predatory at times. We can be brutal. I have. I've killed people. Some deserved it more than others. There's no erasing the past. All we are is a reminder of what once was. All I can do is make amends. Dilute the bad with a little more good.

We're prey. The Tracker hunts us, relentlessly. He's done it for three thousand years. He is many, like us. I killed one of them. Mother took another one with her when she ended her life to save mine. But evil is like the mail. It keeps coming and coming. The one I killed said we both come from a dying world. That *I*, my ancestors, hid something from them, a device of some sort. If they had it, he said, they could call home and save "our" people by bringing them here. Lies, perhaps. The devil is full of deceit and trickery. As always, we don't know.

We don't know where we're from. We don't know why we do what we do, only that we chose to do so a hundred generations ago. Some version of us, of me, chose to. Would I make the same choice now? I don't know. *We* don't know—I guess we would as we keep on *making* that choice.

Take them to the stars, before evil comes and kills them all. That's what I was born for. That's what my daughter has to look forward to. If we're to believe the Tracker, that evil is "our" people—talk about irony. Then again it might be giant squids, little green men, Bible salesmen. We. Don't. Know.

My ancestors started with nothing, before science, before anything. They didn't know what a star was, let alone how to get to one. It took us three thousand years, but we have made progress. We found people to help. I did. I got Wernher von Braun out of Germany after the war. The US wanted him bad. They turned a Nazi officer into the poster boy for space exploration. From SS *Sturmbannführer* to hosting Disney specials. That's some major-league redemption. Von Braun will return the favor and take them to the moon. Even steven. I helped the other side, too. Sergei Korolev and I built the R-7 rocket in Russia. I did more than help. I married the man. But the Tracker found me and I had to disappear. Korolev is a widower now, but he did send the first satellite into orbit, the first man into space. All in all, I think I did my part.

We *do* know a few things, six to be precise. We live by a handful of rules we set for ourselves when we knew who we were.

Fear the Tracker. Always run, never fight.

Preserve the knowledge.

Survive at all costs.

Don't draw attention to yourself.

Don't leave a trace.

Last, and certainly not least: there can never be three for too long.

I bent a few of those rules in my youth, just a little, and we all paid the price. I lost my unborn child. I nearly died. My mother did, spectacularly. After that, I followed the rules like God handed them to me himself. It worked for a while. I had a life. I don't know if it was mine to have, but I took it. Lola and I had a home. We had . . . a beach we called ours, *our* café, *our* used bookstore. I had . . . a friend. Let's call her a good friend. Don't get too attached. It's not one of the rules, but it might as well be. I learned that one the hard way.

It's gone now, all of it. Because we are the same, and different, predator and prey. No matter how hard we try, there is only one thing we truly know, one inescapable truth.

We are the Kibsu.

# 3

## *Gimme Shelter*

### 1969

We came here to hide. They came to flaunt their resistance, daring to be seen. Outside, the streets are filled with students, poets, dancers. Inside, a hundred revolutions are brewing. Agitators, rebels, insurgents. Subversives. The Pan-African Cultural Festival is in full swing and, for a few days, Algiers is the Mecca of revolutionaries.

They've fought their oppressor for over a century, but things are different now. They started winning. Kwame Nkrumah in Ghana, the Mau Mau movement in Kenya, and, of course, the Algerian war. Their fight was the longest, the bloodiest, but no one counts bodies on the winning side. They prevailed, and they inspired a whole fucking continent.

Down with imperialism! Down with colonialism! Intellectuals cerebrate the -isms in smoky hotel rooms while musicians and fire-breathers take to the streets. Everything here is a weapon: guns, words, rhythms. Seditious minds and pulse-pounding drumbeats. This city's electric. And hot. Fucking hot. Everything here smells of sweat and defiance.

Our apartment is mostly sweat. Beige, bare, with a view of the same. We have plenty of money, but money draws attention. Our place most definitely doesn't. Remember the rules.

Lola's a lot braver than I am. I'm still scared shitless, like I was in Germany. I see the same shadows, hear the same footsteps. We stay inside most of the time, away from the unknown, the dark alleys. But not tonight. Tonight is different. I found us a shitty bar with a good breeze to watch the moon landing. A small show of defiance, taking my seven-year-old child to a bar at three in the morning.

This is our moment. This is why I risked my life to save von Braun, so he could build the biggest rocket ever and put a man or two on another world. I was still breastfeeding when Kennedy made his moon speech. "We set sail on this new sea because there is new knowledge to be gained, and new rights to be won, and they must be won and used for the progress of all people." He used the right word: "knowledge." I've had dreams about tonight ever since. I should be ecstatic, jubilant. This is what we all died for. I *should* be . . .

Our bar filled up about an hour ago. Some Tuaregs, SWAPO guerrillas from Namibia, Angola. Tough. Not your average tough, the kind you rarely see in public spaces. These people have seen shit that can't be unseen. I feel a great swirl of pity for the poor soul who comes into this bar looking for trouble. Half a dozen Americans walked through the door moments later. Black Panthers, as is turns out. I think everyone here came straight from a Nina Simone concert.

This is a weird night.

My daughter is playing darts with Angolan freedom fighters. I asked if she was bothering them and they told me to leave. Just me. Lola feels right at home in all this. Another day, another dollar. That's her allowance. Me, I'm neck-deep into all kinds of strange. Right now I'm having a drink with Eldridge Cleaver. Let's just say he's not really into the moon thing.

—I don't see what benefit mankind will have from two astronauts landing on the moon while people are being murdered in Vietnam and suffering from hunger even in the United States.

I don't think he and I will be best friends, but he's right about one thing. We're not doing anything. Well, *I'm* not. Lola's seven;

she gets a pass. The point is I'm not helping anyone and I sure as hell am nowhere close to saving this world. Take them to the stars. Ha! We've gone from Earth to . . . the area around the Earth. The closest star is a hundred million times farther. A hundred million. "Baby steps" doesn't begin to cover it. We don't even know what's in our solar system. Americans just walked on the moon, but it's the Russians doing most of the exploring. They crashed a probe on Venus three years ago and they've been gunning for Mars for almost a decade. Years of development. Hundreds of millions spent on a few minutes of data. Those are the easy ones. Then come the outer planets. Jupiter is first, then . . . Then I don't know if we can reach that far with the engines we have. There's still so much to do and every second I spend with these people is a reminder that I'm not doing it.

I'm on the sidelines, watching. Everyone else is playing the game, whether they're leaving footprints on the moon or planning a revolution. Everyone in this room came to Algiers with purpose. Their ultimate goals vary slightly, their methods vary wildly, but they all—Mother was particularly fond of that Roosevelt speech—they all strive to do the deeds. They spend themselves in a worthy cause, and if they fail, they will fail while daring greatly. I'm afraid my place is now with the cold and timid souls who know neither victory nor defeat.

I thought I was protecting my daughter. Maybe it's me I was hiding from on that island. Whatever fear I've spared ourselves, one of us will have to pay for it down the road. Every step I don't take is one I add on my daughter's journey. If not her then her daughter, or the Hundred and Three. I may never meet my grandchild, but I've wasted seven years of her life already.

No more.

The moon was a small step, but we will take another, and another, and a hundred million more. Like the students chanting on the street, the fire-breathers and the freedom fighters, we will not cower. We will have *our* revolution. Ours will be around the Earth, the sun, the galaxy. Like my mother, I will die fighting for it, but others will follow. We'll win because we're many. We'll win because we have to.

# 4

## *Space Oddity*

If you ask the universe how to get from point A to point B, it will inevitably answer: "What's wrong with point A?" The universe wants us to stay put. Every subatomic particle of it does. The Earth is an overbearing mother. It wants us close by and it is remarkably good at keeping things down. We can pull, throw a tantrum, but even if she lets go of our hand, the sun steps in and says: "Where do you think *you're* going?" That tug-of-war will never stop, and the farther we go, the more energy we have to spend. That means more fuel. That fuel is heavy and so we need more fuel to help carry *that* fuel, and fuel for that fuel, and so on until our head explodes. Rocket science is fighting planets and stars and none of them fight fair.

Von Braun had to build a rocket taller than the Statue of Liberty to get to a rock in our own orbit. I tried to imagine a rocket big enough to reach the outer planets, or to leave the confines of the solar system. I couldn't, so I did the math. The math said it was impossible with the technology we have. I'd hit a brick wall, so I followed the advice of my grandmother. She said there's only one sensible thing to do when you find a problem you can't solve. Eat something.

I went to the place across the street. The food was barely edible, but I hated walking in the heat and they served a half-decent milk shake. For some reason, the owner liked to trade barbs with me. He asked what was wrong with my hair; I told him I'd just slept with his wife. I ordered the usual. I think better with a milk shake. I really do. I finished it in one sip, and that's when it happened. No apple falling on my head, just Nassim the waiter walking by with platter in hand. The place was crowded and I couldn't reach the counter from where I was, so I put my empty glass on Nassim's platter without him looking. I was standing still, but now my empty milk shake was moving at full Nassim speed towards the kitchen.

We don't need the fuel to go all the way to Neptune or Pluto. We only need to reach Jupiter. That's it. She'll give us the speed to make it the rest of the way. I should have figured it out sooner; the Soviets showed us how a decade ago when Luna 3 photographed the far side of the moon. Everything moves, the moon around the Earth, the Earth around the sun. If you fly close enough to anything, it veers you in and alters your course. A tiny bit if it's small, a lot more for something like a planet. If you come in ahead of it and escape gravity in the opposite direction the planet is moving, it resists and slows you down. If you come from behind and leave in the *same* direction, it drags you along and speeds you up. Like a cowboy hopping on a running horse, or a dirty milk-shake glass dropped on Nassim's platter. It's a trade in energy. Tit for tat. For something as big as Jupiter—the king of the gods is massive—the momentum we'd take from it wouldn't mean anything, but for a tiny probe . . . Jupiter flies around the sun at forty thousand miles an hour. If we can steal even a fraction of that speed, we'll come out fast and furious towards our next stop.

That's the pickle. The planets kind of need to be where we want them to be. We're flying hell for leather because we just picked Jupiter's pockets for speed. If we want to visit Saturn next, Saturn has to be on the same side of the sun, and ahead of Jupiter because that's the direction we're in. We can pick up speed again when we get there and visit Uranus, but then *it, too,* has to be on the same side of the sun, ahead of Saturn. Then Neptune, Pluto. What are the odds they'll all just line up for a photograph?

—When can we see *all* the planets, Mom?

—I don't know, honey. Probably never.

Lola's question stuck with me like an earworm. It doesn't matter whether we can see them or not, but are the outer planets *ever* in the right position for us to jump from one to the next? It's not that complicated when I think about it. It's a school problem. A horse, a cat, a turtle, and a snail are going around a racetrack. How often do they line up?

Our world takes one year to go around the sun. We're the horse. The outer planets march to a completely different beat. Jupiter takes nearly twelve years to make one loop. Saturn about thirty. That means these two can wave at each other every twenty years or so. Uranus is a long-distance runner. It takes eighty-four years to go around the sun, which is still only half the time it takes Neptune to run its marathon. If my math is correct, these four planets should align in just the right way . . .

. . . every 175 years.

Once every seven generations. It's not never, but it might as well be. I'll tell Lola her great-great-grandchildren can go on a grand tour of the outer realms.

# 5

## *Everyday People*

—Mom, that was the best ice cream, EVER. Right? Right?

Butterscotch with chocolate and nuts. Mom even let me put cherry syrup on top. She never says yes to the red one, not before we have our Coca-Cola. She says too much sugar makes me talk too much. I don't think that's true. It's just I don't know anyone in Algiers, so I talk to Mom a lot. If I had ten people to talk to, I'd talk ten times less to each of them.

—Mom?

—What?

—The ice cream. It was amazing, right?

—I don't know, Lola. I had a milk shake.

—You do know. There's ice cream in a milk shake. You should have had butterscotch like me. Why do you always get vanilla?

— . . .

—Mom?

[*Bonsoir, mesdames. Par ici. J'insiste.*]

Three strangers just walked up to us. I think they want us to go into the alley with them. Mom just squeezed my hand. I don't know what's going on, but she doesn't like it.

—Stay close, Lola. . . . Guys, my daughter's with me. How about you just let us through?

They're forcing us in. I don't want to go there. It's dark. And it smells . . . bad. It's the garbage containers. We keep stepping on things. Broken wood, broken glass. Mom is squeezing my hand harder. I think she's afraid. Me too.

—What's happening, Mom?

—Not now, Lola. . . . Guys, I have . . . eighty dinars, that's all. Here. Take it.

[*It's a nice necklace your daughter has there. Approches, ma petite. Laisses-moi le voir.*]

Oh no. Not my necklace. He can't have that. Mom lets me wear it sometimes, but it's not mine. Grandma wore it before Mom did. She said it belonged to the first one of us. It's her most precious thing in the whole world. I can't let that man take it. OUCH! The bad man grabbed my arm. It hurts!

—DON'T TOUCH HER! . . . LET. US . . . GO!

No. No. No. He pulled a knife from his pocket. The other two men are holding my mom. I'm *really* scared now. I don't know what to do. I'm . . . hot. I'm really hot. And dizzy.

—Mom . . . I'm not feeling well.

—Don't be afraid, Lola. Just do as he says.

I can feel the sweat running down my dress. My head hurts. It's burning. I don't know what's happening to me. My whole skin is on fire. . . .

—Mom, make it stop!

—What you're feeling is perfectly normal, Lola. Give him the necklace. Just give it to him.

*I'm* burning. I think I'm dreaming. I'm in my room. Something is holding me, something big. A giant claw. I think it's a dragon. I can feel its scorching breath on my back. I try to move, but I make it angry. The whole room fills with flames. My bed is on fire; my stuffed animals are screaming. I'm burning alive. There's a knife. I have a knife. I'm . . . I want to stab the dragon, but my arm burns and turns to ash. I hear more screams, horrible screams. I think they are mine. The dragon flaps its wings and the walls disappear. We're flying. I watch our home burn from above. We fly higher. Higher. Higher, until our home looks like a dollhouse. I stab at the dragon and it opens its claws. I start falling into the fire below. I'm burning up, like a rocket in reentry. I keep falling and falling and burning.

—SOMEONE MAKE IT STOP!

—Just breathe, Lola.

[*What is wrong with you, little girl?*]

Breathe. Breathe. The dream's over. I can see. . . . It's so clear, colorful . . . like Alice when she gets to Wonderland. The bad man is still in front of me. He's a lot stronger than I am. Too strong. I need to make him . . . *less* strong, and I think I know how. *Human Anatomy*, volume 1. It's next to the dictionary in our living room.

There's an old wood nail on the ground. He won't notice if I kneel down and pick it up.

—Please, sir. Please don't hurt my mom.

One prick to the chest. Hard.

—LOLA! What are you doing?

I see a tiny red dot on his shirt. It's growing now, like a small flower.

—It's okay, Mom. I'm okay. "The solar plexus is a bundle of nerves." The nerves in his diaphragm overloaded. He can't breathe right now.

Mom kicked one of the men in the knee. His leg bent sideways before he let go of her. Gross. I can crawl between the bad man's legs and get behind him.

—Run, Lola! Let's get out of here!

The two men who were holding Mom ran away. It's just us and the bad man now.

—If I put the nail below his third vertebra . . .

—LOLA, DON'T! Let's go!

It will sever the cervical nerves. Loss of motor function. His lungs won't work on their own anymore. . . .

—Mom?

—Come here, honey! It's over now. It's all over. Just breathe.

—Can we go home now?

—Yes, Lola. We're going home.

—I'm sorry, Mom. I didn't want to give it to him.

—Don't be sorry. You did nothing wrong.

—I'm sorry.

—You did what you had to do. I'm proud of you, Lola. Mama's proud of you.

— . . . Mom, I—

—What is it? Are you hurt?

—I'm okay. I just—

—Come here. One big hug. Now let's go home and have our Coca-Cola.

# 6

## *Across the Universe*

I'm going to miss Algiers. I don't know why—we barely leave our apartment—but I will. I'm going to miss . . . people. No one in particular, just all of them combined.

—Yes, baby. We have to move again. We're going to California. You'll like it there, I promise.

—Is it because of what I did?

She thinks she did a bad thing hurting that man. I'm just glad she didn't kill him. She stayed in control, somehow. I don't know how, but she did. She might be stronger than I am.

—Of course not. We're moving because of the ancient gods. According to my charts, Uranus is catching up to Neptune now. We're just waiting on Saturn; then Jupiter will follow. It's happening, Lola. That really rare planetary alignment I told you about, it's happening *eight years* from now. Can you believe it?

—We can see all the planets?

—We can visit them! The Greek and Roman gods are all coming together as in some prophecy.

—Like that book series we're reading.

The Chronicles of Narnia. I read her a chapter every night before bed. "Tarva, the Lord of Victory, salutes Alambil, the Lady of Peace. They are just coming to their nearest." I like how optimistic she is. My first thought was the return of Cthulhu.

—Better than the books, Lola. We can send a probe and see

all the planets up close and personal. We can see what they're like for the very first time. We can take pictures.

—Wow.

—I know. But it's going to be hard, and we don't have much time.

—How hard?

—Can I get a sip? Thank you. Imagine that Coca-Cola bottle is the Earth. The moon is the dime we used to buy it, six feet behind us inside the vending machine.

—The moon is in the vending machine?

—Yes, it is. Mars . . . Mars is our bottle cap, about three blocks down the road. But we're not going to Mars. Our first step is Jupiter.

—Where's Jupiter?

—Jupiter is a . . . a beach ball, those big ones—red, white, yellow, green, blue—about two miles from here, and we have to shoot our tiny tiny probe at it.

—Tiny like a grain of sand?

—Oh, much smaller than that.

—Like a molecule!

—Yes! We have to shoot a molecule at this moving beach ball two miles from here, and we have to hit just the right distance. A bit too far and our probe will just fly by; too close and it'll crash into the planet.

—Oh no!

—We don't want that. But if we hit it just right, it's going to take us along for the ride. You see, Jupiter is moving really fast, many many times faster than a bullet. If we can steal even a fraction of its speed, we'll have enough to reach the next planet, and the next.

—We can see the rings of Saturn.

—Yes, another beach ball a couple more miles away.

—With rings.

—Hula hoops! We'll need to leave Jupiter's orbit at just the right time to be in the direction of Saturn. Our probe will be flying a lot faster. That means we have to fly really close to Saturn and make a haaaaard left turn on our way to Uranus. No! No laughing! No Uranus jokes!

—How far is Uranus?

—Ha!

—MOM! You said—

—Sorry! About two billion miles away. In Coca-Cola scale, Uranus is the size of a Frisbee, almost ten miles from here. Neptune is another five miles down the road.

—Then Pluto!

—Tiny Pluto, smaller than our moon.

—You mean our dime. Then what?

—Then we leave the solar system, I guess.

—What's out there?

—We don't know! We've never even been to Jupiter. What do you think? How hard will it be?

—Really hard.

—It's more than that, Lola. It's impossible. But we're going to do it anyway.

—What if it doesn't work? Can we try again?

—Not after the alignment, no. But maybe we can try before. It's a good idea, honey. We could use a guinea pig.

—Oh, I'd love a guinea pig!

—Not a real one, Lola. A trial run. We've never been to Jupiter and we'll have to fly pretty close to it for this to work. Maybe . . . maybe there's too much radiation; maybe the whole place is—I don't know—too hot, or full of space bugs that eat probes for lunch.

—Dragons!

—Giant Jupiter space dragons! We have eight years to get ready, but maybe we can send something to Jupiter first, just to be safe. We won't get another chance at this, not for another one hundred and seventy-five years!

Unfortunately, we don't have anyone at NASA working for us. The best I can do right now is drop my calculations on someone's lap and hope to God they have enough pull to get a project approved. They will. I know they will—this is too good to pass up—and we'll be there to help when they do. This is it. This is my project, my final contribution before Lola takes my place.

I don't believe in fate, or destiny. I don't believe there is a predetermined path for me to follow. I believe in chaos, in the impossible odds of life forming anywhere, the one-in-a-quintillion chance of there being a me, a here, a now. I believe in falling apples and vanilla milk shakes changing the course of history. I believe in the most extraordinary of coincidences, and this one will do just fine.

# 7

## *Ziggy Stardust*

### 1972

March 2. An Atlas-Centaur rocket launched from Cape Kennedy carries a nine-foot-wide parabolic dish with a hexagonal base. For seventeen minutes, the three stages of the rocket hurl the probe away from Earth until it reaches a speed of over thirty-two thousand miles an hour. Eleven hours after launch, *Pioneer 10* has passed our moon.

On July 15, the fastest thing humans ever built becomes the first to enter the asteroid belt between the orbits of Mars and Jupiter.

Trial run. Guinea pig. To prepare for what is known as the Planetary Grand Tour, NASA chose to use the existing Pioneer program to send a pair of twin probes to explore the interplanetary medium and the asteroid belt. They would be the first to approach Jupiter and study its environment as well as the effects of radiation on the probes' instruments.

*Pioneer 10* visited Jupiter and its moons. It flew behind Io and took pictures of Ganymede and Europa. Ion radiation from the planet caused some instruments to malfunction, but the probe escaped the Jovian system intact. No probe-eating space bugs. No dragons.

The probe slingshotted around the planet and continued on its journey towards the edge of the solar system. The successful maneuver served as proof of concept for future missions, just as Mia intended.

Her calculations had landed on the desk of one of NASA's senior staff. He marveled at the level of detail and the palpable excitement buried in the equations. In the end, Mia's work had absolutely nothing to do with the approval of the Grand Tour or the launch of the *Pioneer* probes.

A wise man once said: "When it's helicopter time, you get helicopters." Or in this case, space probes using gravity assist. A JPL engineer had discovered the rare planetary alignment five years earlier in 1964. He examined possible trajectories towards one or more of the outer planets using Jupiter's gravity. His results served as the basis for the Grand Tour missions.

# 8

## *Papa Was a Rolling Stone*

*Get up, Samael. Kill the little shit.*

I will not. I am stronger than the urge. It does not control me. Breathe.

*Kill him. Snap his neck. Rip his fucking tongue out.*

Breathe. Breathe. I am stronger than the urge. It does not control me.

*You pathetic little man.*

Breathe. Think.

I don't need to fight. I scored two tries today. Father will be proud of me.

I spit the grass out of my mouth, run my fingers down my shin. Wet, thick, and warm. Damned cleats. I hate this sport, even when we're winning. The sun is too bright, the air too hot. I could get up, but I don't. I need another minute in the cool dirt while I wait for the whistle to blow. Come on, ref, make the bloody call.

There you go. Now let's finish this stupid game. Why are you looking at me, you gormless git? You tripped me; deal with it. Oh sure, try screaming at the ref. I'm sure that will help. It must run in the family; I can hear your father whining all the way from the stands. I wouldn't do that if I were your father, not when he's sitting next to mine.

My dad is bigger than your dad. I didn't understand when I heard that for the first time. Kids looking up to their parents' violence, aspiring to it even. I suppose I did, too. I wanted to be tall like him, strong like him, but I thought it was because we were different. I *was* him. If I could have been anything else, I would have wished for that even more.

—Come on, guys! Let's play!

Your father is still at it. I can't make out the words, but I see his hands waving, his fingers pointing. Your dad is screaming louder than his voice can handle, foaming at the mouth like the warm beer he's spilling everywhere. He's not the first. Cheap plastic cups are not meant for squabbles and those stands are sticky like fly tape.

Peacocking. I wonder why people do that. I doubt a chest puff ever impressed anyone. Most people would do just about anything to avoid a fight. If it really comes down to it, they'll eat a cockroach, lick some boots, shove their own head down a dirty toilet rather than throw a punch. The problem is they all know it, so they push each other to see who will cave first. Driving head-on at each other until someone swirls away. The working assumption is that someone always will. Not this time. Your dad would sit down if he knew what was good for— Too late. He picked the wrong shoes to spill his wallop on.

My dad is meaner than your dad.

It was only a matter of time. Your dad poked at my dad's chest and now his finger is broken. It hurts, I'm sure, but I think seeing it bend backwards was the worst part. He'll spend a few more seconds looking at it. He thinks of nothing else, as if everything will be fine when the throbbing is over. It's more bearable now, so he looks up and sees my dad is still there. It just dawned on him. This is far from over. My dad will not stop just because yours is crying. What comes next is . . . inevitable. The sun will come up tomorrow, we are going to win this game, and my dad will keep punching long after yours is on his knees. It's a matter of principle. "If you teach a lesson, Son, teach it well so you never have to teach it again." My dad believes in being thorough.

You should thank him. If your dad were merely humiliated, he might take it out on you. He might hurt your mother, your sister, your little brother just to reassert his manhood. He won't be merely humiliated. You can take my word for it. There will be no manhood to reclaim, no ego to rebuild. Your dad will never raise his voice again. He will keep his head down, be polite, apologize. He'll appreciate the small things. Talking. Solid food.

More dads joining in. They think they can stop him, but they won't be able to. Real conviction is a rare thing. Chances are they've never seen it. One more kick to the teeth while they hold his arms back. My dad just rolled yours off the stands. It's a ten-foot drop, but I bet your dad is happy to take it if the kicking stops. Lesson learned. My dad will educate the others now.

This is turning into an all-out brawl. Fists flying. Everyone screaming. Sixteen-year-olds are playing a contact sport and it's the parents doing the fighting. My dad *is* intense, but he's the only one in control at the moment. He is punching heads and guts, not hearts and throats. I don't know how it is possible, but I am both ashamed and proud of him at the same time. My dad is efficient, but for once the real violence is not ours. The rest of the parents were eager to join in. They've been waiting for it, throwing insults all season. "Get off the field! You suck!" "Your son's a fucking loser!" Manly men doing manly things.

Here come the cops. Good timing. My dad just shoved someone headfirst into a trash bin. I think that will be the end of it. No harm, no foul. Well, no one died. Maybe we won't have to move this time.

I hadn't noticed, but the sun is gone. One tiny cloud giving us two minutes of reprieve. The air is cooler already. It's nice. I don't think my dad will be allowed to watch the games anymore. Good. I hope I get kicked off the team. I only play to make him proud. He's nicer to me when he's proud.

# 9

## *All the Young Dudes*

—CAN'T YOU DO *ONE* THING RIGHT, YOU STUPID COW?

Go to your room, Uriel. You can't talk to your mother like that. I'm sure that's what he expects me to say. That's what a good mother would say, but I won't. I'm not going to say a thing—not one word—because that would keep him here a few seconds longer and all I want is for him to be out of this house, with his brother and his father. I want them gone. I want . . . anything but this. I catch a glimpse of it sometimes. There are moments, hours even, when I have the house to myself and I feel . . . happiness. It's not mine; it's someone else's glee. What could have been. Another me living a life I almost had.

Red smudges on the kitchen floor. I must have stepped on a piece of glass. They're everywhere. Little specks of crystal turned into diamonds by the morning light. It's pretty. Maybe that's what God is. Beauty seeping through the violence, finding its way into broken cups and spilled tea.

He missed my head by an inch. My son did. The porridge was too hot, or too cold. I forget. It's on the wall, the porridge, clinging for dear life. It was something else yesterday, but I forgot that, too. I forget a lot of things, like what I did to deserve this. I have done *something*, something horrible enough to anger God beyond reason. Dear Lord, please forgive my sins and bring me back into your fold. The wicked one lives inside me. He spawns in my womb.

I give birth to monsters. My children are cruel, evil. So is my husband, but I *made* my children. They came out of *me*. They were born—why do I feel awful for thinking "normal"? They pooped; they ate. They smiled when I tickled them. They were babies, regular babies. They were my children. I'd like to blame it all on George, but he was barely there for the first few years. I took care of them. They were with *me*.

I knew soon enough that my husband was a bad man. One too many drinks, the wrong team winning at rugby, chicken when what he wanted was beef. I'd have left his anger behind, but my family wouldn't have it. What God had joined together let no man—and certainly no woman—put asunder. Catholic for "You broke it, you bought it." I swore to myself, our children—*my* children . . . things would be different, better. I named them after angels, so *God* would look over them. Raphael, the healer. Uriel, the angel of repentance.

Raphael stabbed his little brother with a steak knife when he was two. My little angel. The doctors did all the healing. Uriel still has a scar on his shoulder, but he worships his older brother. They're like twins, carbon copies. One's just as mean as the other, but as Raphael barely knows I exist, Uriel takes everything out on me. Words, mostly, a sore arm here and there, a broken cup of tea. As for repentance, Uriel never felt sorry for anything in his life. I don't think he'll start with me. I . . . I gave up on them. It's a terrible thing for a mother to say, but I did. I want nothing to do with them. Except for Samael.

I didn't want another child. Ha! I would have gouged my eyes out rather than have another child. Raphael was a very demonic three, Uriel not far behind. I had already glimpsed what my life would be like. My husband felt differently.

Samael was eager to be born. He would have clawed his way

out if he had to. I remember when they first put him on my chest. I cried; I couldn't stop. He had the same face, the same cold eyes as the rest of them. They had done a poor job wiping the blood off him. He looked like the devil himself had torn through my body. But he didn't cry like his brothers. He braved through the cold and the bright light and he stared, at everything, at whatever blurred shape I was to him. I thought: maybe this one didn't hate me as much.

I chose to help him, just him. My son would never be good, or kind. I knew that. He was filled with rage, violence, like everything that comes out of me. But if I could reach him somehow, perhaps I could focus all that rage and violence somewhere else, somewhere better. My son was a killer. I knew I could never atone for my sins, but maybe he could atone for his by doing God's work. I named him Samael, God's venom, the Angel of Death.

He will stay with me today, like most days. I take him to the garden and teach him what I can. Patience, mostly. A bit of self-control. He can be so precise, gentle even, when he puts his mind to it, but it doesn't come easy. Truth be told, he's not much of a gardener, but he hasn't hurt anyone tending flowers yet. That will have to do for now. I don't know how much longer I can teach him. He's a young man now and his father won't leave him behind forever.

I nearly gave up, many times, but I won't take my own life. God hates me enough as it is. I stay because of Samael. I don't know how much he listens. I don't know if I'm getting to him or if I'm fooling myself, but I keep at it. It's all I have, that and some broken glass in a puddle of tea.

# 10

## *Old Man*

You hurt her for the last time, Father. I promise.

I wonder if you will see the irony. I sure do. Me, the weak link, the wuss, the softy. The one who never measures up. The one who's never good enough, fast enough, cruel enough. Why is that, *Dad*? If we are the same person, why can't you love me like you love my brothers? If I am you, why do you hate me so much?

Is it because of Mother? You take my brothers on the hunt and leave me behind. Who do you think I will spend my time with? I don't have friends; you made sure of that. I have her, and you know what? I am grateful for it. I *am* you, but if I could hack my limbs off and be like her instead, I would not hesitate. She's better than us. You can't see it, but she is. She's stronger, in her own way. Is that what scares you? That she rubbed off on me somehow? I think it is. And who knows, maybe she did. Maybe genetics is not all it's cracked up to be. True or not, I think you see a tiny bit of her in me and it scares the hell out of you.

Maybe the only difference between us is that I love her and you never did. It doesn't matter in the end. You were right. I am not as strong as you are. I'm not even as strong as my brothers, not as ambitious, not as eager to show the world how powerful I am. But they are. They are very much like you.

I am, too, like it or not. I can never *not* be like you. Maybe that is why I can do this. I am everything you are. You say committed, I hear heartless. You say efficient, I hear vicious. Po-tay-to po-tah-to. Everything I loathe about you is in me. I am you. It only takes one look in the mirror to know that. It goes beyond our genes. I share your cravings, your temper, your likes and dislikes. I can't stand weakness any more than you. My brothers feel exactly the same. You taught us well, Dad. We can smell weakness a mile away.

Weakness. Like that of a man more concerned with himself than his whole species. Every time we train, every time you leave on a hunt, you speak of us being heroes to our people, as if that were the prize. As if they wouldn't see us exactly for what we are: a mistake. We do what we do to save others, not ourselves. We . . . *died* three thousand years ago. What's left is . . . I don't know what it is, but I know our people will want nothing to do with it. You are selfish, arrogant. Do you know what these things are, Dad? Let me give you a hint. They are not strengths.

Weakness. Like that of a man who let the traitor escape on Mallorca. Countless generations tracking them across the globe and you could not even find them in a small town on a bloody island. Why did you go alone? I bet my brothers would have found them.

Weakness. Like that of a man who could not save his own kin. They had found the traitors. They had one tied to a chair! Your brothers would be alive if you had gone with them. This would all be over. We could stop running. We could rest, live, die, do whatever we want. I could paint, or garden, play the guitar, any of the thousand things you said were a waste of our time.

Can you smell it now, *Dad*? Because my brothers do.

It's funny when I think about it. You taught me to fight, to hunt. You taught me to kill, but it was my mother who showed me how to get rid of *you*. We spend countless hours working in the yard, she and I. Best part of my day, really. It took me a while, but I started to like the quiet. It's hard work. You bought us a house with bad soil, did you know that? We have to choose our plants carefully because most things will die back there. The far end of the garden is all Creeping Bellflower. Heart-shaped leaves, tiny purple flowers. You would know if you saw it. It's an invasive species, kind of like us. You have to control it or it will spread like ragweed. It doesn't look like much, but it is insanely resilient. It spreads through its seeds, through its root system even. If you plant it, it will find ways to grow.

And planting it is easy. You would not believe how easy it is. Drop the seed to the ground, gently. "Damn! Dad was so close on Mallorca! I bet he even walked by them a few times." Just like that. No need to dig it in, you can just drop it in passing. "Oh, Uncle Charles loved that song! I miss him sometimes. . . . Too bad he was alone when they killed him. Bloody bad luck if you ask me."

Behold the Creeping Bellflower. If you plant it, it will find ways to grow.

I could not undo what I did if I tried. It took about a week before my brothers smelled blood in the water. Your blood. You're too full of yourself to notice, but they have been circling you for weeks. The funny thing about us all being the same is that it makes us all replaceable. Standard parts. You can just swap one for the next.

You should not have treated her that way. Not ever. She didn't deserve any of this, and you sure as hell didn't deserve her. I may not be as strong as you are, not as *committed*, but there is one other thing you are that I'm not.

You are prey now, Father. We're coming for you.

# 11

## *Mother and Child Reunion*

My sons were sitting quietly. Smiling. Civilized. The sun was just in the right spot, peeking through the corner of the stained-glass window. Yellow stripes of light racing on the walls. It was so perfect I kept waiting for the birds to sing. They all lined up on one branch, silent though, almost solemn. They weren't the only ones. There was no screaming in my kitchen. Nothing thrown, nothing broken. One of those rare . . . blissful mornings when I feel awful for resenting them.

But I do. I resent them for making me resent them, chipping away at a mother's unconditional love until there's nothing left but unreasonable conditions. I resent them for making me think I'm wrong, that they didn't take anything away because it was never there to begin with. I resent them for making me think I'm incapable of love, for making me feel empty, defective, like a lioness who gives birth and eats her cubs without pause. I resent them for making me think *I'm* the monster.

The house is empty now. I should be happy, but I can't even stand my own company.

Oh. I hear footsteps upstairs. I could swear Samael left with his brothers.

—Samael? You're going to be late for school.

—I'm not going.

—What?

— . . .

He's not in his room.

—Samael, where are you?

—In here.

He's in mine. None of the others care, but Samael always respected my space. Whatever brought him here, it must be important, to him at least. What in God's name is happening here? The dresser drawers are open. There are clothes all over the bed.

—What are you doing?! Are these my clothes? You know I don't like you touching my things.

—You have too many clothes. I don't know which ones you like.

—You're not making any sense, Samael. Put those back where you found them, please. You can still make it to school in time if you hurry.

—I was going to pack all your things, but I only found this one suitcase. It won't all fit and I don't know what you like. I just . . . You need to tell me what you like.

He's upset, genuinely upset. I don't think I've ever seen him like this. There is this . . . boldness in them, in all of them. Not now. All the bravado's gone. He's a scared child asking his mother for help.

—Why would I pack a suitcase? Where are we going?

—We're not going; you are. As far from here as possible. You don't have much time. Take this.

—What is this? Where is all this money coming from?

—Some of it is Dad's; the rest is what I saved over summer. It's all I have; take it.

—You stole your father's money? Samael, you're scaring me now. You need to tell me what's going on.

— . . .

—Samael!

—THERE'S NO TIME!

He's angry. He had this all planned, whatever this is, and now I'm ruining it by asking too many questions.

—I'm not going anywhere before you tell—

—They're going to kill you!

There is a right answer to this, a normal answer. Who is? Of course they're not. You're imagining things. How I would give anything to say these things and mean it, but the truth is I know who. And I know he's right. Deep down, I've always known this day would come. I only hoped Samael would not be the one to do it.

—When?

—This afternoon, before Dad comes home. You have to go. You're free now, Mother.

—Free? I don't want to be free from you, Samael. Never.

What kind of mother abandons her children?

Am I that kind of mother? I know I don't want to be. I can leave *them* behind. They're adults, legally, and I know they won't miss me. Him, he's . . .

—I'll be fine.

—You're sixteen!

—I have my brothers.

That is exactly what I'm afraid of. I know now that I can get through to him. Barely, but I can. Without me, he'll— They'll change him. They will squeeze what little light is in him until he is nothing but darkness, until he's just like them.

—Come with me, Samael. We can leave together, you and me.

—I can't. They'll look for us. They're not gonna stop until they find us. But they . . .

—They what?

—They won't look for *you*.

— ...

There's shame in his eyes when he says it. I'm not worth the effort. They'll kill me if it's convenient, but they don't care enough to chase after me. I believe him. What truly hurts is that this is not why he's staying. I wish it were. I so desperately wish it were, but he's not doing it for me. He's staying because he thinks he's one of them, like his brothers and his father. Whatever insanity gets them up in the morning, he believes it, too. He's staying because I've failed.

—Say something, Mother.

— ... They are not *going to* stop.

—What?

—They are not going to stop until they find us. Not "gonna." Speak clearly, Samael, so you're always understood. Say what you mean, always, and say it clearly.

—Yes, Mother.

—And don't try to be something you're not. Be ... be the best version of yourself.

—I know. You need to—

—Is it okay if I hug my son for a minute?

He's so strong, but he still hugs like a child, like he's hiding from the world in my arms. Maybe I'm wrong. Maybe he'll turn out ... different. I don't know, but this is as far as I can guide him. If I had half a heart, I would scold him, tell him to put all my clothes back in their drawers. I'd face whatever storm is coming like normal people would. Like a mother would. I know now that I am neither of those things. As horrible as it is, I can't help but think Samael is right. I'm free now. Lord, please forgive me and protect my son.

# 12

## *Children of the Revolution*

—Boys, I'm home!

. . .

I'm starving! I wonder what's for dinner. I just hope it's not quiche. I should have said something the first time she made it, but I had educated her about something else the night before. You can't scold people all the time; it loses its impact. You have to let some things slide. I let quiche slide. Quiche. Even the name is stupid. I could tolerate it for breakfast—it's a snobbish omelet, really—but dinner should have meat. Visible meat. I don't think that's too much to ask. That's right. She can cook something else if it's quiche. I won't get angry. I won't yell or throw things. I'll just calmly explain that from now on quiche is not an acceptable evening meal, period.

Why is it so dark in here? And what's that smell? Is that wax? Goddamn it, if this is another one of her craft projects, I'm going to chain her in the shed. What in the living hell? There are more candles here than at an Indian wedding. I don't know if there are candles at an Indian wedding, but if there were, it would be fewer than this. Oh, good, the boys are here. Maybe one of them can explain this nonsense.

—What's with the candles, kids? Which one of you has a hot date?

— . . .

There's something off with them. Their clothes, I think. Yes, that's what it is. Tucked-in shirts. They look like they're going to get their driver's license pictures taken. Job interview, maybe.

—Don't just stare at me. Our living room looks like a meeting place for a seedy cult. Seriously, what are we doing? Summoning demons? Calling for rain?

— . . .

They're up to something, that's for sure. They've never been this quiet their whole life. A surprise? It's not my birthday. At least, I don't think it's my birthday. Hers? One of theirs? Shit . . . I'm going to look like an asshole again, aren't I? I keep telling myself to mark a calendar, but I never look at the damn thing anyway. It's bad enough we have to celebrate this stupid thing. Coming out of . . . *them* isn't something I want to think about every year. No wonder it's the women who make a big deal out of it. It rubs off on the kids, and before you know it everyone thinks you're a bad person because you didn't bring home a fucking gift. The least people could do is tell you theirs is coming up. . . . Ten days beforehand. Etiquette. That would be the decent thing to do. None of this "Oh no! You forgot! I'm not going to say anything because that'd be rude, but you're still a jerk."

Why would they be in the dark, though, with a bunch of candles? Also, they'd be smiling or something if this were a birthday. They look like someone stole their lunch money.

—Why the long faces? Did anyone die?

— . . .

Oh fuck.

—Oh, come on, boys. Seriously? . . . Uriel, answer me when I'm talking to you!

—Raphael is the prime, now. I answer to him, not you.

—Raphael the prime? He can barely tie his shoes! Enough with this nonsense. Whatever you're pissed off for, I'll make up for it. I promise. Wait. Is it because of that girl? Raph, she was bad news; trust me on this. Self-righteous bra-burning Gloria

Steinem bullshit. Can you see yourself changing diapers? Cooking your own meals? God save us all! Anyway, she'd have dumped your sorry ass before you knew it.

— . . .

—Oh for fuck's sake, this isn't my time, boys. You know that. What about you, Samael? Did they rope you into this, too? Did they threaten you?

— . . .

A smile. Not really, it's more of a smirk. I know pride when I see it. Noooo, he couldn't have. Or could he? Ha! He did this. I can't believe it, but the little shit did this.

—Please. Not now. Not . . . today!

—Don't beg, Dad. It's unbecoming.

Am I begging? I guess I am. I don't know why I bother. You don't do something like this on a whim. *I* wouldn't. They've been planning this, probably for weeks. Their minds are made up, and there's no unmaking them. Samael, though. I didn't know he had it in him. I never thought I'd say it, but I think his mother finally made a man out of him. Good for him. Good for her, I guess. For me, not so much, but still.

I suppose I should have seen it coming. I was a year younger than Raphael when we did it. What a fucked-up day that was. We did it in the yard. Horrible weather, but this isn't the kind of thing you can reschedule. It was wet, and cold. Fucking cold. The wind was so strong it was raining sideways. I remember Father's hair flying everywhere like some cheap toupee. I kept wanting him to fix it. I thought it was . . . unbecoming. I loved my dad. I wanted him to die with some fucking dignity. It didn't matter in the end. Everyone looks like a fool with their throat slit open. Still, it was my turn to lead, finally. I was so proud of myself. Young and dumb. I remember hoping he was proud of me. I think he was, that stupid old fool.

—Where will you kids go?

—What makes you think we're going anywhere?

—No tarp. None of you ever clean up your room. Can't even pick up your damn towel from the bathroom floor. I don't see any of you scrubbing the carpet when this is over and done.

— . . .

They're right. Small talk is cheap. I told them a million times. It's nice to see they were listening. So this is it. No more me. I just . . . Fuck! Forty-five years old. About 45 *billion* regrets. Mostly I wish I'd been born second. I'd still be hunting, or I'd have caught them. I was good at it. Real good at it. Raising kids is a lot harder. And look how they repay you.

I guess I'm never going to buy that boat after all. I'd been saving for that thing since . . . since Samael was born. Shit, that long! A boat. I don't know what I was thinking. Me and the boys, a big old lake somewhere. Dad and I used to fish together. I liked that. We never caught anything, but that was our time, just the two of us. No brothers. I haven't taken Raph in . . . Oh, to hell with it. He can buy his own goddamn boat if he wants one. Ingrate little prick.

—All right, boys. Let's get this over with.

—Any last words?

— . . . Yeah. You dimwits have no idea what the hell you're doing.

# ENTR'ACTE

## The Fox and the Hound

### AD 415

**The Fox**

Hypatia sought to bring the future closer, but every night she dreamed of olden times. She saw herself walking the aisles of the Great Library. She smelled the old parchment, basked in the light of the world's brightest minds. Hypatia had never seen the Library, of course. Its last remnants had been destroyed half a century before she was born. The end of a five-hundred-year-long agony that began with Ptolemy VIII. Still, Alexandria held on to its past. Memories, thick as honey, seeped through its walls, running through the pavement once walked by Euclid and Apollonius of Rhodes.

A student of Theon of Alexandria, a man she called Father, Hypatia had become one of the foremost mathematicians of her time. She was also a philosopher and an avid astronomer. More than anything, Hypatia was a great teacher. She taught Christians, Jews, and pagans alike. She taught in school and on the streets. She engaged anyone willing to listen, whether they wielded a sword or a broom. Hypatia was well liked and respected. Over time, she gained influence within the city, attended political meetings typically reserved for men, and became an advisor to Orestes, the Roman prefect of Alexandria.

The march against science that began with the last pharaohs had picked up the pace under Roman rule. Hypatia fought against it as best she could, for herself, of course, but mostly for the city. Knowledge, she thought, was the fabric of Alexandria. People of various creed, color, or ambition brought together by curiosity. Philosophy, mathematics, things that stretched the limits of the human spirit formed an invisible thread that held her city, her world, together. Now the Church sought to unravel that thread, pretexting the word of God. A blatant excuse if there was ever one. This was about hate, Hypatia knew. Hate of the Jew, of the pagan, of anyone different, of those who dared to question.

## The Hound

Peter was waiting to die. His nephews had already killed their father and would soon come for him. This wasn't a bad thing, Peter thought. He had found his life unrewarding at times but always tried to make the most of it. He had traveled the world, seen things most men only dreamed of. Peter thought himself lucky. He didn't try to hide, didn't run. He did his best to enjoy what he called his retirement. Live every day as if it were your last, that sort of thing. Peter had a big mouth. He talked and talked, and talked. It only seemed fitting that he was offered a position as a lector by the new bishop of Alexandria. Peter was not a religious man, but he liked reading from scriptures as they lent themselves to adding dramatic effect, something he enjoyed immensely.

In exchange for the opportunity, Peter would, from time to time, perform "services" for the Church, services he was uniquely suited for. The newly appointed bishop had wasted no time in his efforts to rid the city of Jews and pagans. All the synagogues had been closed the year before. Jews were being expelled from the city, their belongings confiscated by the Church. The manner in which these things were accomplished was of little concern to the bishop, and there were no questions asked whenever Peter's more violent instincts reared their heads. A good arrangement for all parties, Peter thought. He was a lucky man.

And so when the bishop told him of a pagan philosopher, a woman, who practiced dark magic and "beguiled people through her Satanic wiles," Peter did not make much of it. The bishop always talked nonsense. For dramatic effect, Peter thought. Allegory aside, this was a simple request. This woman was a thorn up the bishop's arse and Peter was to remove it. Easy.

It was an odd day. No ship in port. The city filled with empty space. Even the wind blew the wrong way. No matter. Peter had a plan. He would observe his prey for a day, find a suitable moment in her routine, and stealthily disappear her the next day. It was a simple plan, which was how Peter liked them, but one that did not allow for contingencies, such as Hypatia approaching him on the street, moments into his stalking.

What Peter had truly not planned for was how charming his prey turned out to be. She was smart, obviously—witches often were—but also stood taller than most, exuding strength and confidence the likes of which Peter had rarely seen. She was enthralling, not in the sexual sense—stories of Hypatia showing her menstrual pad in response to men's suits had made it clear romance was not in the cards. She was just . . . interesting, in the way most people weren't. The fascination ran both ways. Though he had little interest in philosophy or mathematics, Peter was of keen intellect, his wit sharp as a scalpellus blade. Hypatia liked him immediately. They walked for hours, from the gates of the moon to the gates of the sun. No one disappeared the next day, or the next.

Dark clouds moved over the city. Peter was restless. Rain meant no walk; no walk meant no Hypatia. He decided to visit her school, unsure if the invitation he'd received was sincere or had been extended out of mere politeness. He arrived, soaking wet and oddly diffident. Hypatia met him with a large smile and asked him to take a seat. She was teaching her students to build an astrolabe. Peter knew nothing of astronomy. He did not know Hypatia had written commentary on Ptolemy's Handy Tables or that she was known for making star charts of her own. The term "astrolabe" had come out of the bishop's mouth along with words like "witchery" and "demonism," but never in Peter's mind had it suggested such a beautifully precise and complex instrument.

Asked what its purpose was, Hypatia explained how it could be used for computing the altitude of celestial bodies, identifying planets and stars, et cetera, et cetera. The astrolabe, Hypatia added, was a practical instrument derived from a mechanical model of the heavens, one she called an "armillary sphere." Peter's lack of reaction only increased Hypatia's manifest enthusiasm, and she dragged Peter into her office where another device lay on her desk. Peter immediately understood Hypatia's passion. Nine graduated rings of metal moving in all directions around a smaller orb. Whatever its purpose, this "sphere" was the most awe-inspiring contraption he had ever laid eyes on. That's when it happened.

Eureka. Neurons firing in all directions, dots connected in a flash. An epiphany. Hypatia was brilliant, strong, taller than most. She knew of distant stars and planets. She built devices used to navigate the heavens. She had a sphere in her office. Could it be *the* sphere? Could fortune favor him enough that he would stumble upon the traitor on the street, that she would invite him into her office and show him the very device they had been chasing for more than a thousand years? Peter stormed out without saying a word.

Peter didn't feel the rain on his way home. He could end his family's ordeal. He could end the chase. He would be a hero, perhaps with the added bonus of being allowed to live. Peter knew he was getting ahead of himself. First, he had to get the device. Kill Hypatia. He didn't want to do that. Think. He needed to think. He did not know how to use the sphere, and neither did his nephews. Hypatia did. She would have to teach them. Then, maybe, she could die. One thing at a time. Peter rushed inside his home and found the bishop sitting in his kitchen.

Why was Hypatia still walking the streets, still teaching, still breathing? The bishop was unaccustomed to having his wishes denied. Peter promised he would take care of it in the evening. The bishop said that he would send a group of men to help Peter with his task. *Parabolani,* an order of zealots founded to care for the sick, now just thugs doing the bishop's dirty work. "That won't be necessary," said Peter, but the bishop made it clear this was not an offer one was at liberty to refuse.

Peter needed to think, again. There was still a way to make this work. He would convince Hypatia to recant her beliefs and pledge allegiance to the Church, a greater victory for the bishop, and a chance for her to teach Peter how to activate the sphere. A simple plan. That was the way Peter liked his plans. That night, he and a small group of *parabolani* stopped Hypatia's carriage on a narrow cobbled street. Hypatia smiled when she recognized Peter, but her grin quickly faded at the sight of the mob behind him.

Peter set his plan into motion. He told Hypatia she only had to recant her be— Hypatia spat in his face. The next few seconds are fuzzy in Peter's mind. His right hand hurts. Hypatia's on the ground, moaning. Peter's plan vanishes into thin air. One small act of violence sends the *parabolani* into a violent frenzy. They drag Hypatia into an abandoned pagan temple and strip her naked before hacking at her with oyster shells until she is nothing but pulp. Frenzy turns to demonic rage. The men remove her eyeballs, cut her into parts, each man carrying a bloody limb through the streets. Hypatia's mangled pieces are thrown into a mound in a public place. Peter watches, horrified, as his hopes and dreams are incinerated, filling the air with the smell of burning flesh.

Hypatia was no Kibsu. She died fighting the Church, but her last thought was of Peter. He was her friend, and he betrayed her in the end. Hypatia's murder lasted thirty-seven minutes in total, 2,220 seconds of violence that would eclipse a lifetime of attainment. One of the most brilliant minds of her time would be remembered for the way she died, and not for how she lived. A martyr for philosophy, a symbol of paganism, of Christian virtue, of the struggle for women's rights. Hypatia's death would be used by all to further their agenda, but few, if any, would remember the woman who discussed philosophy with strangers on the street. Extraordinary, yet unabashedly human.

As for Peter, his nephews found him two weeks after Hypatia's death. He said he had been waiting for them.

# ACT II

# 13

## *Time in a Bottle*

### 1973

Dear Sarah,

I doubt this letter will reach you. It has been more than a decade since I last heard from you. I cringe at the notion that my returning to China has changed your image of me and that you chose to end our friendship. Despite my misgivings, I can only hope you are ignoring me, for I cannot bear the alternative. I refuse to entertain the notion that your light stopped shining, and so I write, hoping these letters find you in good health and spirits.

I am doing relatively well under China's perpetually changing circumstances. I have navigated the Cultural Revolution as best I could, though some of my chosen allegiances were, in hindsight, unfortunate. I suppose my writing this letter is evidence that I have at least moderately succeeded. I have been little more than a teacher here, but what credit I get for my student's achievements is apparently enough to keep me in the party's graces.

I sometimes take pride in all that we have done in such a short time. Our first satellite launched in '70, heavier than all of the other nations' satellites combined. Astronauts for our first manned mission have already been selected, though I do not know if the program can move forward in our current state of affairs. Surprisingly, at least to me, my work on systems engineering is also getting renewed attention. Some of *my pupils wish to apply those principles to human systems. I find the idea intriguing, though somewhat unsettling. Whatever successes I enjoy also come with a proportional feeling of guilt. So many in academia have been purged, an entire generation of educated children sent to work in rice fields and textile factories. I kept working through it all. I spent time and resources splitting the atom and sending machines to space while my people died in the great famine. I survived when others did not. I am hopeful that Nixon's visit will help restore a modicum of trust between us and the West. Relations with the USSR are becoming increasingly hostile and this country can hardly afford another decade of isolation.*

*As I read these lines, I realize I must sound like a man on the brink of depression. I am, all things considered, happy and cautiously optimistic about the future. I picked up pen and paper not to complain, but because I have been thinking of you a lot these past few days. The human mind is a wondrous thing. My friendship with you runs deep, but it is always the smallest, most inconsequential thing that reminds me of it. A cloud that looks out of place in the eastern sky. A sudden craving for coffee. Or in this particular case, a bow.*

*I have returned from a visit to Xinjiang, along the northern route of the ancient Silk Road. Archaeologists discovered several Scythian-style bows that have, somewhat miraculously, been preserved underground for more than three thousand years. All have been crafted with Chinese materials and techniques. All but one. It was carved with unknown symbols that match the ones from what you called our "side project" to a T. I know our friends in Berlin have not received anything in fifteen years, so I presume you have since lost interest, but there are enough symbols on the bow* to form a coherent text. Perhaps it even tells a story. Whether or not these symbols are still of interest to you, I thought you might enjoy seeing the bow and have enclosed a picture. It is a beautifully crafted instrument.

I truly miss the excitement I felt during this small quest of ours, the sense of wonder that came with each find. Seeing those symbols again reminded me of the necklace you showed me the day we first met. I can hardly believe that was more than three decades ago. I was so young and insecure, certain I would never find my place. And there you were, more curious and bright than anyone I had ever met. One bad meal in the MIT commons and I knew I would never again be truly alone. I hope that is still true, that you are well and that we remain friends. I wish it with all the ardor you can conceive.

Yours faithfully,
Qian Xuesen

# 14

## *Higher Ground*

I don't know what I missed about California, but it wasn't the traffic. I guess San Diego's not as bad as LA. And Lola likes it here, so there's that, but I'm going to lose it if this car doesn't start moving.

—Who's this Xuesen guy again?

—I told you, Lola, he's a friend of your grandma. He's a very important man. He founded the entire Chinese space program. He lived here before, but the US accused him of being a communist. He actually helped found the Jet Propulsion Laboratory back in the day. That's where I worked when we lived here.

It's too bad I can't work at JPL again. It's been fifteen years, but someone's bound to recognize me there. I know Sue Finley's still around. Hell, I bet half the women I worked with are still there. Regardless, I need a way into that space probe project. I'll find a subcontractor somewhere. Close by if I can. I don't want Lola to lose her friends again, not so soon. She's lost too—

—Mom, can I see the picture?

—Not now, Lola, I'm driving.

—But I—

—No buts. You've looked at the bow a hundred times already. It hasn't changed in three thousand years. I bet you the picture hasn't either. Oh, before I forget, we're going out for dinner tonight. Where do you want to go?

—Tonight? No! I'm supposed to help Heather with her homework.

—You can watch TV with Heather tomorrow. Tonight is girls' night out. Us girls, not you and Heather . . . Come on! It'll be fun! You can have anything you want. Steak, lobster, five courses of ice cream if that's what you want.

—For real?

—No. I meant it about the lobster, though. We're celebrating. They're having their first science meeting today, Lola. At JPL. They call it the Mariner Jupiter/Saturn 1977 project. Horrible name, I know, but it's happening. They're doing it.

—Did they use any of the math we did?

—I don't think so, no. But that's not the point.

—Well, that was a lot of work for nothing.

—This was never about us, Lola. It doesn't matter where the math comes from.

—And why Jupiter and Saturn? I thought the idea was to visit *all* the planets.

—Oh, the name. It's a . . . trick, Lola, to get the budget approved. They start with two planets; then they'll say: "We've come all this way, might as well keep going." Like you, when you want to go to the library.

—What? You're the one who wants me to read more.

—Nice try, Lola. "But Mooooom, we're here already. The record shop is just around the corner!" It's the same thing with NASA. They've launched a probe to Saturn in April. Everyone knows this is about the Grand Tour.

—If you say so.

—Wow, Lola. Try to contain your enthusiasm. I thought you'd be happy.

—I am. I just don't think they need our help, that's all.

—They need some help, that's for sure. They're barely doing anything. Back in '69, Nixon was given a plan for the next phase of space travel. A huge American space station in orbit. Several spaceships. They even talked about a manned mission to Mars.

—That sounds cool.

—It does, doesn't it? Do you know what they budgeted for in the end? A reusable space vehicle.

—It can go to Mars?

—No, no. It can't go to the moon either, just low orbit like everything else.

—So what does it do?

—It's reusable. Well, part of it is. No one seems to care about space anymore, Lola. Except for this, this mission, the Grand Tour; it's a real step forward.

—Fine. I'll tell Heather I can't go. Why are we stopping?

—We have to get gas.

—What, here? But the line goes all the way around the block!

—It'll be the same everywhere.

—Why don't we get gas tomorrow then? I don't want to be late for school.

—You won't. And we can't get gas tomorrow. Tomorrow's the twelfth. Odd-numbered license plate, remember?

—Oh, that. That's just stupid.

—I know. But we still have to wait.

—Fine . . . Let's wait in line with all the odd people. Now, can I see the bow?

—The picture's in my purse, but—

—But what? I just want to look at it!

—Okay! But there's something else in there. I didn't have time to wrap it. I was going to give it to you tonight.

—A gift?

—Yes . . . Go ahead.

—Thank you, Mom! I— What is this?

—It's a calculator.

—Does it work?

—Of course it works, Lola. Why would I get you a calculator that doesn't work?

—It's so small, it . . . This is rad, Mom. Thanks!

—Better than an old bow?

—I don't know, Mom. Where's the pictu— Never mind, I got it. Are you sure the symbols are ours?

—Definitely not sure, but the alphabet looks a lot like what's on your necklace. It's quite possible one of us carved that bow.

—And you can't tell me what it says?

—Can you?

—Well, no, but you told me what's on the necklace!

—I told you what my mother told me. The symbols are somewhere in our journals. We can look for them together if you want, but they're just sounds. We'll need to know the language if we're going to read what's on the bow. I'm not sure there's enough on that picture to decipher anything, but we can try.

—We should go see it.

—The bow? It's in China, Lola.

—So what? You're not even curious?

—Of course I am, but it's in China! The Grand Tour is happening right here. I'm more curious about why your grandmother never mentioned her pen pal, or that "side project" he's talking about.

—You don't know what it is?

—I didn't even know my mother knew him. I still have some of her personal things. I know she kept some letters; maybe some of them are his.

—He called it a small quest. That sounds kind of fun.

—I guess it was because she kept writing to him long after we moved. In Russia, back in California.

—Isn't that against the rules?

—Good point. I'm not worried about the letters—they go through half a dozen mailboxes before they make it here—but yes, it's against the rules. If I'm honest, we broke that one too many times, your grandma and I.

—You did? What did you do?

—It was war. We thought . . . Mother thought we couldn't just watch, so we got involved. We did some things, things that leave a trace.

—Like what?

—Like they have your grandma's picture in her OSS file. They have mine. There's no reason for anyone to look at them, but there's one of me standing next to Wernher von Braun's brother in Germany, him and a bunch of American soldiers. That one might get some attention. I'm sure there's more I don't know about. It's all in the National Archives with the military personnel records.

—Is that how the Tracker found us? Is he going to find us here?

—No, Lola. He won't find us with that. I don't like loose ends, that's all. You and I are not going to make the same mistakes. We're going to be careful.

—No school picture, I know . . .

—Exactly. What are the rules, Lola?

—Now? Really?

—Yes really.

—Preserve the knowledge.

    Survive at all costs.

    Don't draw attention to yourself.

    Don't leave a trace.

    Fear the Tracker. Always run, never fight.

    There can never be three for too long.

—Good. We're going to follow the rules and do what we came here to do. You're going to start a journal and—

—What?

—Yes, you are. First rule, Lola. And we're not going to waste our time thinking about a bow. We have to get a job and—

—Mom, I'm eleven.

—Well, you can help me. Your math is just as good as mine. There are other ways to help. You can start right now, actually. It's our turn at the pump. Hop! Out of the car!

# 15

## 20th Century Boy

[*I'm a good-looking guy, aren't I?*]

Raphael is the prime, the one who gets to have children. Unfortunately for him, and future generations of us, he is unable to listen to anyone for more than ten seconds. This, along with some of our least endearing dispositions, has made finding a lasting relationship somewhat challenging. For all of us.

—You need to give it time, Raphael. You will find the right woman, eventually.

[*I meant that. Seriously, if you were a broad, you'd find me attractive, wouldn't you?*]

—Guys, I think all of us should go to Egypt.

Thank god for my brother Uriel. He wanted us to meet, said he had something to share. It was time, I suppose. We have not seen much of each other these past few months. We had to relocate, find jobs. Raphael still needs a wife. He chose New York. I was skeptical at first, but I like it here. This silence is getting truly awkward. I suppose one of us has to ask.

—Why do you think we should go to Egypt, Uriel?

—Ah! I'm glad you asked. I found some ancient Greek translations at the library. This place has a huge library, did you know?

[*Is that where you've been spending all your time since we got here? Uriel doesn't have a job yet, so he keeps asking me for money. Now I know why.*]

—Can we let Uriel finish his story?

—I'll pay you back, Raph, I swear. My point is, I found this thing written around 550 BC, 552, something like that, by some Greek guy. Somewhere in there he tells the story of how he met a priestess near Thebes, the Egyptian Thebes, not the Greek one. That confused me for a while. Why would you use the same name for two different places? Anyway, the whole thing lasts for less than a page, and on that page only a few words are about the priestess herself. "Her name was Mer-Neith-it-es." That's pretty much it. The rest of the page is devoted to her daughter Hemut-Taui, who is twenty years old and looks "like her mother saw herself in a lake and summoned her reflection to life." I think the Greek guy had a crush on her.

[*Don't take this the wrong way, Brother, but there are a few girls who look just like their mother in this café right here. Why would you waste your time looking for one on the other side of the world? One who's been dead for—I don't know—*]

—Please, Raphael, let him finish.

I should have said something nice. This is probably the longest Raphael ever went without interrupting.

—Thanks, Sam. I didn't make much of it either, not at first. Then I read this other thing, by another Greek. A philosopher. Older fellow. This one is from 490 BC. That's like . . .

—Sixty years later.

—Right. I forgot the guy's name, something something. This old guy, he also traveled to Egypt. He mostly writes nonsense about the meaning of life and shit, but at some point he starts rambling on and on about a priestess he met at the temple of Sekhmet, in Thebes. Same Thebes. Not the other one. She also has a daughter, but he doesn't say anything about her. That priestess, though, he says she's a *hundred years old* but looks to be thirty.

[*That doesn't mean anything, Uriel. She could be—*]

I'm still not done! What do you think is the priestess's name—the mother, not the daughter? That's right. Mer-Fucking-Neith-it-es. It's the same name. Same . . . priestess.

[*You think it's the daughter.*]

Granddaughter, actually. I think they stayed there for three generations and pretended to be the same person.

Interesting. They would have found a way to use their resemblance to their advantage. Turn a liability into an asset.

[*Even if you're right, Uriel. That story's twenty-five hundred years old. Our uncles found them in California not fifteen years ago. I say we go from there.*]

—If I may. I think what Uriel is trying to say—

—What I'm trying to say is we're not really looking for them now, are we? What we want is that sphere they have, or had. I don't know much about radio waves or whatever it is that thing would send out, but if it's going to send a signal way the hell out there, it probably wouldn't fit in their purse. I mean, if it were me . . .

—You would hide it.

—I sure as hell wouldn't carry it around everywhere, not with us chasing after them and all.

[*You think they hid that sphere in Egypt?*]

I have no idea. But they were there for over a century. Three generations in one place. That's got to leave some footprint, records, something. It's not much, but it's . . . different. Anything different is good, right? We don't need them. We just need that thing to call home. Fuck them.

—He has a point, Raphael. We should at least consider it. I know you were hoping to find a wife here, but I am willing to venture that there are plenty of eligible bachelorettes in Egypt as well. Perhaps—and I say this with the utmost respect—perhaps a bit of a language barrier might even be to your advantage.

*[All right, if both of you want to go to Egypt, we'll go to Egypt. Women here are all stuck-up, snobbish, toffee-nosed . . . smarty-pants anyway. We'll just need to make a quick stop in Prague along the way.]*

What's in Prague?

*[This.]*

A letter. I know the handwriting, it's from—

—Is this from who I think it is?

It's from our mother.

*[Can you believe the old lady was dumb enough to put a return address on it? The letter's for you, Samael.]*

—You didn't open it?

*[Well, no. I mean it's your letter. There might be some personal shit in there. Maybe you should wait until the deed's done before reading it. I know you two were close.]*

     . . .

*[Don't just sit there, Sam. Say something.]*

I . . . I was about to tell you I found a house in Miami that was purchased by a lady whose death certificate is dated forty years ago. I doubt it will lead to anything, but I would like to cross it off the list. I think we should split up. You should go to Prague and take care of Mother; I will go to Florida; then we can both meet Uriel in Egypt. That will give him time to find us a place to live.

*[Why don't we—]*

Unless, of course, you don't think you can handle our mother on your own. I would understand.

# 16

## *Dream On*

Dear journal . . . Hi, journal! How are you today?

What do people write in these things? My name is Lola. I'm eleven years old. I'm like my mom, like a copy. I'm a Kibsu, but if you're reading this, you know that already. Mom said I'm to keep this to a minimum since we have to carry these journals with us every time we move. Just the science and things that are important, she said.

There's a psycho killer chasing us. Pretty sure that's important. I have nightmares about it almost every night. He and his brothers killed my grandmother, almost killed my mom and me when I was six. I guess they're also chasing you.

I don't know what else to say. I haven't done any real science yet. Mom wants me to start, but I'm not sure what I can do. To be honest, I'm not really sure what we're supposed to do. Take them to the stars, I know. But we can't take *everyone* to the stars. How many people can you fit on a spaceship? A thousand? Maybe we can build a hundred spaceships, but we can never fit everyone. If this evil comes and wants to kill everybody, most people will die no matter what we do. Mom said we need Russia and the US to compete. Space race! Space race! Sometimes I think they might get further if they worked together instead. We can't keep sending people to space two at a time. We'll need big ships, like big big. We can't send a really big ship from down here, so we'll need to build it up there, on a space station or something. Who's going to build that? And if we go super super far with the ship, it's going to run out of gas at some point. I don't think we can take anyone to the stars with something that guzzles gas like a Chevy Monte Carlo.

I don't understand a lot of what we're doing and what my life is supposed to be like. Maybe I'm just too young, like Mom says. All I know is I don't really fit in anywhere. I'm pretty sure I'm not into boys, and I don't have any real friends. I don't know what I'm trying to say, but I want . . . more than this. There has to be more than this, right?

Maybe there's something I don't know. Maybe I'm supposed to know. Like, maybe our ancestors wanted to tell us something. They sent a message and we just never got it. A message in a bottle, except bottles didn't exist. Like that golden record they're making for the Grand Tour mission. Mom only talks about the probes, but I really dig that record thing. They put a plaque on the last series of probes, with a drawing of naked white people to show aliens what we look like. People complained about them being naked. This is a lot better. No nudes, but they put lots of photographs on it, a drawing of DNA, some sounds from Earth, and an hour and a half of music. Music! They'll stick the record to the probe, and if anyone ever finds it, and they have a record player, they can learn a whole lot about us. Here, listen. This is who we are. So cool. Mom said I could write to the man who's making the record, Dr. Sagan. I sent him this wolf picture I found, one of a dolphin. I like dolphins. I told him about my favorite songs. I doubt he likes Chuck Berry as much as I do, but it was worth a shot, and it was way more fun than calculating optimal magnitudes like Mom asked.

I can't help thinking maybe we made our own golden record at some point, something just for us. Maybe one of us wrote it down a long time ago so we wouldn't have to feel sad all the time. It wouldn't have to be fancy or gold, no music. A few words on a bow might do it.

Here, listen. This is who you are.

# 17

## *She's Gone*

*As ever, your obliged and affectionate friend,*
*Sarah*

I replied. I sent a letter to Xuesen and I signed my mother's
name.

So much for following the rules. Lola and I have been trying
to decipher that bow. It's pretty much the only thing she wants
to do with me nowadays. Still, I don't know what I was thinking.
Well, I *do* know. My mother was keeping things from me and
I'm dying to find out what it was. I woke up in the middle of
the night. I grabbed a pen and paper and started writing. I ran
outside at sundown and mailed the thing before I could change
my mind. I try to rationalize it—the man runs the Chinese space
program; that could come in handy—but I know that had nothing to do with it. It had nothing to do with a bow either. I wonder
what else Mother didn't tell me. I guess I didn't know her as well
as I thought.

I miss her, so much. This—I don't know—it felt like I could
bring her back. As if, somehow, if she wrote to her friend, she'd
still be with us, and I'd still be the person I'm supposed to be.

I startle myself sometimes. When I come out of the shower
and I wipe the fog off the bathroom mirror. When I catch a
glimpse of myself in a storefront window. I have this *idea* of me,
this skin I put on every day. That's who I think I am, but the

bathroom mirror disagrees. Small wrinkles. Fine lines where there shouldn't be. Those are hers. That's how I remember her. All the subtle ways her face was not mine. Those differences meant the world to me. I saw wisdom in her small wrinkles. I was insecure, scared shitless, but she wasn't. I could tell. Now I know what I saw didn't mean anything. Just the world leaving a mark when it bumps at you, all of us bowing to the caprices of time. I feel . . . guilty for changing, blurring those differences. It feels like I'm *erasing* her, so I keep her alive in any way I can.

I continue her research. There are only a handful of people dabbling in climate science nowadays. Most of them are forecasting global warming, but we knew that a hundred years ago. The media, for some reason, will only talk about the weirdos predicting another ice age. Nevertheless, we have a lot more data to play with now. I've started measuring other gases. People are pouring all sorts of new things in the air. Things that didn't even exist a few years ago. I was watching Lola choking on hairspray the other day. They put chlorofluorocarbons in the aerosol cans. It makes sense. It's stable, nontoxic, nonflammable, won't cause cancer, et cetera. It all sounds great. The problem is, CFCs are *so* stable they'll stick in the atmosphere for a hundred years, and if my calculations are correct they're something like ten thousand times better than $CO_2$ at absorbing heat. I found a couple people at UC Irvine working on chlorofluorocarbons and sent them what I had. It turns out they were looking at something else entirely. CFCs will apparently release chlorine in the atmosphere under sunlight, and that chlorine eats away at the ozone layer. That's not good.

Then there's methane. It won't stay for long once it's released, but it's much more potent than carbon dioxide. The Earth's population is growing fast, and more people means more farming. Farming means manure. Manure means methane. This whole thing could happen ten times faster than we thought. It's all speculation right now. There are just too many variables to consider. When we have enough computing power for a good model, we'll know what we're up against. At the rate we're moving, Lola might still be around for that. Either way, Mother would be happy that we're making progress.

I wonder what she'd think of me. There are times, still, when I feel completely lost without her. Like the child who let go of her mother's hand at the fair. Everything is new, and exciting, until she realizes her safety's gone and she's all alone. Only I'm not the child; I'm the mother keeping my daughter close in the crowd.

I have this dream. I'm by the ocean on this long, gravelly beach. The sky is gray, the air thick and misty. Mother's head emerges as she slowly walks out of the water. She wears a white dress, the one she wore when we landed in New York, the one I buried my face in when I learned my grandmother was gone. I want to run to her. I want it so bad my whole body aches, but I can't move my feet. She smiles as if to say everything is going to be okay. Another head crosses the threshold, my grandmother. Then her mother. Her mother . . . Her mother. Suddenly we're all here. All one hundred of us. And I should feel good, relieved, because it's not all on me anymore. It's a good dream, I think. But I don't feel good, or relieved. I feel like my mother never really was. Just another link in the chain.

Lola, she— I was in complete denial when I was her age. I didn't want any of it to be true. I thought I could just *wish it away* and be a regular kid. Not her. Maybe I'm wrong, but I think she's *accepted* it, always has. She knows she'll never be like everyone else. She just wants . . . something else. The universe is this giant letdown and she keeps yelling at it: "Is that all there is?" That's why she cares so much about that bow. She's clinging to this idea that we're just "missing" a piece of the puzzle. If we only knew more about who we are or where we come from then all of this would feel different.

I wish it were true. I wish two dozen words carved on a wooden bow held the answer to all our questions, about life, the universe. I wish my daughter were happy, that she weren't chased by murdering men, that I were a better mother. I wish for a lot of things, just like I did when Mother was alive. I wanted things. Mother and I broke the rules because we *both* wanted things and I lost a child, and Mother died before she could hold her granddaughter. There can never be three for too long, but there should have been three for a little while.

# 18

## *Let's Get It On*

—Our ancestor wrote smut? Like, seriously. She wrote porn on a bow!

—Lola! It's . . . poetry.

—Sure, Mom. Poetry. Are you sure that's what it says?

—Pretty sure. I know for a fact it's written in Akkadian, just like your necklace. I suppose I could be wrong about a word or two but . . .

—Read it again.

—"From the underworld, she emerges in . . . wetness." Something wet?

   "I touch her elbow, then her mouth.

   She speaks after a cold silence.

   Desire awakens and I reach for her breast."

—That's it?

—Well, there are symbols all over the bow, but that's all we can see on the picture. The next line says something about salt. I can't see enough of it to translate. I asked Xuesen for more pictures, but it might take a while before we hear back.

—Did you ask him about that "side project"?

—No.

—Why?

—Because I'm writing as my mother, remember? It's *my* project. I'm supposed to know what it is. I found some of his letters in your grandma's things. Maybe there's something there.

—If you say so . . .

—I know that poem is not what you were hoping for, Lola, but—

—How do you know what I was hoping for? You don't have the faintest idea! But you're right; that wasn't it.

—You're upset. It's okay. I get it. But it's really "rad" when you think about it. That bow was probably the most important thing to her. She'd have hunted with it, fought with it. That bow was the difference between life and death. Whatever it says, whatever those words mean to us now, they obviously meant—

—Oh, stop it, Mom. For all we know she had two bows. We just happened to find the one she wrote sex stuff on. I'm— This was stupid. I feel stupid, okay?

—It wasn't stu— Where are you going? Lola, wait!

I should have known this would end badly. I'll admit I didn't see *that* coming. I was almost certain we'd get bits of the bow's owner's biography, her lineage, maybe a list of things she'd killed with it. Lola was looking for the meaning of life.

For a while I thought this might actually bring us closer. She dove headfirst into our journals looking for clues on how to read that script. I think she half expected our journals to be in English. She kept going, though. She was so eager to find what she was looking for. And she did. She practically dragged me to the library to pick up everything they had on Coptic when she saw those symbols in the Sixty-One's writings. No stopping at the record shop. She carefully reproduced every symbol on a piece of paper and pinned them to the wall. Our kitchen looks like one of those evidence boards on crime shows. She stared at it over every meal waiting for some sort of eureka moment. She was obsessed. She kept asking questions about her ancestors, what it was like for them, as if I knew any more than she did. I kept telling her, but she wouldn't take "I don't know" for an answer. I'm the mother; I *have* to know. Finally, I gave up. "High school," I said. "It must have felt a lot like high school."

It's the best I could come up with. I can't begin to imagine what their lives were like, but the science . . . They were studying something they couldn't interact with in any way, things they couldn't see or touch. With any luck, they could predict where a star would be on a given day, but they didn't know what a star was. It could have been a giant muffin for all they knew. They could theorize, but they would never know whether they were right or wrong, not in *their* lifetime. In many ways it must have felt like calculus to a sixteen-year-old Kibsu. Pure theory with no practical application whatsoever. "But Mom! I want to hunt deer!" "Finish your orbit calculation first, honey." I'm sure they all hated every minute of it. I'm sure their moms felt as helpless as I do.

Needless to say, my high school answer wasn't the resounding success I hoped it would be. High school is still a couple years away, but she knows it won't come with sudden contentment. She'll feel just as out of place, awkward, and she can't imagine anyone else feeling like she does. Not me, certainly not some warrior three thousand years ago.

Lola's not asking for much. She's not being . . . unreasonable. I know that. She just wants the one thing I don't have to give her: answers. I have questions. Tons of them. I have enough questions to last her a lifetime. Watching her struggle makes me realize how much I've changed. I don't know exactly when or how. I suppose that's how it works.

And who knows, maybe Lola was right all along and all we really need to know is written on that bow.

"I touch her elbow, then her mouth.
She speaks after a cold silence.
Desire awakens and I reach for her breast."

I still think of Billie sometimes. Not as often, but there are times when I tell myself a quick trip to Moscow wouldn't hurt anyone. She buried me. I won't put her through that pain again, but I still wish I could see her face, catch a glimpse of that careless smile one last time. Deep down I know that wouldn't be enough. Even after all these years, after everything I've been through, I've never felt so whole, so utterly alive and vulnerable, as I did lying beside her. Maybe that's what our ancestor is trying to tell us. Watching the small of her lover's back, she realized the one thing that truly mattered to her. She got up in the middle of the night and carved her feelings on her most prized possession.

# 19

## *Mind Games*

The blanket is folded in just the right way. The pillows are fluffed, carefully placed. I lit a Yankee Candle by the bed. Everything smells of . . . I don't know what that smell is. Whatever; Lola's room is straight out of a magazine—well, almost. It sure is cleaner than it's ever been.

She didn't come home last night. I knew she wouldn't. Not because I know my daughter like I know myself, certainly not because she said anything. I knew because Heather's mom called to make sure I knew Lola would sleep over. I said, "Yes! Of course! Lola's been talking about it all week." My daughter was upset. The least I could do was let her have her small rebellion.

I spent the night calculating how much fuel we'll need for the Grand Tour once we clear orbit. It's amazing, really. We need a tanker's worth of fuel to fly up two hundred miles, but the next ten billion only cost a suitcaseful. As for the instruments, a canister of plutonium dioxide should do the trick. The heat from radioactive decay will generate a few hundred watts of power. Plenty enough if we stick to the essentials. I'd done some of the work before. This would have been quick if my mind hadn't kept wandering. I read all of Xuesen's letters and there weren't any clues about what he and my mother were working on, except maybe for that one line: "I am intrigued by the boundary in Iraq." That's what he said. The boundary with what? First Berlin, then Iraq. What were they doing?

I was on my second pot of coffee when the sun came up and was fairly certain I wouldn't survive a third. I finished reading *Solaris*. I'll have to read the end again. I was way too tired for Lem. Antsy. I don't know if it was the coffee or the fact that Lola rarely leaves my sight. Too awake to sleep, too sleepy for anything. There's plenty of accounting to go through. People to pay, money to move. I made a list of things I could do in my head. It's still growing.

I cleaned Lola's room. I thought she'd be happy to come home to a clean bed. But she didn't come home. Not this morning, or afternoon. It's almost nine now. Heather's mom called twice already looking for her daughter. "I'm sure they're fine," I said. I am. I really am.

Now I'm exhausted, but I can't close my eyes. I don't like what I see. A dozen cars parked in front of a beach house. Drunken kids crowding the place while the parents are out of town. Cheap beer. Plastic cups. The kitchen counter wet from another game of beer pong. More cars, older boys. This party's getting out of hand. The owner's kids know it, but they won't say anything. Being popular is worth a load of pain.

Dim the lights. Some boy I've never met sticking his hands inside my daughter's shirt. "Let's go upstairs; we can't hear ourselves down here." "Oops. Sorry! Let's try the other bedroom." More cheap beer. "How about a pink lady?" Bad gin and pasteurized egg whites. Head spinning. Throwing up in a strange bathroom while someone bangs on the door.

Heather's mom probably has the same thoughts. We're overreacting, I know. It's only nine. They've come home much later before. It's our job to worry, I suppose. Kids will be kids; mothers will be mothers. I bet she'll call again soon. I won't mind. Anything to stop the B movie playing in my head.

More cheap beer. The music gets louder. Louder still. The whole room smells of sweat and raging hormones. Someone picks on Lola. Maybe that someone's jealous, just looking for attention. They laugh at what she's wearing, the way she dances, or talks, or laughs, or eats, or cries. Bad memories stirred. The being mocked now mixes with the being mocked before, until her whole life tastes of rejection. Sadness doesn't last. It ferments and turns into something stronger. Lola feels warmer. Warmer still. At first she doesn't know if it's the dancing or too many kids crammed into the living room. Someone pushes her. She's angry now, sweating up a storm.

I'm thinking too much. I need to clear my head. She might have fallen asleep watching TV. I try to do that, watch TV, but I get . . . distracted. The house feels like it's a mile wide, foreign. The refrigerator hums louder than it ever has. Walls cracking. A dripping faucet going off beat. I stare at shadows I've never seen on the kitchen ceiling. Finally, I look up at the clock and five long seconds have passed. Repeat the process a million times and it's been a minute. How can my coffee be so cold already?

Don't think.

A pack of Trackers chasing their prey down the alley. No lights. My daughter races to the sound of her own breath. Heather runs face-first into a chained fence. She shakes it with both hands. Again. Again. They scream for help into the empty void and the only answer is the sound of laughter. Hyenas fending lions off a found carcass. Machetes fly, painting the dark walls with more black. Silence. Dead fucking silence as pubescent monsters sort through body parts to see which ones belong to us. Cut. My daughter's head brought back as trophy to the devil who sired them.

It's 9:04 and I've already watched everyone die in my head. I need to find something to do if I don't want to refine that nightmare for hours. I can make more coffee. Plenty of accounting to go through. People to pay, money to move. I make a whole list. Only I can't do any of it. I can't reach that far. The rest of the world is on the other side of an unbreakable window.

Lola's missing. There's nothing else to think about.

It's just me.

An empty room.

A phone. Decidedly not ringing.

# 20

## *I Can't Stand the Rain*

—Let's make like a prom dress and take off.

That's what Brent said when he showed up early at Heather's in his Chevelle convertible. Then he went on and on about living on the wild side, going where the wind will take us. I was all over that. Heather too, I was surprised. I think she might have a crush on him. Supergross. Brent put down the roof and spun his tires for two and a half seconds until Heather's dad came yelling out of the house.

—Let's go to Mexico.

That's what *I* said. It's superclose and they wouldn't be able to find us once we crossed the border. Brent headed east. Still, we were free. Rebels. For a good five minutes, we stared at the valleys in silence—you can't hear a thing with the roof down— our hair blowing in the wind. Then it started pouring. Brent pulled over and put the roof back on. We were still free, though. Wet rebels. We were in Phoenix by the time I finished working out the knots in my hair. I didn't tell them I'd already been to Phoenix. I didn't want to ruin the moment.

This wasn't the most well-planned escape; I knew that going in. Brent barely had enough for gas and Heather's dress doesn't have pockets to put money *in*, not that she had any. We spent half of my five dollars on Googles and Banana Flips. That's when Heather started freaking out about the cops. I told her this was the sugar rush talking, but she wouldn't listen. Brent didn't help with all his talk about us being like Bonnie and Clyde, and another Bonnie. Somehow the Grand Canyon came up in the conversation and we were headed north before I could say anything. I was cool with it. I'd never been to the Grand Canyon.

It started snowing somewhere in the mountains. Then it started *really* snowing. Brent was driving five miles an hour, his face glued to the windshield. It was really pretty, but I told him we should turn around. Brent agreed immediately. He didn't want to be the one to chicken out, but I could tell he was relieved at the suggestion. The road was too narrow for a U-turn and we couldn't see anything, so we drove to the nearest town. Strawberry. For real, that's what it's called.

So we're in Strawberry, Arizona, and we find the first parking lot big enough to turn the car in. We're about to head back when two Smokey cars pull right in front of us. I hear some crying and I turn to Heather to calm her down, but it's not her; she's sound asleep. I ask Brent if he's okay. He clears his throat a couple times and says he has allergies. A state trooper gets out of the car and straightens his collar to hide his face from the snow.

—What can I do for you, Officer?

If you'd asked me what the Chain Act was a day ago, I'd have guessed a state law from 1864 paving the way for the Thirteenth Amendment. Maybe something to limit the number of Woolworth stores they could open in one city. Anything but a law that says you can't drive your car without actual fucking chains on the tires. As luck would have it, our car was already in the parking lot of the only restaurant/bar/hotel on the main road. I woke Heather up. We all got out of the Chevelle wearing flip-flops and ran inside. I told Michelle—superfriendly waitress—we only had two dollars and sixty cents to our name. She sat us down and brought us back three bowls of hot soup, a basket of biscuits, and a bill, for two dollars and sixty cents. That was nine hours ago, which may not seem that long, but a lot has happened since then. Like, a lot.

Really good soup, for starters. Halfway through the biscuits we realized the whole town was in our restaurant/bar/hotel, and staring at us. Just in time to see Brent turn into a hysterical four-year-old. He'd been trying to look cool in front of us this whole trip, but Heather and I had moved way down on his list of priorities, along with things like self-respect or dignity. He collapsed under our table in a sobbing heap. With Michelle's help, we managed to decipher a few things through the crying. There wasn't enough gas to get home. His dad would kill him for taking the Chevelle without permission. Something about crossing state lines with two minors. This snowstorm would never end and we'd all die here wearing flip-flops. Brent eventually curled into a ball on a bench by the pool table and Michelle found him a blanket so he'd stop shaking. She also let Heather use the phone to tell her mom she was staying at my house for the night. I called *my* mom and asked her to come get us. I think it was the soup that made me change my mind, or maybe I didn't *really* want to run away and live with Brent for the rest of my life.

Mom was angry. I knew she'd be angry, but she wasn't livid. I'm alive. No one died. I've never done anything like this, but our standards for what is considered bad are not like most people's. There's bad, and then there's *bad* bad. This fell into the first category and I figured she'd save the worst punishment for the second. She was *way* more angry when she got here. I forgot how much she hates driving.

I offered to pay for gas. I thought it would help my case. I'd made sixty bucks playing darts. I sucked at first; then I got sort of semiangry. It happened before. Happens a lot, actually, but I usually rein it in like Mom taught me to. I don't know if it's the cold, or how much of an asshole that guy was. I just stayed angry a little. I could hear his heart skip every time he missed. I could see the darts move in slow motion. The bull's-eye looked as big as a house. I'd have never guessed, but I'm really fucking good at throwing darts when I put my mind to it. Pete—that's the guy's name—wouldn't pay up at first, but the whole town stepped in, especially Thomas, who is Pete's girlfriend's older brother. Also works here. Ruth the mayor even apologized for him. "No Strawberry folk will stiff an eleven-year-old." These people live by a code.

Mom stayed in the car for a good ten minutes when she arrived. No way I was coming out. For one thing, I'd lost Heather. Last I saw her, she was making out with the town's only teenage boy. Mom had had seven hours to prepare whatever hell was coming my way. I had had seven hours to turn every single person in Strawberry on my side to soften the blow. Mom versus Town. We lost, of course, but the town did their best. They wouldn't let her drive without at least having a bowl of soup and some biscuits. It's *really* good soup. They told her I felt superbad for what I'd done, how I fixed the restaurant bathroom door handle all on my own with a fridge magnet. Ruth even gave Mom an official Strawberry hug. She might have been a little drunk by then.

We found Heather and the boy in a broom closet, so I think we're ready to go. Brent won't leave without the Chevelle. Mom insisted I give him my sixty bucks, right after she asked him what an eighteen-year-old man was doing all the way out here with eleven-year-old girls. The town agreed with her on that one. Mom had already called Brent's parents. I don't think we'll see him for a while. Still, with Heather in the car, and Brent bearing his share of the blame, I think I have a good chance of surviving the ride home.

# 21

## *Midnight at the Oasis*

It's so hot the air is wiggling, but I can see the Valley of the Kings. The traitors would have seen it, too. If my brother is right and they spent a century here, they could have stood in this very spot and stared across the Nile. Some of these tombs were a thousand years old already. Just as impressive, I guess. Old is old. Maybe not. I need to find some shade before I get heatstroke.

These gardens are stunning. It must cost a fortune to maintain. I'm amazed the plants even survive out here. Water lilies. Irises. Chrysanthemums. We tried planting some once, Mother and I. I don't think we watered them enough. Mandrakes! I'd never seen them up close. Their roots look like a tiny person. They were used in magic rituals because of it. Wow. When I heard "Winter Palace," I thought it was just a clever name for a hotel, but it *is* a palace, or at least it's meant to look like one. I wonder who—

—Sam!

Is that Uriel? I've never seen us with a full beard. It suits him well, I think. He looks more mature, less . . . Uriel. I'm not sure I could wear it that long, if that makes any sense.

—Good to see you, Brother. I said you didn't have to come all this way. I could have met you at the apartment.

—I'm sorry, what? What apartment?

—House? Whatever accommodation you found for us, Uriel. How are you not sweating, by the way?

—Oh, you mean this place.

—Winter Palace? This is where you live?

—Where *we* live. It's nice; you'll see.

—Oh, I'm certain it is, but it looks expensive.

—Yeah. Kind of.

—What did you do, Uriel? Did you rob a bank?

—No, nothing like that . . .

—Uriel?

— . . . Do you know Led Zeppelin?

—I don't see—

—They're a British band. I'm sure—

—I know who Led Zeppelin is, Uriel. I just fail to see what this has to do with—

—I took their money, some of it. . . . What?! You asked how we can afford this place. I robbed Led Zeppelin. That's how.

—You . . . How? At gunpoint?

—No! No one walks around with that kind of money. I emptied the safe-deposit boxes at the Drake Hotel. Theirs had like two hundred K in it.

— . . . Why did you rob the Drake Hotel?

—I went to buy some warm-weather clothes. I saw it on the way back.

—I meant why did you rob the place, not why you chose the Drake Hotel.

—Oh. Raph was gone and I needed money. For this, you know. Traveling money. I spent everything I had on clothes. These pants, right here! Nice, right? They dry so fast. And a hat. I have to show you the hat.

—We said we weren't going to kill anyone in New York. That way we can go back.

—And I didn't! I swear! Wait, did he die? If he did he must have had some preexisting condition or something. I didn't hit him that hard. Don't tell Raphael, okay?

—You haven't told him?

—Well, no. He hasn't shown up yet. I thought he was with you. Come! Let's have a drink. Wait till you see the pool.

I cannot say no to that. I will faint if I don't cool down. I gather Uriel hasn't found anything yet. Knowing him, he probably hasn't looked. It doesn't matter; we'll have plenty of time for research while we wait for Raphael.

I wonder how long we should wait. . . .

I found Mother in Prague right away. She lives above a small jazz club just off Charles Bridge. I walked to her door, stared at the bell for— I knew I wouldn't ring it, but part of me hoped she'd open the door while I hesitated. I rented a room at the inn across the street and watched her through the window. I watched her for hours. She seemed happy in her own quiet way. It hurt. I feel selfish for thinking it, but it did. I'd never seen her this way. She went to bed early. I stared at her dark window until . . .

It was always about her. That should have been obvious. My brothers knew; they had to. What were the odds she would pack her things and leave without word, on *that* day? They knew I told her. This . . . charade—"we have to make a quick stop in Prague"—was just to remind me of who's in charge. It was me who made them kill Father. They knew why. I didn't *trick* them into anything. Manipulated, yes, only because they let me. They were waiting for it.

I saw his silhouette just before sunrise, my own shadow stretching across the street. He must have come straight from the airport. No shower, no nap. Straight to business. Typical Raphael. He stopped a few feet from her door. Then he heard people in the distance. Drunken laughter. He recognized them cussing without knowing the language. "You! Can you spare some change?" one of them said. Raphael dug a few bills out of his wallet. He was always generous with his money. He didn't see the knife, not until it had gone in a few times. They were long gone by the time he realized the damage they'd done. Raph didn't cry for help. That's not his style. He leaned against the wall and waited. It took about five minutes until his legs gave up on him. He just sat on the sidewalk holding his empty wallet. Then, he smiled. Big, heartfelt grin. He'd have burst into laughter if his body had let him. Yes, Brother, it was always about her.

I feel guilty. It doesn't change anything, but I do feel guilty. I didn't with Father. I don't know why. In most ways this was no different. Raphael was just as bad, but he loved us, Uriel and me. He got between Father's hand and my face more than once, paid a hefty price for it every time. Maybe that's why I couldn't kill him myself. In the end, it doesn't matter. There are plenty of us left alive.

# ENTR'ACTE

## *Scenes That Are Brightest*

### 1844

It had rained that morning. Emily feared she could see nothing but gray, but the clouds had vanished just after dinner and the night sky was as clear as it had ever been. Emily stared at the heavens waiting for Venus to appear where her math said it would. She felt certain of her calculations, but each tick of the watch nibbled at her conviction until she felt foolish for indulging in such a futile exercise. Other people had made those calculations before her and one could simply look at their published work to know where and when Venus would be seen. She was searching for something that was already found, discovering the known instead of the unknown.

For most of her adult life, the Ninety-Six had pondered the nature of knowledge. Five plus five equals ten. Every particle attracts every other particle in the universe. A planet would soon traverse the heavens before continuing on its merry dance with the sun. These were some of the things Emily knew. That knowledge, *her* knowledge, was based on that of others: Kepler, Newton, who themselves used knowledge other people possessed, and so on. The equations in her notebooks were hers, but, in many ways, they also belonged to Galileo, to the Sumerians, who developed the first counting system.

Two thousand years before Emily was born, a man named Aristarchus of Samos *knew* the Earth and planets spun around the sun. Or did he? Did he suspect? Suppose? Surmise? Knowledge takes many forms, some more resilient than others. Aristarchus published his work—it even received the attention of Archimedes—but it was the knowledge of Aristotle, that of Ptolemy, that survived the passage of time. For another eighteen hundred years, most people *knew* our planet was the center of the universe and everything else spun around *it*. Did they know it any less? However imperfect, that *knowledge* led to more knowledge, and some of it would hold long after Copernicus came along and made the world know a different truth.

Through it all, Venus kept on spinning. It cared not for Aristarchus any more than it did for Aristotle, and tonight it would appear on the horizon when it was time for it to do so. Emily's calculations had absolutely nothing to do with it. Nothing she knew could make it appear sooner. The rules told Emily to preserve the knowledge, but what was it, exactly, that she was meant to care for?

When Venus peeked its head over Memorial Court, Emily allowed herself a fleeting grin. She stared at the slow-moving dot, her mind wandering somewhere along its path.

—You were looking for Venus, were you not?

— . . .

The words were enough to disturb Emily's train of thought, but not enough to get her full attention. The voice belonged to John Couch Adams, a lanky undergraduate who, despite being admitted as a sizar, was as sure of himself as Cambridge permitted young men to be. Women, of course, were not admitted, but Emily liked strolling around campus. So many brilliant minds concentrated in so little space. It sent out an energy that gave her thoughts more clarity. That was something she felt, not something she knew.

—If you want to see Mars, it is hiding behind King's College Chapel.

Emily did not care much for people, but even on Cambridge grounds, knowledge of, even remote interest in, celestial bodies was thinly dispersed. She introduced herself and agreed to a stroll along the River Cam. Both quickly realized they had found a kindred spirit. When they stopped to rest on a lonely bench, John took out a notebook full of barely legible equations. He almost cried when Emily recognized them for what they were. John's obsession was Uranus. For all the progress that had been made, even the latest tables on the position of planets erred slightly when it came to the last known planet. Perturbations in its orbit resisted an explanation. Those perturbations, John was convinced, were caused by an unknown object. Something big. A planet.

The thought of discovering an entire world filled Emily with unbridled excitement. She offered her help and urged John to obtain the latest data on the rebellious planet. While confident enough to approach a lady on college grounds, John could not imagine astronomers of renown being interested in the mathematical ramblings of an undergraduate. It was only after Emily threatened never to see him again that he reluctantly asked George Airy, Cambridge professor and Astronomer Royal, for the latest data on Uranus.

Every day after class, Emily and John broke new mathematical ground over high tea. Newton's laws of gravitation had been used to describe the effect planets have on one another based on their mass and position. Emily and John turned the formulas on their head, attempting to predict a planet's mass and location based on the effect it had on another. Poetry, by any standard, using words in ways they were not intended to be used.

John, true to self, refused to share their predictions with anyone and, this time, no amount of threat could make him yield. He suspected nothing when Emily agreed to visit his home in Cornwall in September of '45. It was only when she made him stop by George Airy's home on the way back that he understood he had been played. Unfortunately, Emily's ruse failed, as the Astronomer Royal was in France at the time. A month later, they visited Airy again. He was absent, again, but this time they left behind a manuscript of their predictions for the new planet. Airy would later write asking for clarifications, but John did not reply, nor did he tell Emily of the letter. Adams chose, instead, to search for the planet himself.

Neither John Couch Adams nor the Ninety-Six would discover the planet Neptune.

Knowledge is like spring, Emily's mother once told her. It will surely arrive, but it will do so in its own time. Unbeknownst to Emily and John, Urbain Le Verrier, a French astronomer, had made the same hypothesis concerning the orbit of Uranus and come to similar conclusions. Le Verrier's predictions made their way to George Airy, who immediately realized they matched what John Couch Adams had left him. At Airy's request, the director of the Cambridge observatory searched for the planet in its predicted location. He even observed it on August 4 and 12, 1846, but mistook it for another star. He would not discover Neptune either.

Around the same time, Le Verrier sent his predictions for the location of the new planet to a German astronomer by the name of Galle. It took Galle less than thirty minutes to find what he was looking for. On September 23, 1846, Johann Gottfried Galle became the first person to look at the planet Neptune and know what he was looking at. Two days later, Galle wrote to Le Verrier. The letter said: "Monsieur, the planet of which you indicated the position really exists."

Knowledge is like spring. It arrives in its own time.

# ACT III

# 22

## *The Passenger*

"Everything is proceeding right on time," said the voice in the speakers as people scurried around like ants in preparation for countdown.

The probe stood atop its launch vehicle, impervious to the dangers ahead, or the fact that, despite launching first, its creators had labeled it with an inglorious "2." The machine had no fear, no pride to wound. It did not care that the press only spoke of the gold-plated record it carried. It also had no recollection of the double computer failure it suffered earlier that day. Every human in the control room wished they could perform with the same detachment. A decade of their lives was sitting on top of that rocket. This was more than a machine; it was myriad intimate triumphs and failures, an assemblage of daring dreams. With any luck, it would carry those dreams where no thing had gone before. Today was the day of the voyage, and *it* was the *Voyager.*

The rocket began to growl as the numbers got smaller and smaller. Soon there were no numbers left, and the *Titan's* engines roared like thunder. Hands and knees trembled in the control room as the rocket left the ground. After 117 seconds, the Titan III-E jettisoned its boosters, but the trembling didn't stop. The rocket was shaking, pitching, rolling. Onboard instruments told the robot something terrible had happened as it swayed in the darkness inside its Centaur upper stage, but *Voyager* was not in control. It was only a passenger.

Entire minutes passed. Aeons for all concerned. When the rocket's final stage separated, Voyager's systems told it the rocket separated too soon. The robot switched its altitude control to a backup system, assuming it was the one malfunctioning. When that failed, it tried another system, and another. Something was wrong, or so said every sensor. What exactly that was, it did not know.

Robots do not panic; they experience an unspecified low-level error their operating system isn't equipped to handle. *Voyager* turned everything on and off, its program desperate for the numbers in its brain to make sense. Commands came in through the robot's antennae, but the robot had long stopped listening. This was mutiny.

The upper stage finally shut off and set the robot free. The trembling stopped. *Voyager* was now traveling alone in the vastness of space, but it was derelict, having shut down half of itself while it probed the other half for answers. After a few billion attempts, the probe did what it was programmed to do when all else fails: it repositioned its high-gain antenna towards Earth and waited.

Critical failure. *Voyager* would reach the same conclusion every eight milliseconds for the rest of its battery life. It would do so two hundred trillion times before the plutonium-238 it carried decayed enough for power to run out.

Out of the darkness, a signal. A deluge of ones and zeroes rushed through the robot's brain, rewriting its program. Reboot.

*Voyager* turned itself on again and checked its status. The robot was ready. It would perform its duty with the exactness and detachment ascribed only to its kind. All on Earth breathed a sigh of relief, for their dreams were still alive. *Voyager* 2 was en route to Jupiter.

# 23

## *Sweet Emotion*

—Slow down, Mom! You almost ran that woman over!

—SORRY! I love this song. Best rock-and-roll song ever. Well, maybe not ever. Come on, Lola, sing with me!

—I hate that song.

—No, you don't. You only think you do.

—What does that even mean?

—You know what it means. I see you tapping your foot. I bet you didn't notice you were doing it. . . . Here we go! You're ready? Sweeeeeeeeeeeeeeeeee—

—MOM!

—eet emoooootion. Sing with your mom. Sweeeeeeeeeeee-eeeet—

—Emooootion.

—That's my girl.

—We're here, Mom. Turn it down! Turn it down!

—What? What's wrong? Ashamed of your mother? I'm fifty-two, Lola, not one hundred. I'm still cool!

—I'm fifteen and my mom still drops me off at school. You know what I mean? That's not exactly ringin'. Oh, almost forgot. I'm going to H's tonight.

—To do what?

—Just chillin'.

—Well, you've got to come home first. You have some approach vectors to calculate, young lady.

—Why?

—What do you mean why? You know why. In case there are more problems with the probes. Maybe we can help.

—They don't need our help, Mom. They did it. They launched *Voyager 2*, and they did it without us. We had nothing to do with it. Nothing. *You* had nothing to do with it.

—Watch your tone, Lola. And yes, they got this far on their own, but things go wrong. They ran into trouble on their first day! The second stage separated early. If it weren't for the Centaur figuring it out and burning longer, *Voyager* would have been lost. Not to mention the probe went on the fritz before it even cleared orbit.

—Are you saying you worked on the exact thing that saved *Voyager 2*?

—No. I helped with the *Centaur's* guidance computer. It could have made a difference.

—But it didn't. Whatever went wrong, they fixed it, Mom. *They* did. They also ran a test flight for their "reusable" space plane. They do what they want, Mom. We're . . . useless. If you want us to work on something, we should work on the next probe, not the one that's already out there.

—Fine. Then work on that.

—I . . .

—I what?

—I started doing the math on something. An engine. It's electric.

—Moving charged atoms with a magnetic field?

—Yeah, kind of like socks pushing each other when they come out of the dryer. I got the idea from your friend, von Braun.

—He's not my friend.

—Whatever. He said: he wouldn't be a bit surprised if we flew to Mars electrically.

—He was talking about the work of his mentor, Oberth. You

know they actually *built* ion engines. The US tested two of them in low orbit when you were a baby. The Russians even have a handful of satellites that use ion thrusters for stabilization.

—I know, but obviously they're not that good or they wouldn't have strapped a gas tank onto the *Voyager* probes. Going really far is exactly what these engines are supposed to be good at.

—Then make a better one.

—Mom, it's just scribbles in a notebook. I'm not going to actually build the thing.

—How about we buy you a computer? Would that help? We can go to RadioShack on Saturday.

—You're serious? That would be so cool! And so much faster. Maybe I can make it work, my engine. Will you help?

—Of course! You see, we're not useless after all. And you still have to come home. You haven't cleaned your room in a month. Your grandmother's friend sent another picture of that bow, by the way.

—Again? I bet we can't see anything new on that one either. Who takes a dozen pictures of something, all from the same side?

—These are just the ones he could find, but we *can* see a bit more of the inside edge on this one. We can translate it together if you want.

—Sure, Mom. Can I go now?

—You come home right after school.

—All right! All right! See ya!

—Later, gator.

 . . . Useless. Ha! I'm not useless! I'm . . . behind, ever so slightly. Things are moving fast. Six years on an island is an eternity nowadays. I think it's a good sign. Besides, we might not have done much ourselves, but our money sure did. Mother would have been mad. Spending this much money on a semiconductor company. She didn't want to be the one to dilapidate what others spent a hundred lifetimes accumulating. In all fairness, there wasn't much to spend it on until now. Most of our expenses were bribes or endowments for professorships in the name of wealthy families that never existed. It didn't even make a dent in the interest we made. Now that women can teach, we don't even need the puppets, though I still prefer to let others put their names on things. The smaller our footprint, the easier it is to move on. Ironically, every dime I spent is bringing in a hundred times more. I don't really care about the money, but our interests now seem to align with everyone's when it comes to computers. More profit to be made means more people doing the work, and Lola is right about one thing. When they put their collective minds to it, people can move a lot faster than we can.

And I did *something*. Well, I don't know how much I helped, but that paper on the ozone layer made a splash. They're sending a satellite up next year to measure it from above. We'll know a lot more soon. We'll know a lot more about a lot of things, and Lola will be around for all of it. I envy her.

I'm also scared for her. She's going through those years where we think we're not us. I know because I've gone through it. She is me. But things are different now; at least I think they are. The war had just started when I was Lola's age. We learned the jitterbug, went to the drive-in. We hung out at the soda shop. We didn't drink, didn't do drugs. We didn't have sex until . . . Let's just say I was a late bloomer. I think my mother had a lot more fun than I did. Whatever she's going through, Lola's more rebellious than I ever was. More stubborn, too. She won't budge an inch. Then again, maybe she's exactly as I was and it's me who's getting old.

# 24

## *Sound and Vision*

—Lola, when's the last time you wore shoes?

— . . .

We're translating more of what's on that bow, but all I see are Lola's black feet swinging to whatever song is playing in her head. Something upbeat, judging by the foot speed. Maybe her mood's improving.

—Lola?

She can't hear me. I used to be like that. If I focused on anything, a book, even a thought, I'd get into that weird headspace. A million miles from the rest of the world. I was like that with Billie. I'd lie with her and stare at the back of her neck until she pinched me. "Of course I've been listening," I'd say. She let me get away with it. God knows for how long she'd been talking, but she always let it slide.

—I found it, Mom. *Samāne*. Sa-maaa-nay. I don't know how to pronounce it, but it means eight. Do we have it all now?

—Yes, we do. You're ready? This is what it says.

"I am eight. I am one and many.

Perhaps you are also me."

—That's it?

—Well, yes. It's just one line. We'd need more pictures if we want the whole thing.

—Wow.

—What do you mean, wow?

—I mean, there's a whole day of my life I'm never getting back.

—Lola, you don't understand. This is . . . This is extraordinary!

—My mistake. There's an extraordinary day I'm never getting back. I'm going to watch some TV now. I am the Hundred and One and I will watch TV. Perhaps later on, you will join me.

—She was the Eight, Lola! The Eight!

—And?

—You know how you keep saying you feel lost, not knowing who you are or why we're doing all this? I always give you the same answer.

—We're the—

—Not that. I tell you that you're not alone, that we all felt that way. Well, that's a lie, because she didn't. As far as we know, her granddaughter is the one who lost the knowledge. But she knew, probably. There's a good chance the woman who carved that bow knew who exactly who she was and where she came from. Close your eyes.

—Why?

—Close your eyes. You're all alone in a barren field. The heat is pressing on you like a ton of bricks. You look around. You can't see her yet, but if you listen carefully you'll know she's coming. You can hear the hooves of her horse stomping the ground in the distance. The sound gets louder and louder. You try to look up, but the sun is behind her. She gets closer. It was too bright a second ago, but you can see her now. Dark hair blowing across her face, her skin and will hardened by the elements. She stops, right in front of you. It takes nerve just to meet her gaze. Her brown eyes pierce into your soul, and yours into hers. The rush hits you like a freight train, and for an instant you understand.

Her horse nickers, restless. She keeps reining it in until she finally lets it run wild. The feeling leaves with her, nearly tears your heart out. You try to catch her. You know you won't, but you try anyway, until your lungs give out and your legs fold like paper. You watch as she rides hard into the steppes and fades into the horizon.

And when she's gone, all you want is to feel that strength again. You'd do anything for one more second of it. You try to hold on to the memory, to remember the completeness you felt when you held the knowledge you and I have been missing all our lives. You feel it disappear like sand running through your hands until you're not sure any of it was ever real.

Do you get it? She knew, Lola. She was the Eight and she knew everything! She knew about the One.

—And wetness.

—Oh, for fuck's sake. All right, you're in a bad mood. Go watch some TV. We can talk about this when you're done pouting.

—Pouting?

—Take a look in the mirror. Muh, muh, muh. Pouting. And wash your feet, will you?

—My feet?

—I don't understand you, Lola. You were hoping for something life-changing when you first heard of that bow. Well, this is it. This is as close as you get.

—It's a fucking poem, Mom. It doesn't change anything.

—Watch your tongue, Lola.

—You said "fuck" not five seconds ago.

—I said "for f"— Never mind. I thought you'd be—I don't know—interested, excited, something.

—Why? So she was a single-digit Kibsu. Good for her. But I'm not. I'm me. And I still don't know shit. I'll still get up tomorrow, go to that stupid school, and pretend I'm like them. And it won't work because I'm not. They might all suck at math, but they're smart enough to know I'm different, Mom. They all are.

—I'm sorry. I'm really sorry you see it this way. We all have to do things we'd rather not do.

—Do we? I mean, I could just . . . not go.

—No, Lola. You couldn't.

—Fine. I'm leaving now. We're watching a movie at Brent's. I told Heather I'd pick her up.

—After you finish your homework.

—I'll do it tomorrow.

—No, Lola. Now.

—Why? What difference does it make? Why do you get to decide?

—Because we're the One Hundred. When you're the Hundred and One, you can do whatever you want.

—Then maybe I should just get pregnant. There can never be three for too long.

# 25

## *(Don't Fear) the Reaper*

I probably have a few years before she says it and means it, but that time will come, sooner or later. Mother was three years older than I am when she died. I'm fifty-two. *Fifty-two.* That's like a hundred in Kibsu years. It sounds surreal when I hear myself say it. I don't know how old I see myself as, but I know it's not that. I'm a mother, but I'm still the child in more ways than one. The Ninety-Nine never truly went away. I'm still thirty-five, watching my mother die. I'm twenty-four, mourning my unborn daughter, saying goodbye to Billie for the last time. I'm twenty years old, sitting in that truck with Wernher von Braun. I'm ten, sneaking into Mother's bed because I'm having nightmares, seven, holding my grandma's hand when we got on that boat. I guess that will never change. Soon I'll be the grandmother, the mother, the daughter. We are many. I suppose that's true of everyone, not just us.

I should be upset, angry. I'm not. That's for Lola to feel. It's her anger. I won't take it from her. I get to feel something else, something like self-doubt, only not quite. It's not helplessness either. I don't know if there's a name for it. It's the absolute certainty that you are doing everything you can, but that it may not be enough. I *do* know what it's called now that I think about it. It's motherhood. I watch my daughter hurting—a slow, nagging hurt that makes the world look dull, pointless—and I can't do a thing about it. I felt something like that once, but that was *my* feeling. I can't experience hers, nor can I really understand it. I'll never know how someone else experiences cauliflower, a headache, hot sand under their feet. You think it would be different with us, but it's not. I haven't the faintest clue. I haven't lived Lola's life. I was there, that's all. I trust that if I had lived her life, I'd be just as angry with the world as she is. And right now, I'd be feeling like an ass for what I said. . . .

I hope she's feeling it, thoroughly.

I *might* be angry a little. I'd be a lot more angry if my mind weren't busy with something else. Lola was obsessed with the carvings on that bow. I told her it was a bad idea to put this much hope into anything, but she didn't listen, and she got hurt. Now she couldn't care less. It's me who can't stop thinking about it. I'm setting myself up for disappointment just like she was, obviously, but I can't help it. I want to know. I want to know the Eight. I want to know how she felt, how it felt being her. I want to know how different that was from being me. Someone left a puzzle box on my doorstep. I can't just leave it alone.

We carved that bow; that's what is driving me mad. It should make sense to me. It's *my* bow, except it's not. I can hear the words in my head. She says them with my voice. "I am eight. I am . . ." *I* is her talking. But who is *she*? From the underworld, she emerges in wetness. *She*, not *I*. That's someone else but who? Someone dead, or sleeping, or in a coma. A wet coma . . . Dead in the water. Ba dum tsss. Come on, Mia, you can figure this out.

A fallen Kibsu, a lost lover. She could be talking about virtually anyone, even her own daughter. Whoever "she" is mattered to the Eight, that much is clear, but I know absolutely nothing of her life. I don't know what mattered to anyone then, let alone to her. There might be more clues at the burial site. More writings, drawings, bodies. Maybe "she" is lying next to the Eight for eternity.

I touch her elbow, then her mouth. She speaks after a cold silence. Is that the same "she"? You would think so. A cold silence, the underworld. She's talking about someone dead, someone who's been dead for a long time, but now speaks. A zombie. This is about zombies, and desire. Let's not forget desire. Sex and necromancy. You do you, I guess. It was three thousand years ago; maybe that's how they rolled.

This is pointless. I need a bath; my head's about to explode.

Ewww. That bath needs a good scrub. Not today. I'll just add bubbles and pretend I can't see that big line of soap scum. That's probably what I hate most about growing up. All the small things you realize don't happen magically. Clean clothes, a spotless bath. It's a wonder Mother found time for research after all this. I wish she were still with us. That bow was just her kind of thing. She was great at riddles, and baths. Mother loved to take baths. She'd take three a day when she could. I think she was hiding from me. Thirty minutes of solitude. She always said she liked running her bath more than taking it, that the water was talking to her. It sounded really profound to five-year-old me. I think she liked that it was loud enough to mute everything else, including my nagging high-pitched voice. She had a point, though. There's something soothing about running water.

Maybe she used that time to think about that project with Xuesen. Boundaries in Iraq and their Berlin friends, whatever that means. I don't know why it still bothers me, but—

AAAAH! This water's freezing! This isn't one of Lola's thirty-minute showers. Her feet looked like she worked in a coal mine when she left. No bath for me, I guess, unless they can install a new water heater the same day. I'm not getting that thing fixed again. It's way past its expiration date. Kind of like me, soon. Ha! I'm telling dead jokes to myself now. Bad ones at that.

Am I afraid of dying? Is that it? I used to be. I haven't given it much thought since Lola was born. I save my fears for her. I never thought I would live forever, I know that. I could just lie in that bathtub if that's what I wanted. I can see the headline: "Body Found in Freezing Water, Preserved for 3 Million Years."

Freezing . . .

A cold silence. Her elbow, her mouth.

Fuck me. I need to find Lola. She said something about a movie.

# 26

*Marquee Moon*

I didn't tell Uriel I killed a man today. I don't know his name. I'd seen him before, in bars, in restaurants all over town. I'd seen him at our hotel. He seemed to know everyone no matter where he went. A *respected* man. They call him Baba, Father. When I asked what he did I was told he did favors for people. A gun here, a passport there, but mostly Baba procured young boys for rich old men. He was a monster. He deserved it. I have been repeating those words to myself all day. I killed him because he was a bad man.

Uriel and I were having tea on the terrace this morning. Baba arrived a few minutes after we did. As soon as he sat down, a little boy—he could not have been more than five—walked up to him. Baba dug into his satchel and handed the boy . . . something. Candy, a few piastres. I couldn't see. I only saw the boy running away smiling. Uriel had already gone. He likes his tea scalding hot. Baba left before mine was cool enough to drink. I saw him again an hour later in the passageway behind the apothecary. It was once an alley, but every building encroached on it over time. What remains is barely wide enough for one man to zigzag his way through. I leaned sideways against the wall to let Baba pass. I felt the wetness of my shirt when his chest brushed against mine. His breath reeked of *shisha*, though I could still smell the mint from his morning tea. He was about to apologize when I saw my hands wrapped around his throat. There was no room for him to struggle or even lift his arms. He lost consciousness after a few seconds and I kept pressure for a minute or two before I stepped to the side and let his body fall. I remember thinking I would have to change shirts because mine was now soaking wet from rubbing against him.

I might have let someone else pass through—he was not the most sympathetic figure—but I know it was not a sense of justice that made me do it. It was the heat. I leave our hotel room early, hoping for a morning breeze, but there isn't one. There never is. It's too hot at eight o'clock in the morning, too hot at ten, at noon, at three. Even the pool is warm; it feels like stepping into soup. I wash my hands fifty times a day, but they are always moist. I can't even stand my own hands; they disgust me. Everything does. Chairs too hot to sit on, drinks that taste like melted ice. The heat won. I capitulated. It wasn't rage. I did not hear the voice. I did not see myself dismembering him or feeding him his privates. Call it a heartfelt annoyance at the world. I didn't feel remorse. That's not entirely true. I felt guilty for letting Mother down. She would be ashamed if she knew.

What's done is done, I told myself. I went back to the hotel and changed. It was eleven thirty. I wasn't hungry, so I took a cab to the museum. I still had five hours to dig through the archives and saw no sense in letting the incident ruin the entire day.

Uriel and I had found nothing in the three months we'd been here. That afternoon in the archives was no different. Ironically, our first clue had been staring me in the face the whole time. I walked by it twice every day, on my way in and on my way out. Second stairwell to the basement, alone on an otherwise barren wall.

*The Priestess*. Wax painting on limewood. Unknown artist,

circa 500 BC. There she was. The great Mer-Neith-it-es standing in front of a captivated crowd, hands hovering above a metal orb the size of a hubcap. We were right to come here. For all we knew, we had been chasing a dream for three thousand years. We caught up to our prey before, but this is the first time we have ever seen the sphere. It exists, and if my feeling is right, she will tell us where to find it.

Whoever painted this was awed by her. He made her three feet taller than everyone else. A gross exaggeration, but I have no trouble believing she stood tall, proud. She didn't cower and run. She didn't hide what we were hunting them for. She put it on a pedestal, right in the middle of the temple for all to see.

She wasn't afraid of us.

I would not be surprised if her entire life had been meticulously crafted with us in mind. She ascended to a position of power, advising pharaohs. She spent her days in a public place, guarded by soldiers she could no doubt command. Like a spider casting her net, she was daring us to come after her.

The more I learn about the traitor, the more I want to know them. I see now they have more depth than the shallow creatures we've always painted them as. My uncle talked to one of them, but he had her tied up. That's not entirely conducive to an honest discussion. I would like to sit with them over tea. Even if we manage to find the sphere on our own, there is so much we can learn from them, so much they can teach us before we kill them all.

The sun is about to set, but I am sweating just the same. The buildings, the streets, every piece of rock or concrete soaks up the heat, so it never lets down. I don't know how people stand it. Look at them. Happy couples dressed sharply for an evening in town. This one is wearing a suit. Buttoned-up shirt and tie.

How is he not drenched? And what has he got to be so happy about? I need to hide in the air conditioning. I am getting irritable again.

I turned twenty today. Why does it feel like a hundred?

# 27

## *White Rabbit*

It must be getting late. There's a clock in the kitchen. Shit, it's past midnight already. How can that be? We were just talking. Talkin'. Chillin'. Drinkin'. Rhymin'. Maybe I shouldn't have had that last drink. Time to be responsible, Lola. Or . . . I can have one more. No, I need to go. Mom'll be worried sick. She'll be— She'll be fucking pissed, and worried. I shouldn't have said it. I was just angry. She knows that. Right? Right? She has to. Maybe she still needs some time. I can hang a little longer. Chicken. No shit, I don't think I can face her right now.

I don't know why I got mad. It's that stupid bow. "I am eight." So what? Go back to where you came from, with your elbow fetish and your cold silence. You're dead; leave me alone. As if she could help me. Writing weird sex stuff on her hunting weapon, I'm gonna take a wild guess and say her life wasn't all that peachy. I bet she chewed the fuck out of her nails.

Of course, Mom's all psyched about the whole thing. Figures. She makes me so— AAAAAGH! "What are the rules? Tell me what the rules are, Lola!" It's . . . too much, or too little. Whatever it is, it's not for me. Don't draw attention to yourself. I *wish.* My whole life I don't think anyone's really noticed me. I might as well not exist at that school. Preserve the knowledge. What knowledge? I don't know shit! I have *no clue.* Those rules, they're for her, not me. I'm not her. I have absolutely no idea who I am, but I'm not her. I'm something else.

—Hey, Lola! Did it kick in yet?

—What? Did what kick in?

What did they give me? I didn't ask. I just took it. Be there or be square. Everyone thinks I'm this huge dork. Even my friends. I'm the weird girl who's good at math. They're all smiles, but I think they're making fun of me. They're all laughing. Why are they laughing?

—Here. Have a drink.

I'm not supposed to drink. Another rule. Rules. Rules. Rules. Well, fuck the rules. I can have some fun. Oooh, this one's fizzy. It tastes just like cherry cola. I feel the tiny bubbles bursting on my tongue. Thousands of them distinctly screaming while they die. Pfff. Aaaaah! Pfff. Aaaaah! I can almost count them. Maybe I can. One two three— I—

I'm in the kitchen. Again. It feels smaller, somehow. Maybe there are more people. Brent sure has a lot of friends. By "friends," I mean people willing to raid his parents' bar. I shouldn't judge. I don't have that many friends. We don't have a bar. Maybe it's the room. It feels . . . small—

A mirror.

The room looks bigger on the other side. Whoa. It's like the real world's shrinking, but the mirror world is the same. I'm the same. I'm not shrinking. I'm . . . reversed, though. My right hand is mirror me's left hand. Her right hand is my left. She's staring at me. I'm staring back. There are two versions of me observing each other. We're the same, but we're different. It's like Mom and me. Mom's like the mirror, except her hands aren't reversed. At least I don't think they are.

—Are you okay, Lola? You're maintaining or what?

— . . .

My right hand is mirror me's left hand. What if I turn around? I can't see myself in the mirror anymore. My hand is . . . I can't tell without looking, but if I look . . . It's like Schrödinger's cat.

Maybe if I look in the mirror with another mirror, then my right hand . . .

—Lola!

— . . .

Shit, it's not the mirror. My right thumb points left and my left thumb points right. My hands are mirror images of each other in the *real world*. I love this. This is awesome. Commutativity. I'm—

—LOLA!

—What? Come here, give me a hug.

—Wait! STOP! Stop! You're too strong! I'm not the world's most physical guy, but damn!

—Can I see your hands?

—Oh, Lola. You're tripping.

—Tripping, why? What did you give me?

—Lucy.

—Who?

—In the sky, with diamonds.

—I don't . . . Just give me your hands, okay? Something I gotta see.

Mirror hands. If I put mine out, it's like two mirrors at a right angle now. Four hands, all reflections of each other. Left is right. Right is left.

—Can I go now, Lola?

Go where? Why am I in the kitchen again? I was just here. Why do I keep coming back? Oh, I found my drink! I'm not sure how long it's been sitting here, but it's still fizzy. How's that possible? All the little bubbles are bursting on the surface. It should run out. It should be flat by now. Unless there's something at the bottom making more. More bubbles, always more.

—Brent, what'd you put in my drink?

—What? Too much rum?

Rum doesn't make bubbles. Why would he say that? I— I was

going to say something. I forgot. I wonder what time it is. . . . Oh shit. Mom's going to throw a fit. I don't want to go home, though. I can't face her right now. Well, I definitely can't face her *now*, but even if I were sober, how do you apologize for saying something like that? She wouldn't have said it. She's heavy sometimes, but she's never mean. *I'm* the jerk. We're not the same. There's something wrong with me. Something ugly inside. If people saw— If my friends saw . . . Maybe they do. Maybe that's why they're all laughing.

I should book; I'm not feeling so well. It's probably past midnight anyway. Why am I still in the kitchen? I keep trying to leave, but I end up back here every time. Why can't I leave the fucking kitchen?! This is all wrong. Everyone's walking past like they can't see me. I can't leave. I can't— Shit. I think the walls are . . . breathing.

# 28

## *Lola*

I see my reflection in the kitchen mirror. There's a katana on the wall behind me. Mirror katana. What's katana backwards? An . . . atak. Whoa. . . . But from whom? From where? I know everyone here, but it's still not safe. I'm in danger, even among my friends.

Are they, though? My friends? Maybe they're just pretending. Maybe they're not real. They look like my friends, but their eyes . . . They're all empty. Vitreous. Fuck. I think it's a disguise. My friends aren't my friends and that's not their eyes. They're all wearing masks with fake fucking eyes. Who are they? I can't see. Their real selves are hiding, peeking through the hair on the back of their heads. They're demons. Evil.

They're the fucking Tracker.

*That's* why they're laughing. They brought me here to kill me. Twenty-five Trackers with their heads on backwards. I can't run. I can't hide. I'm sweating up a storm. I'm too scared to move, but me in the mirror isn't. She wants to fight. I can't. All I can do is watch her.

The katana.

Gravity shifts as I walk on the wall where the long blade hangs. I pick it up from what is now the floor. I draw, silently, careful not to slice through the wood of the sheath. The blade vibrates like a tuning fork. I feel its warm song spreading inside me. My hands, my arms, my chest.

The Tracker feels it, too. He turns his twenty-five masks away from me. They form a circle and stare through the backs of their heads. My move. I crouch. I *leap* off the wall, flying over their heads. Vertigo. My world makes a ninety-degree turn and I land on one knee, smack dab in the middle of them. My sword is now the dial of a giant clock. I strike at midnight.

The blade slides on the Tracker's neck. I should hit bone, but there's nothing there. His head falls, but the mask keeps staring. It smiles at me while ten of him grab me from behind. They grab my arms. My hands. I can't move. I turn up into down. I let my feet fall to the ceiling while they stand upside down over me. I swing from left to right and two of their heads drop high above mine.

I spin back to the floor and extend my right arm to the devil at three. The tip of the blade grazes his neck. He moves his hand up, feels the drop of blood on his Adam's apple. He opens his mouth to scream, but I can't hear a thing. They all scream in deafening silence. And they come for me

I pirouette, blade drawn. Faster. Faster. I draw ancient symbols with the tip of my blade. Body parts fly, spit through the mouth of my tornado. I add more steps to this ballet of death. Chassé, châiné, fouetté. Heads fall with each new French term. Attitude.

Full stop.

I look around. Only one of them stands. I bow to my enemy and throw the katana at his feet.

Wrist bent forward. Index finger drawn, thumb to the side. I am the weapon now. I am the praying mantis.

I watch myself star in my own B movie. Flashback. Exiled from my village, I am attacked by brigands. Left for dead in the woods, I watch the strange insect fight. I observe. I learn. Fast-forward. I return home with new skills and avenge my honor.

The Tracker strikes first. Sticky hands technique. I parry and lock his arm into my claw. Backhand to the neck. I release his arm and gouge his eyes out.

Side elbow to the solar plexus. Up elbow to the chin. Again. His feet lift off the floor with each blow. He tries to grab ahold of me, but I steal his magic and I turn into smoke. He stumbles forward, latching on to nothing, and I return to solid form behind him. I grab his hair and pull his head back. Front kick. I break him in half like a matchstick. I blow my nose and toss his limp body to the side.

I walk the kitchen floor to finish off the wounded. There aren't any. The Tracker's all dead. It's over now.

I was too scared to fight, I couldn't move, but my reflection killed them all. I'm still in the kitchen. We both are. She wipes at the blood on her face and turns towards me. Her gaze swallows me whole. I can still see her, but the blood on her face is gone. She's sitting in the kitchen with her friends. I think I crossed over.

I look down. I stand in a circle of his headless corpses. I pick up one head, push aside the hair on the back of it. I want to see the Tracker's face, but there is nothing there. Nothing. Just hair, and my friend staring at nothing on the other side. I look at all their faces. A friend. Another friend. Where's Heather? I need to find Heather. It was the Tracker. I swear it was, but now . . . What did she do? Did mirror me kill my friends?

Did I? I don't know which one I am anymore.

So much blood on the floor. Always more. I don't know where it's coming from. The blood's rising above my feet. It keeps rising, rising still. I climb on a corpse, on the table next to it. Only an inch of air left at the top. I tilt my head backwards, push my nose to the ceiling. Half an inch. I hold my breath and dive. Bodies floating in a sea of red. I don't know how much longer I can hold my breath. I want this to stop. I just need to look away from the mirror. It will all be over if I look away. My lungs are burning. I keep turning, but all I see are bodies. Why can't I look away from the mirror? I can't breathe. I want to get out! I WANT TO GET OUT OF THE FUCKING MIRROR!

# 29

*Psycho Killer*

My head, holy fuck. My mouth's so dry my lips are fused together. It's like I've been chewing on sawdust all night. Not sawdust, cat litter. That's what my mouth tastes like. I feel . . . like someone filled my skull with hot sauce before they kicked me in the face a hundred times. I'm dying. Someone make it stop.

Bright lights. Oh shit. Too bright! *Way* too bright! To hell with this, I'm just going to lie here with my eyes closed and wait to die. . . .

Where *is* here? I'm on a foam mattress. Thin. I can feel concrete underneath. This isn't home.

I guess I'll need to open one eye. Brick wall in front of me. Off-white. Another brick wall. A little sink. It looks like . . . No, please. Please, please, please. Tell me it isn't.

Metal bars. I'm in fucking jail.

What happened? There was a party. I know that. I don't remember leaving. I . . . I was upset. I said something mean before I left home. I had a drink or two, or three. What did I do?

—Helloooo!

God, that hurt. Like I woke up a thousand pissed-off bees in my brain with that one word. No more talking. There's no one here anyway. Two cells in a small room. The one next to mine is empty; so is the desk in the corner. I'm alone.

What did I do? I get angry sometimes, but I always rein it in. I do exactly what Mom showed me. What the fuck did I do to get here?

Keys ringing. Dead bolt sliding. Someone's here. It's . . . Mom?

And a cop.

—I don't want to hear one word coming out of you, Lola. Not one word.

—Okay.

No talking. I'm fine with that. I'm so glad to see her. I just want to sleep. She's mad, though. I knew she'd be mad yesterday, but now . . . I don't know. How mad is she? I can't tell if this is drunk and disorderly mad or something worse. Did Heather and I have a fight? Did I hurt her?

—Can I take her home now, Officer?

—Yes, please!

That's all I want. I get angry at Mom, but she's the only person I feel safe with. Please take me home. I want to go home.

[*In a minute, ma'am. We'll need a blood sample from her.*]

Shit. That's not good. No one can look at our blood. Not a rule, but Mom said we'd be lab rats for the rest of our lives if they did. That was good enough for me. I can say no, right? Religious grounds, something. I'm not talking. Mom will think of something.

—Is that really necessary, Officer? She really hates needles. She takes after me. I get woozy just talking about it. Besides, I think she's learned her lesson already.

[*I understand, ma'am. But there've been some bad drugs going around lately. I'll do it myself. She won't feel a thing, I promise. I just need to get the blood kit. I'll be right back.*]

—I'm sorry, Mom.

—Not a word, I told you. You just do as I say.

—What did I do? I don't even know why they arrested me.

—Arrest you? They didn't arrest you, Lola. You "surrendered" all on your own—your words. You walked through the front door, asked them to cuff you, then confessed to killing every person you knew, with a sword no less. Seventeen people, I think. You gave them a whole list of names.

—My friends. Did I—

—They're fine, no thanks to you. They said you were doing tai chi in the living room, some kind of dance, then you started screaming and ran out. Heather called me. She was worried sick about you. I think they all are.

—Oh God. Everyone at school will know. I don't think I can show my face again.

—Good. You won't have to. We're moving.

—Wha—

Oh shit, the cop's coming back.

[*Sorry to keep you waiting. I just need you to sign these forms and we—*]

—About that. You know she's a minor. Don't I need to consent before you can draw blood?

Consent. Right. I like that. I just want to get out of here.

[*I can get a* warrant *if you prefer, ma'am. It'll just be a lot faster if you give your—*]

—WHAT THE HELL, MOM!?

She threw a right hook at the cop's jaw. She punched his lights out! Like, Mom punched a cop! She's up on his desk now. What is she— Oh, she's pointing the camera at the other cell.

—Shut up, Lola.

—Mom . . . What are you doing?

—What does it look like I'm doing? I'm busting my daughter out of jail. Well, technically, this is processing, but let's not quibble over details, shall we?

— . . .

I just wanted to vent a little, have some fun. How did things get so messed up? Mom took the keychain from the cop's belt. She's opening my cell now. Holy shit. We're really doing this.

—Help me drag him in here, will you? Cuff him to the bars.

And . . . we're dragging a cop into a jail cell. I just wanted a good night's sleep. Some aspirin. Maybe she'd ground me for a week. Fine, I'll take a month. Now Mom's burning my file in the garbage bin while I handcuff an unconscious cop to a steel door. This isn't happening, is it?

—Mom, why do we have to move?

—You're asking me now?

—I mean before you punched a cop.

—Because you were high as a kite and you told your friends all sorts of crazy stories. You talked to the cops. Some of it they won't believe; some they might. Either way, I told you I'm done taking chances. This is drawing all sorts of attention. Oh, and I figured out what's on the bow.

I'm sorry I asked. This *is* a bad fucking dream. I'm fifteen. I don't bust out of police stations. I didn't even do anything. I steal candy sometimes, but fuck . . . I can't do this. I'm not sure if it's my head that will explode first or my heart, but— Oh crap.

— . . . I think I'm gonna throw up.

—Not now, Lola. Give me *one* more second. See if the cop has a dime in his pock— Never mind. I got one.

A dime? She's unscrewing the plate over the light switch. I think she wants to trip the breaker.

—Mom!

—Damn it! That stings! Pull the fire alarm, will you?

— . . .

Lights just went out. She's opening the door. I think we're making a run for it.

—LOLA! Fire alarm.

Right. The fire alarm. Let's make as much noise as we can.

—Got it. Oh shit, that's loud!

We're walking. I think we're in the lunchroom. Only about a thousand cops between us and the front door. Four of them heading for us right now.

—Now you can throw up. And scream "Tommy" as loud as you can while you're at it. Scream like you mean it.

What is she talking about? We're totally fucked. Don't think, Lola. Just do as Mom says.

—HHHHHLLLL . . . TOMMY! TOOOOMMMYYYYY!

—Officers, please! I can't find her little brother. He was back there when the fire started. Four years old. Blue overalls.

*[Just take her outside, ma'am. We'll find the boy.]*

I can't believe they went for it. We probably have a minute or two to get out before they find their friend chained to a cell.

*[Hey, wait! That's the girl who walked in stoned out of her wits and confessed to murder. Weren't you in a cell?]*

Or not. Fuck this. I'm done. I'm going to lie down, put my hands on my head, and wait for— WHOA!

Mom threw some sort of powder at them. She just fanned her arm like a fucking wizard! What's in her hand? I think it's the saltshaker. They're four *half-blind* cops now. I don't even think they know they're missing two of their sticks. God, she's fast. Baton swing at a pencil holder. Incoming red stapler. Coffee cup. Another salvo of blue ink pens. Oh shit. I'm throwing up again.

What's happ— Oh. That escalated quickly. An office chair kicked to the knees. Another one coming, but Mom is riding this one. Holy cow! The onslaught is on. Their guns are coming out, but not fast enough. Mom's chair is swiveling furiously. She's like a butterfly, a badass, a ninja, a wrathful butterfly. Batons and teeth flying everywhere. I'm getting dizzy just looking at it. I don't think I'm done puking.

I just wanted to blow off some steam. Have a few drinks. Maybe do the funky chicken. How the hell did we get to this? God, she's just whaling at them now. Foot sweep. Front kick. Front everything. That's my mom, for Christ's sake. She does math and bakes lasagna! Now she's a raging berserker with sticks for arms. Ewwww, that's gotta hurt.

I don't see anyone moving. Is she done? I think she's done.

—Mom?

—WHAT?

—Are they dead?

—I don't think so. Come on. Let's get out of here.

How is she so calm? I suppose my instincts would have kicked in if I weren't still half baked. I'm sweating like a pig, but I'm pretty sure it's just the hangover. I swear to God, I'm never having another drink in my life.

We're walking out the front door. Oh good. Our car's right here. . . . And we're gone. Just like that.

—What did you mean earlier? About the bow?

—Oh. It's not poetry she wrote on it; it's a map. The bow is a map.

— . . .

—What has elbows and a mouth and stops moving when it's really cold?

— . . .

—It's a river, Lola. It speaks after a cold silence. It's a river at springtime. She's going downstream. Her elbow, then her mouth. Whatever the river runs into, that's where she's going.

—Her breast?

—I didn't get that far. But these are instructions. She's telling us where to go.

—And where are we going?

—Russia. We're going to Russia.

—Now?

—No. We have to make a stop in Berlin first.

# ENTR'ACTE

## *Something in Your Teeth*

### 2014

Ania grabbed her third coffee of the day and ran up to the lab. She had high hopes for that one. A bit more caffeine and a triple dose of ibuprofen might do the trick. She scanned the faces of her colleagues. About half were sporting the same hangover. Today might not be the greatest day for science, she thought. Still, lessons were learned. Last night's data strongly supported several hypotheses. Vodka and Red Bull was for the young. Birthday parties should not be held on Thursdays. She crossed her fingers hoping her advisor wouldn't come. Her headache didn't show, but the lab smelled like a frat house on Sunday. It was a fun night, though. Theirs was a close-knit group. They would say it made them more efficient, hangover or not. It certainly made staying late or coming in on weekends feel like less of a chore.

Despite the godlike powers of ibuprofen, today would be a tedious day. Every science project is one part exciting brain prowess, nine parts boring clerical work. Logging, labeling, yawning. Ania always saved the true boring for Friday. She was in the middle of an Excel-induced trance when Adison tapped her shoulder.

—Ania, there's something in her teeth.

— . . .

—Something blue.

Ania made a face. The one her friends always laughed about.

Half-puzzled, half-annoyed. Eyebrows seemingly moving of their own volition. Something in her teeth was exactly what Ania was expecting. Something blue was most certainly not.

The teeth in question belonged to individual B77, an otherwise unexceptional woman who lived approximately a thousand years before her skull and femur were unearthed in a small German town. Ania, Adison, et al were looking at old teeth, searching for living things preserved through time. Like the Jurassic Park mosquito stuck in tree sap, only the mosquito was bacteria and the tree sap was dental plaque. The icky stuff on our teeth is full of living things, some good, some bad, and when plaque hardens into tartar those things get trapped, like an insect in amber. The fun part about teeth, Ania and her friends knew, is that the bacteria that causes tooth decay need a living host. After we die, teeth become the most resistant part of the entire body, and things that get trapped *stay* trapped. By examining calculus, a.k.a. tartar, they could learn a lot about the person the teeth were attached to: what they were eating, diseases they were exposed to, what kind of immunity they had developed. They were looking for a wide range of pathogens with almost nothing in common, except for one thing. None of them were blue.

Ania knew many things about the teeth in question. Radiocarbon dating placed the death of the owner between AD 997 and 1162 with good enough degree of probability. The subject was determined to be biologically female. B77 had relatively good oral health. Prior to her death, she had only lost two of her teeth, both of which molars. The site in which her remains were found was an old church-monastery destroyed by fire in the fourteenth century. B77 might have been a nun.

There were, of course, many things Ania did not know. She did not know those blue-stained teeth belonged to a woman named Agnes and that they were once part of the most endearing smile. Agnes loved to smile. She smiled all the time, even when she was alone. She smiled for no reason other than it made her feel good. The chicken came first, she said; smile and happiness will follow.

Agnes had lost her mother to the Tracker at the age of eleven. A year later, she gave birth to her daughter, Eila. For eight years, they traveled through Europe, begging for food and shelter, until they stumbled upon a small religious community in Dalheim. Mother and daughter already looked very much alike, and when the barren door of the monastery opened, Agnes introduced Eila as her little sister.

Eila wouldn't stay long. She left when she turned sixteen and found herself a husband in the nearby village. Agnes stayed. The life of a nun was a lot simpler than what she'd experienced and highly compatible with the rules she'd sworn to follow. She became a scribe, copying the works of saints and philosophers for future generations. Agnes's hand was precise, surgical. She had a vivid imagination and a strong sense of aesthetics. By the time she was a grandmother, Agnes had become an illuminator, producing the most beautiful manuscripts as both painter and calligrapher.

Agnes didn't kill herself when her granddaughter was of age. She knew there shouldn't be three for too long, but she didn't care. There were too many books to transcribe, too much knowledge to preserve. Eila did not insist. She just packed her things and took her daughter with her. There was no anger, just a difference of opinion. In the last centuries, the Church had grown in power and science had all but disappeared throughout the continent. Both of them had observed the same thing, but the facts led each of them towards separate conclusions. Agnes wanted to preserve what little knowledge was left in Europe. Eila wanted to create new knowledge elsewhere. The Muslim world was pressing forward making giant leaps in mathematics and astronomy. Knowledge wasn't lost, she thought. It simply moved south.

Agnes hadn't seen her daughter in twelve years. Her granddaughter would soon turn twenty, but Agnes only had memories of the little girl running through the aisles, hiding behind bookshelves. One rainy summer morning, a small package was delivered to Agnes's desk. Agnes opened it with great care, for she knew what it contained was worth a lot more than gold.

Inside the small box was a substance the likes of which Europe had never seen. Ultramarine was made by grounding lapis lazuli stones into a fine powder. The Earth, as it turns out, likes to hide its blue. The Egyptians once developed a process to manufacture large quantities of blue pigment, but the secret to its fabrication had been lost for five centuries. Now only a handful of minerals could produce blue and all of them needed to be mined. Hard, expensive work. Ultramarine was the deepest, most brilliant blue on the planet. The blue to end all blues. It had been produced in Asia for ages but had waited this long to make its way to Europe. Within decades, it would change the European color palette, and Agnes's world in the process.

Because it was so precious, ultramarine, like gold and silver, was reserved for the most important manuscripts, which, in a world controlled by the Church, often meant portraying the Virgin Mary. Agnes, in what would be her most rebellious act, besides living, set aside a small amount for a different kind of treatise. Buried deep in the library, she had found an old, barely legible transcription, work by a man named Seleucus of Seleucia who died in 150 BC. A follower of Aristarchus of Samos, Seleucus had used logic to demonstrate a heliocentric model of the solar system. He was centuries ahead of his time, believed in an infinite universe, that the attraction of the moon was causing the tides, and that their height was dependent on the position of the moon relative to the sun. None of his original work was thought to have survived, until then.

Every night, Agnes made her way to the library and for precisely one hour she copied the words of a dead astronomer in secrecy. She completed her work thirteen years later, mere months before her death. The Seventy-One died of old age, a rare feat for her kind. She died in her sleep, happy, dreaming of her granddaughter running through the library aisles. When the monastery was set ablaze three hundred years later, several lifetimes of meticulous work were lost. Hidden behind the book of Genesis, a mathematical model of the heavens turned into ashes, including the most beautiful depiction of the moon circling a bright blue planet Earth.

Agnes was a talented artist and a brilliant woman. Her entire life was spent preserving knowledge for posterity, and yet not once did it occur to her that her teeth might be the only thing to last. Had she known, she would have taken better care of them. She certainly would have washed off the pigment she licked from her fingers while working.

While all the knowledge she sought to preserve was lost, Agnes would unknowingly help create new insight, a thousand years later, in a room full of hungover people in white coats. Old teeth, as it turns out, can teach us about a lot more than diseases. They are a window into the lives people lived, their work and passions. Some knowledge, however, is lost forever, and no one will ever know just how much Agnes loved to smile.

# ACT IV

# 30

## *Let's Go*

Mia saw it in her dreams a thousand times. It starts with a dot. One pixel becomes four, then a thousand. The largest planet in the solar system soon fills the entire lens. Tonight, the dream would be the same, but this time it would come true, a few hundred million miles away.

The probe wasn't the first to enter the Jovian system. *Pioneers* had come five years before it launched. Even the robot's twin brother had overtaken it and reached the gas giant four months earlier. None of it mattered to Mia. She knew firsts would come later if about a hundred trillion other things went right. The robot had crossed the asteroid belt unharmed. Almost. Its primary receiver had failed in the spring of '78, but the backup system was working smoothly.

Before its date with the king of the gods, *Voyager 2* would meet some of its children. First came Callisto, the ancient. The robot looked for a moment before it turned to Ganymede. The entire control room held its breath as the probe flew a mere sixty thousand kilometers from Jupiter's largest moon. Ganymede is massive, larger than Mercury, but at this distance it felt even bigger than the sun. Scientists pressed their fingers against the computer screen. They could almost feel the ridges and furrows on the surface, the complex set of grooves that tell epic stories of the moon's tectonic past.

On approach for its Europa flyby, everyone watched intently.

Light pixels, dark pixels. A pattern emerged as thousands of them combined. Irregular, intersecting lines striated the moon's surface over thousands of kilometers. Red paint strokes on a bluish white canvas, or maybe they were the canvas. Not anything but the absence of something. Europa is the smallest of Jupiter's moons but one of the most reflective objects in the solar system. Like a mirror. Like ice. Perhaps they were looking at cracks in the ice above a hidden ocean. An ocean spanning the entire moon, moved around by the planet's gravity. A frozen layer bent by titanic forces until it buckled, scarring the moon surface. Could there be life beneath that ocean?

The tiny moon Amalthea looked like a red pebble. Barely anyone noticed it, awestruck by the gas giant behind it. It was time for *Voyager* and Jupiter to meet. A deluge of spectrometer data flooded its eleven senses. The atmosphere shined in ultraviolet light. Plasma ions danced in the magnetosphere while the planet broadcasted its song in long radio wavelengths. Jupiter loved to sing. Had it been a few times bigger, it might have been a star.

The robot's camera turned to a giant storm on the surface below. With no solid ground to slow it down, this red hurricane, twice as big as the Earth, had been churning gas for over a century. Jupiter pulled at the tiny probe like a siren calling it to sea, but this was as close to the planet as *Voyager* would get as it began the outbound leg of its encounter.

It would fly by Io on its way out, a slight course change it owed to its twin brother. Months earlier, *Voyager 1* had seen something no one expected on Io, the planet's closest moon: active volcanoes spewing sulphur dioxide five hundred kilometers into the air. To confirm its brother's findings, the robot spent ten hours of its own watching the moon's insides get pulled apart as the planet and its largest moon played their tug-of-war with Io, opposing forces dissipating as heat inside Io's crust, creating and erasing mountains higher than Mount Everest. A multicolored hell, painted with lava flows and a dozen shades of sulphuric dust.

The machine was the fourth of its kind to enter the Jovian system, but it had its fair share of firsts. *Voyager 2* helped change the way we thought of moons, any moon: from bare inanimate balls of dust to small living worlds with frozen oceans and active volcanoes. It was the first to photograph the rings of Jupiter, thin halos of dust hurled up when small meteors collide with the Jovian moons. It even discovered a moon itself just outside the outermost ring, the first found by a spacecraft and not using a telescope.

*Voyager 2* now had another Roman god to meet. Thanks to Jupiter's gravitational pull, the robot was zooming at a hundred thousand kilometers an hour towards Saturn, where its mission was scheduled to end. Even at that speed, the trip would take more than two years. Seven hundred and seventy-eight more nights for Mia to dream.

# 31

*Sara*

Berlin, again. This isn't the Berlin from the war, not von Braun's or Hitler's. It's not the Germany I met Korolev in, the one where I was scared of everything and everyone. This one is straight from childhood memories. Mother took me here every week when we lived in Berlin. I don't remember much from those years, but this place I remember. My little legs struggled to climb the altar steps. They had just completed reconstruction of the Ishtar Gate when we left. It was the eighth gate to the inner city of Babylon, built by King Nebuchadnezzar II—I loved that king's name. Five-year-old me thought that blue and gold gate was the greatest thing ever. It's fifty feet tall, but to me it looked like it could touch the sky.

I came on a hunch, something nagging me about "the boundary in Iraq." I think it might be a boundary stone—a . . . *kudurru*—from Mesopotamia. They were like . . . contracts, with the king. If he gave you land or freed you from taxes, they'd carve it on a stone along with some depictions of gods. The king kept the stone, and you placed a clay copy on the edge of your land. I've only ever seen one, with Mother, here at the Pergamon Museum.

Boundary stone. Mother. The Pergamon. "Our friends in Berlin."

It sort of made sense. There's an entire building dedicated to the Middle East. That's where we went every Sunday, Mother and I, before she took out the "h" at the end of her name.

Assyrian, Sumerian, Babylonian art. There it is. We'd sit before that fragment of the *Epic of Gilgamesh,* and I'd ask Mom to tell me the story for the umpteenth time. She'd tell me about the astronomers of Uruk and—

Shit . . . Two symbols on a cylinder seal. I've seen them before. Around my neck. On the bow Xuesen happened to find. "Noo . . . Ra." A name, perhaps. One of us. Is there more? I don't— Yes. This must be the *kudurru* from Iraq. "Decorative symbols with cuneiforms." Decorative . . . That's a nice way to put it. What is this? Some sort of printing plate, I think. Whatever it is, it has the entire text from the back of my necklace. Take them to the fucking stars.

—This place is rad, Mom! What are you looki— Wait, are these . . . ?

—They are.

—All of them?

—I counted seven pieces so far. I'm sure there's more.

—I don't understand. What does this mean?

—It means I didn't know my mother very well.

It means she lied. For a minute, I thought this might have been my mother's way of giving back. The Russians pillaged everything that was left inside after the war. It would have made sense for her to find stolen pieces and return them to their rightful owner. But that's not it. She wasn't looking for Akkadian art. She was looking for us.

—Mom, where are you going?

—Away from here.

—You're not even going to look? I mean, this is cool, right?

—I've looked enough already. Don't you see, Lola? Xuesen didn't just *stumble* upon that bow. He and my mother were looking for those symbols. They'd been searching for years.

—And that's bad *because* . . .

Lola's right. I should be happy, relieved at least. I thought we were breaking the rules by doing this. We still are, but we're also just continuing what my mother started. Why do I feel . . . betrayed? Part of it is selfishness, I know. I thought this was my project. The bow. The map. I thought I was doing something, me, and I'm not. *We're* doing it, again. We're the Kibsu, always. I can't help feeling like Mother stole something from me.

It's more than that, though. My whole life, Mother told me that trying to learn about who we are was a waste of time. "No, Mia. We will not waste time indulging personal curiosity. That is not our path." Every time I wanted something different, I reminded myself of what Mother said. I felt vain, self-centered for wanting it. I felt weak, because she was strong. Now . . . I don't know anything anymore. I don't know which of my memories are real and which ones are lies. I thought I knew who I was. I was the mother, the daughter. I was the Kibsu, but I was also me. I held on to my . . . peculiarities, even if they felt like weaknesses, because they set me apart. All of it feels wrong now, blurry.

—I'll wait for you outside by the Ishtar Gate, okay? Let me know if you find anything interesting.

—Mom, I—

—I'm fine, Lola. I just need some air.

# 32

## *Take Me to the River*

We're Russians now. Like, for real. Mom got us some Russian papers and everything. I'm doing my best, but I can't hold a conversation with anyone. I think I'd stand a better chance as an undocumented immigrant than as the one Russian girl who doesn't speak a lick of Russian. I'm not even sure where I'm supposed to be from. All I do is smile and nod. Smile and nod.

We live in Russia, of course, 'cause we're Russians. We live in Stalingrad. Actually, it's Volgograd now, the city of the Volga, but everyone still calls it Stalingrad. I know because it's like the one Russian word I recognize all the time. Not true, I know *vodka*, and *nemtsy*, "dumb" as in speechless; *inostranets*: "immigrant"— that one's easy. I never really belonged anywhere, but here, here they see me coming like ten miles away. Darker skin stands out. Mom said the Russians are sending the first black Hispanic person into space next year. Good for him, but I bet he doesn't live in Volgograd. These people are pasty white. I suppose carrying a dictionary and a piece of paper with the Cyrillic alphabet everywhere doesn't help either. Mom kind of fits in, I guess, in a square peg, round hole sort of way. They say she speaks funny, but at least she speaks.

It's not just me, though; everything is weird here. It's old, but almost everything is new. You can tell it was done in a hurry. I see endless rows of poorly built apartment buildings. Everyone else still sees ruins and blood. Even young people. Igor—he's about my age, works at the library—talks about the war every chance he gets. "My father died in that war, so did my uncle, but we beat the Germans. Why do they live so much better than us now?" Igor's a bit grim, but he speaks English, so I like him. The war ended thirty-four years ago, but it's still here. It's like this bond everyone shares. Even Mom understands it; she's seen it up close. Not me. I know I should feel lucky. I do, most times. I also feel . . . left out. Then again, what else is new?

I don't have any friends, of course. I wonder what Heather's doing. I miss her, but I thought I would miss her more. I think I was already losing her. We hung out, but all she talked about was meeting someone and moving away. I was the backup plan, one boyfriend away from uninteresting. It's my fault, I guess. I was never that nice to her. I wasn't mean or anything, just . . . She was a better friend to me than I was to her. Maybe I'm not built for that sort of thing. Some party that was, though. I bet they still talk about it. The night the nerd girl got high before she broke out of a police station, never to be heard from again. I'm probably a lot more popular now that I'm gone. Figures.

It's not all bad. There's a beach. It's not California, but it's okay. We can go now that it's summer, but we never do. Well, not often anyway. When we moved here, Mom said we'd be looking at archaeological sites. She thinks the Eight lived around here when she carved her bow. I don't know the first thing about archaeology, but I imagined a small brush. Brushing things. That sounded interesting for some reason. What she really meant was we'd spend all our time at the library. There's nothing left to brush, apparently. Just about everything people dug up all over Europe was lost during the war. Not just the artifacts, but most of the excavation notes, so we don't even know what they found. In most places that would be a tragedy, but Stalingrad was completely destroyed. They lost everything, so old pottery from Iranian-speaking nomadic tribes doesn't rank too high on everyone's list. Mom found a few boxes of notes from a site near . . . Berezovka. I don't know where that is, up the river, somewhere. Some German SS guy had stolen them before. He thought Scythians might have been ancestors of the master race. Whatever. I just read notes now. I look at the little drawings. A knife here, a small jar there. I'm not sure what I'm looking for exactly, only that I'll never find it.

—Mom? Can we take a break?

—Coffee already? You've been reading for . . . seventeen minutes.

—I don't want coffee. Coffee sucks, and I have to drink it with a bunch of writers and wannabe philosophers. They call me Lolitochka. Like, seriously. I meant we should do something else, instead of this.

—We still haven't found anything.

—What if we never find anything? It's been five months. . . . Five months, nine days. And seventeen minutes. And you know, we had something before we left. "She speaks after a cold silence." I mean, that's why you dragged me here, isn't it? Spring was three months ago, Mom. We didn't do anything. We didn't touch her elbow, or her mouth—I can't believe I'm talking like that now. Shouldn't we—you know—go?

—What would be the point?

—What? You said it's a map. Call me crazy, but maybe we should follow it. You said this is the river.

—I said I was fairly certain—

—Good! Let's get a boat! Touch some elbows!

—Where would we go? We're at the elbow now. This is it. And we know where the mouth is; it's at the Caspian Sea. What then? It's a big sea. We can't just paddle until we find what we're looking for.

—Well . . . "Desire awakens and I reach for her breast." Boobs, Mom. We need to find a mountain. A hill, maybe? A mound. I don't know, but there can't be that many out there.

—In or out of the water? The Caspian Sea is almost four hundred thousand square kilometers, with seven thousand kilometers of shoreline. Lots of mounds, Lola. Lots and lots of mounds. Besides, it could be something else entirely.

—Fine, then. Let's get the bow so we can read the rest of it. Maybe that will help.

—The bow isn't on display anymore. It's inside the museum vault, in China, and your grandmother's friend said he can't get access. Neither can we, obviously. We've been through all of this already, Lola. Now can we please get back to work?

—Sure. . . .

—And you never told me how that electric engine of yours is coming along.

—Meh. I can only get ninety millinewtons of thrust out of it. That's like the weight of a sheet of paper.

—That's not bad at all!

—Right. . . . You know what? I think I'll have a cup of coffee after all.

# 33

## *The Logical Song*

Burnt oatmeal. Maybe a hint of dirt. Lola was right. This coffee sucks. I came back to this country thinking everything had changed, but I forgot about Russia being Russia. They constantly run out of everything, so they cut coffee with cereal, chicory, whatever else they can get their hands on. We need to be *nomenklatura* nowadays to get the real thing and I haven't gotten around to blackmailing anyone for drinks. It doesn't really matter. I can handle bad coffee. What matters is Lola was right. I was wrong.

I missed an appointment at the bank this morning. I thought it was Tuesday instead of Wednesday. I got the days wrong, the *days*. There are seven of them; it shouldn't be that hard to keep up. I thought I might be coming down with something, but I'm not that lucky. It's just my mind turning into mush, with some chicory thrown in. I don't know why I'm making a big deal out of it. I can reschedule, but it seems to be par for the course lately.

I was wrong about my mother. I thought I knew her, but she was . . . someone else, someone different. How different? I'll never know. There's no rewind button, and even if there were, I couldn't rethink everything, analyze every smile, replay every word she ever said to me.

I was wrong about the ozone layer. Everyone was. It doesn't make any sense. I went over Molina and Rowland's work a dozen times. I went over mine and theirs, and it all checked out. They didn't make mistakes; neither did everyone else who came to the same conclusion. It was good science. So good in fact that when the Nimbus 7 satellite launched last October, we all waited for it to confirm what we already knew: that CFCs were eating away at the ozone layer. There would be sharp variations, some obvious signs of ozone depletion. Nope. Nothing. Better luck next time.

One giant Earth-sized slap in the face. There were quite a few people working on that subject. Some brilliant work. I wonder what they'll do now. How are they supposed to keep publishing their findings when the science says one thing, but the satellite that's up there *looking at it* says the opposite? Truth be told, I couldn't care less about the ozone layer right now. I feel like it's the whole universe that stopped making sense.

I don't know what I missed. I keep playing it over and over in my head and I would do everything the same. And I would still be wrong. It's not the first time. I've been wrong plenty, about life, or raising a child, things with too many variables to consider. This was different. Pure logic. Numbers. I've never been wrong about numbers. I don't even know what to make of it. How do you— How do you get up in the morning if one plus one is three? I did everything right and yet I was wrong. What else was I wrong about?

Was I right to come here? I don't even know if this is the right river. It seemed . . . logical. The writings on the bow are Akkadian, which could mean anything. Akkadian was spoken in the Mesopotamian empires, but it was also the Lingua Franca in most of the Near East. "Wetness" didn't make any sense until I remembered that the bow itself is Scythian. A Scythian bow made the Scythian way. If the Eight were Scythian then Akkadian would have been her second language. In Scythian, the Volga was called Rha, which would translate as "water" or "wetness." It just fit. The Volga was a major trade route for them. There's an elbow in the river not too far from its mouth. It . . .

fit. At least it did back then. Now, now it seems like a stretch. Did it fit because I wanted it to? Did I see what I wanted to see?

I might have dreamed up the entire thing. The river, the map. Maybe the Eight just smoked too much *kannab*. Maybe I dropped everything and dragged Lola here for some sex fantasy she wrote while stoned out of her wits. Hell, for all I know, there *is* no Eight and those symbols are some secret code kids found on whatever the hell they put cereals in back then.

I don't know what I'm doing anymore. I figured, if the Eight lived around these parts, she might have left some clues, something we can use to figure this puzzle out. I thought learning about the people who lived here might help. But in truth I have absolutely no idea what that help might look like. A needle in a haystack, except there might not be a needle, but I'm still looking, just in case.

I know for a fact that what I'm doing *now* is wrong. I'm doing it anyway. Lola's losing her mind in Volgograd. I called in a favor and got her a small programming job. It turns out we're still paying some very old people here and one of them works on the *Progress* spacecraft. It's a nice project: small unmanned resupply ships that will bring food and whatnot to the new Salyut 6 station. Not a huge step technologically, but it will be reliable, and it will make long-term space missions possible for the first time. Smart. Useful. It makes what I'm doing feel like an even bigger waste of time. I'm not even *really* doing that anymore. I find excuses, things to do around the house. I'm only thinking about one thing. The wrong thing.

The job I found Lola is only for a week, near Moscow. Lola gets to spend some time away from me. I get to see Billie.

I know it's wrong, but I'm wrong about *everything*. I might as well go all in.

# 34

## *Walking on the Moon*

She shaved her head. I don't know why that bothers me. I loved her hair, loved burying my face in it. This is a good look, just not what I had imagined. I suppose that's it. I have this idea of her, now, this person I long for, and the hair reminds me that person doesn't exist. She's her, not my version of her.

I wonder who she's meeting here. Fancy café, Victorian furniture. There are so many old books. I think I can smell them. This place was made for men who wear monocles. So not her. Here I go again. Billie never cared much for what people think of her. Billie's Billie. There's no such thing as *not her*. Still, I keep thinking of who could walk in through that door and sit across that table. Girlfriend. Girl friend. Husband. Accountant. Maybe she's not meeting anyone. Maybe she just felt like having a fancy coffee sitting in a green velvet chair. Maybe she'll dig into her bag and take out a monocle.

—You just going to sit there or are you going to come and talk to me?

Shit. She didn't turn around, but I think she's talking to me.

— . . .

—Do you think I'm blind? You don't think I'd notice a crazy lady staring at me from behind for twenty minutes?

—I didn't think you'd recognize me.

—You recognized *me*. Besides, you look like your mother

walked out of a time machine. It's a bit eerie, seriously. Come. Sit your ass down, you ghost.

My heart's pumping like I just ran a marathon. I don't know if I'm ready for th—

—OUCH! Why'd you pinch me?!

—Sorry. Had to make sure.

I don't know how many times I imagined this moment. I've had that talk with her a hundred times in my head. I had it down to a T. Now that she's sitting right in front of me, I don't know what I'm supposed to say to her. I'm the same scared twenty-year-old who took a drag off her cigarette when we first met.

—I like the new look.

—No, you don't, but thank you for saying it. I went to your funeral, you know. Your husband was there. There were something like a dozen armed guards standing ten feet behind, but really it was just him, no one else. Poor guy. I know funerals are supposed to be sad, but yours was fucking pathetic.

—You said you were there.

—I watched from a distance.

— . . .

—Come on! What was I going to say? "Hi! You don't know me, but I used to fuck your wife"?

—Did you know I was alive?

—I didn't know anything. I just . . . Like I said, it was just him. I mean, you weren't the easiest person to be around, but your own mother didn't show. Then there's the whole "Nina the 'interpreter' falls off a platform at some top-secret military site, miraculously survives, only to die in a fire at the hospital the very same day." I mean, that is some serious bad luck. Anyway, I wasn't sure. I figured you were a spy or something, had to leave in a hurry. It was a better thought to hold on to than you burning alive in some ugly hospital gown.

—I was—

—Don't tell me! Shit! I've lived with that spy story for thirty years. I'm not going to change it now! Next you'll tell me Nina's not your real name and I'll feel even more cheated. No, you're a spy. A good one, of course. You hide a small gun in your purse and you travel the world, stealing state secrets.

—No purse.

—It's your day off.

—You're not mad at me?

—Of course I'm mad! What do you think? I'm mad now. I was way madder then! I was crazy in love with you; then you dumped me without saying a word. Even if you'd died for real I'd have been angry as hell. You weren't supposed to die, or leave, or . . . Will you excuse me for a minute? I need to go to . . . you know.

This was a bad idea. I've hurt that woman enough already and now I'm doing it again, sticking my knife inside old wounds for selfish reasons.

—I'm sorry, Billie. I shouldn't have come.

—But you did. "Should" doesn't really play into it, now does it? "Should" is for someone else. You did you. You can't not do you. No point in trying. Certainly no point in feeling sorry for it.

—I don't know what to say to that.

—Why *did* you come? Let me guess. You felt lost, for what-ever reason. You started questioning things, playing what if. You remembered the good old days and you thought a little trip down memory lane might help you fix whatever's broken?

— . . . Something like that.

—Is it working?

— . . .

I know that face. She wants to show me something. She's not giving me what I want; she's giving me what she thinks I need.

—I did that, too, you know, for a long time. I wished I could go back knowing what I know now, but it doesn't work that way.

Face it, you wouldn't want to go back to the way things were. I sure fucking wouldn't. We'd be together, sure, but we'd be the same insecure messes we were back then. Both of us. That's why we found each other in the first place—remember?—because everything else around hurt too much.

She's right. She was there when I needed her. We were there for each other. I remember when she ran outside and made me catch her before she fell off a bridge. I hurt so much then, I wanted to die, but I ran after her. I caught her, and I knew she'd catch me. I needed her more than anything. I think she wants me to realize I don't anymore, that it's okay just to be me.

—It's good to see you. So, what have you been up to these past—

—Oh, hell no. We're sooo not doing that.

—Right. . . . Thank you, Billie. I mean it.

—You're welcome.

— . . . I should get going.

—More spy stuff?

—Yeah. Spy stuff.

I love you, Billie.

# 35

## *Boys Don't Cry*

My brother is the definition of useless, but the Egyptian Museum in Cairo turned out to be a treasure trove of information. Writings, not from Mer-Neith-it-es herself, but from some city official who was obsessed with all forms of gossip about Egyptian royalty and their entourage. I believe three generations of traitors lived here in Egypt under Persian rule, until about 480 BC when Mer-Neith-it-es left for Parsa—a.k.a. Persepolis—and was never heard from again. The timing makes sense. Xerxes I, the king of the Achaemenid empire and pharaoh of Egypt, had signed a decree slashing the moneys devoted to major temples in Egypt. Without adequate resources, she'd have found herself vulnerable, to us and others. I found it interesting that she told someone where she was going. It seemed like an odd way to disappear. There is no mention of the sphere leaving with her, but representations of the temple two decades later show no orb in the main room. I can only assume that she took it with her. If it is what I think it is, she would not leave it behind if she never intended to return.

She and her children had been priestesses for three generations. I would not be surprised if she chose the same profession in Persepolis. Regardless, I have to tell Uriel we're moving to Iran. I don't think he'll be pleased. It will have to wait until morning because he passed out an hour ago after drinking himself into a stupor. Today was . . . difficult.

Uriel finally figured out that Raphael is never coming back. It only took him six years. I wish I knew what triggered this sudden realization, but he was fine yesterday and this morning I found him sobbing on the kitchen floor. I was surprised. He and our older brother were close, but I don't think I have ever seen Uriel cry or for that matter display any kind of emotion besides his usual puppy-like excitement.

It took nearly an hour to get him to speak. When I first asked what had happened, he just kept mumbling the same thing over and over again. I couldn't make out the words at first and my constant probing made him speak louder to drown out the sound of my voice. "I'm not content to be with you in the day-time" is what he said. I did not understand. It wasn't until he started adding emphasis that I recognized the song. "I'M NOT. CONTENT. TO BE WITH YOU. IN THE DAYTIME."

When Uriel was twelve, maybe thirteen, Father educated one of our neighbors a bit too vigorously. He halfheartedly tried to persuade a young Raphael to get rid of the body but soon gave up and agreed to fix his own mistake. Father always said one should use the right tool for the job, and after a brief inventory of the shed, a bruised toe, and some epic cursing he determined that we were lacking the proper instruments for this particular project. We were young and believed our father to be fully competent at anything gruesome, but despite his penchant for violence, he had never hacked anyone to pieces before. He took the car and reappeared an hour later with half a dozen power tools. After some trial and error, the most efficient one was identified and the neighbor dismembered and disposed of. I had trouble sleeping for months, but what truly mattered to Uriel was that we now had a plethora of tools at our disposal.

Days later, Uriel found himself a piece of plywood and some white paint, and locked himself inside the shed. He reemerged at dinnertime with a replica of Dave Davies's Gibson Flying V guitar, complete with a strap made of rope, three bottle caps for knobs, and five crooked strings painted on. Uriel stood proudly in the middle of the yard and gave Mother and me a concert, including a heartfelt guitar solo performed on one knee. The show ended rather abruptly when our father returned home.

Father was never one for the arts. He made Uriel watch his fake guitar burn in the firepit in some sort of "educational" ceremony. In total, the Gibson Flying V existed for about two hours. Uriel didn't cry or scream. He made a better Flying V the next day, this time with a sixth string. He had indeed learned something from the experience and he hid that one in the woods behind our house. Uriel would use a walk as a pretext and play to a crowd of birch trees almost every day. He did so for an entire summer until the sun and rain turned the guitar into a rotten mess.

I believe that deep down, Uriel still fancied himself a rock star. He must have realized a long time ago that a complete lack of musical talent might be a hindrance to stardom, but he could at least live the life. With Raphael "officially" gone, Uriel now has our entire future in his hands, and the lifestyle he so cherishes will, undoubtedly, be difficult to maintain with a wife and three to five children. Uriel misses his brother, I am certain of it, but I think it was the idea of becoming a responsible adult that completely destroyed him.

# 36

*Mother*


I was gone for eight days, but I know Mom will act all weird like we haven't seen each other in a year. "How was Moscow? I want to hear everything." It doesn't matter what I say after that; it won't be enough. She'll want details, as if I remember every single thing I did. It's not like there were that many. I was alone in a small room with graph paper and a pencil. I did some math for a day, then some FORTRAN, on paper. They'd requested access to a computer, but it's Russia, so . . . whatever. Bad food at the cafeteria. Noisy neighbors. I think that's it. I didn't get to see the city at all. Like, we didn't even go. It won't matter. She'll say: "Oh, I'm sure you did a lot more than that. Did you meet anyone?" She asks if I met someone every time I leave the house. Yes, Mom, I got married at the grocery store. She'll want to talk and talk. . . . All right, deep breath.

—Hi, Mom! I'm back!

— . . .

—MOM?

She might still be at the library. I—

—IN THE KITCHEN, LOLA!

Half a dozen books open on the kitchen table. Maybe we can make this short. I wish.

—Hi, Mom!

—Sorry, I didn't hear you come in. I think I've figured it out.

—Figured what out?

—We don't need to know about her life. We know all we need to know about the Eight. She is us, Lola. She's the Kibsu. She couldn't be anything else if she tried.

—Didn't we know that before?

—What is it we do, Lola?

Oh God. Not this.

—I'm not reciting the rules, Mom.

—Not the rules. Before the rules. What is it we do? What's our purpose?

—To take them to the stars.

—That's right. That's what she lived for. She stared at the night sky and dreamed of distant worlds. She looked at the stars, Lola.

—So?

—So she craved knowledge like all of us, and the Babylonians were the ones who had it. She would have studied the works of astronomers of Babylon and Uruk. She wrote in their language; she knew their customs, their beliefs. Science and religion were intimately entwined at the time. Now what did *she* know about the people who could someday read what she wrote? She couldn't know what the future would look like, but she didn't need to. "Perhaps you are also me." She's writing for us, Lola, and she knew just as much about us as we know about her. We're the Kibsu. We look at the stars. "From the underworld, she emerges in wetness." The Babylonian new year begins at spring equinox, a day after the goddess Inanna rises from the underworld. Inanna is "she," "I touch her elbow, then her mouth. She speaks after a cold silence." I think I had that part right. The Volga flows again at springtime. Follow the river at the equinox, all the way to the Caspian Sea.

—No stars.

—Stars are coming. "Desire awakens." That's Inanna again. She was the goddess of sex and desire. "And I reach for her breast."

Her breast . . . Now let's say it's not a mountain but something in the night sky. Inanna was associated with the planet Venus, but planetary orbits wouldn't work for what she was doing. She'd need an actual star, one that shows up in the same spot every year. Preferably something bright, like one of the Royal Stars. Antares, I thought. It says here the Babylonians called Antares the "breast of the scorpion," the heart of the scorpion goddess Ishara. Unless I'm mistaken, she and Inanna became one and the same over time. Reach for her breast. It's a heading, Lola, not a place. Travel in the direction of Antares when it appears on the horizon. That would be somewhere southeast.

—I . . . What does that mean for us?

—It means we need to read the rest of it. We need to get the bow.

—In China?

—Yes, in China.

—Okay. . . . First, can we talk about my trip?

—Oh, I'm so sorry, Lola. How was Moscow? I want to hear everything.

# 37

*Brass in Pocket*

—Dear Xuesen,

I hope you and your family are doing well and that time has been kinder to your health than it has to mine.

Our friendship means the world to me and I have held it close like the treasure it is—private, a gift I dared not share for fear of losing it. I have gone through our past correspondence and I am ashamed of how little I have told you about my family. I write now hoping to make amends, and with a request.

My only daughter, Mia, lost her husband several years ago. She had spent most of her life working in the restaurant they owned and raising my granddaughter. It has been a difficult time for all of us, but she eventually chose to sell the family business and build a new life. At the young age of fifty-five, she is now beginning graduate studies in art history. I could not be prouder of my daughter. When she told me she planned to write her dissertation on ancient jade chimes in the Shang dynasty, I thought of you and hoped you could help give my daughter a small token of my love and admiration.

—What's a jade chime, Mom? And why the whole cockamamie?

—Something I found in a book at the library. I needed a reason to visit Xinjiang. I just . . . I feel bad for lying to the man, but what if he wants to meet? The odds of him being an expert in old chimes are low, I think, and being a student makes me anonymous enough if he decides to look me up.

—Dead husband?

—I know. I figured he won't probe if the story is personal enough. I don't think he'll want to come with us, but you never know. What do you think of that part? It would mean the world to her, and to me, if you could help her obtain a travel permit to Xinjiang so that she could visit the museums in Ürümqi.

—And her daughter.

—What?

—If you could help her and her daughter obtain a travel permit. I'm going with you, aren't I?

—Are you . . . sure? I keep— I took you to Algiers, then we moved to California, then . . . I keep dragging you places and away from your friends and I realize I never once asked you if you wanted to go. I don't want to do that again. I know we don't always get along, so I thought, maybe some time alone, away from me might be—I don't know—

—Mom! You're not leaving me here. Like, I wouldn't mind being on my own in California, but I'm not staying here if I don't have to. I don't know anyone. If you don't want me to come, you can just say so.

—It would mean the world to her, and to me, if you could help her and her daughter obtain a travel permit to Xinjiang. You know what else I realize, Lola? How I forget to tell you how much I love you. I forget almost every day. But I do. You know that, don't you?

—Well, I'm you, so . . .

—No, Lola. I love you for all the ways you're not me. You annoy the living shit out of me when you act like me.

—Geez, thanks! You annoy the shit out of me, too, so . . .

—So . . .

—I don't know, Mom. You're so . . . compliant.

—Compliant? Really? Your grandma would have something to say about that.

—Come on, Mom! Take them to the stars. Follow the rules. What are the rules, Lola? Tell me what the rules are. You're always . . . That's them, Mom. You're always them, the whole fucking hundred of them. I'd just . . . I'd like you to be you sometimes, even a little. Then maybe I can be me.

—Oh, Lola, I don't think there's any way you could not be you. And yes, I try to follow the rules. I wrote those rules, you know. So did you. You wrote them when you were older, and wiser. This is *really* going to annoy you, but there'll come a day when you actually like having those rules. You'll feel stronger for having them.

—Stop it, Mom.

—And I'm not that boring, I'll have you know. I went—

—To Germany, I know. It was war. You told me a million times about von Braun and the Nazis. The V-2, the R-7. I know everything you did in Russia. You were insanely cool, Mom. And I feel like shit because I'll never do anything that comes remotely close to that. But what have you done since I was born? How many adventures did you go on? How many rockets did you build?

—What are you asking, Lola?

—Did you like your life better then?

—I was young. Would I go back to being young again, is that what you're asking? Sure. Maybe not to my twenties. I was a mess back then. Early thirties, maybe.

—Let me rephrase what I said so it's clearer. . . . Would you rather I wasn't born?!

—Lola . . . I wish for a lot of things. I wish I'd spent more time with my mother. I wish I could give you the life you want. I wish you didn't . . . hate me so—

—I don't hate you.

—But never once did it even cross my mind that I'd be better off without you. You're the best thing that ever happened to me.

— . . .

—And I torched the National Archives.

—What?

—I burned it down. How's that for compliant? Remember I told you they had a picture of me with von Braun, my mother's files, all of that? I went to St. Louis. I broke into the National Personnel Records Center and lit the biggest paper fire the world had ever seen.

—When was that? Was I born?

—Born? That was like six years ago. You had a sleepover at Heather's.

—Shit.

—How about we make this trip . . . *our* trip? Spending time together, maybe we can find a way to—

—Not annoy the crap out of each other . . . I'd like that.

—Me too. I'd like that very much.

# 38

## Don't Stop Believin'

Mia had hoped for news of *Voyager 2* before she left for China. The probe's speed had dropped to thirty times that of a bullet and the sun kept pulling, slowing it down bit by bit. It would be another seven months before it reached Saturn, but that's not what the wait was about.

*Voyager 1* had visited Saturn and some of its smaller moons before changing course towards Titan. The second-largest moon in the solar system had long been known to have an atmosphere, and the brass at mission control had made the Titan flyby their first priority. Visiting Titan would take the probe on a different trajectory, away from the plane where the planets travel. Going to Titan meant neither probe would visit Pluto. It also meant Titan would be the last thing *Voyager 1* ever saw up close. Had it failed, *Voyager 2* would have altered *its* course to reach Titan, ending any hope of visiting new worlds. *Voyager 1* discovered a thick nitrogen atmosphere on Titan, making the moon the only known place besides Earth where liquid water might exist on the surface. It even found methane and complex hydrocarbons that made chemical reactions essential to life a possibility. The Titan flyby had been a resounding success. It was, in fact, so successful that NASA was considering an encore.

Lola was still uninterested since other probes had flown by Saturn, but Mia knew another trip to Titan meant neither she nor her daughter would see Uranus or Neptune in her lifetime.

The probe had turned most of itself off, waiting for its fate to be decided. *Voyager 1* had left Titan in November. It was now January and *Voyager 2* was still awaiting orders.

Finally, a radio signal came from Earth. New course. New mission parameters. On August 22, 1981, two years after leaving the Jovian system, the robot began its encounter with the sixth planet.

*Voyager 2* first met with Iapetus, the yin-yang moon of Saturn. Extremely dark on one side, bright on the other, the moon is barely denser than liquid water. *Voyager 2* took better pictures of the ten-kilometer-high mountain range *Voyager 1* had discovered on the equator. It would photograph half a dozen moons before turning its eye towards the ringed planet.

*Voyager* found a large hexagonal weather pattern at Saturn's north pole. It snapped picture after picture, like a tourist in Rome. The rings were majestic. Millions of particles, almost entirely made of ice, ritual dancing around the giant world. The camera spotted some kinks and "spokes" in the planet's main rings. What they were no one knew. The answer would have to come from another probe; *Voyager's* time with the sixth planet was coming to an end.

The robot flew past and behind Saturn before diving through the disc of the planet's rings at forty-seven thousand kilometers per hour.

Poof. A small dust grain hit the robot's antenna and disintegrated on contact. No damage, but the puff plasma it created was enough to slightly alter the probe's course. *Voyager 2* adjusted its— Poof. Another micrograin hit. Poof. Poof. One thruster fired after another. Like sailor through storm, *Voyager* struggled to keep its heading. Eighty-one thousand operations per second weren't enough to keep up with the onslaught of poof poof. For a moment, it appeared as though the voyage might end there. *Voyager 2* had traveled millions of miles, traversed the asteroid belt, and brushed against a world ten times larger than Earth and was now in danger of being sent adrift by things half the size of an average bacterium. And then . . .

No more poof.

The machine had done it. It had completed its primary mission. *Voyager 2* had visited the two largest planets in the solar system, sent back oodles of data and tens of thousands of images. So many images, in fact, that the overused camera platform had run out of lubricant and stopped rotating after the Saturn encounter. A special delivery of ones and zeroes got the camera moving again. A fortunate outcome, since *Voyager's* mission had been extended.

The probe took a screaming left turn around Saturn and zipped towards Uranus with newfound speed and purpose. With any luck, it would get there in a mere four and a half years.

# 39

*Rapture*

Lola was first to notice him. There was this little boy standing on the sidewalk when the taxi dropped us off. Three, four years old, maybe? Short, stalky little thing, with the most stereotypical bowl cut. He looked like a tiny adult in his blue dress shirt and dark pants. I was about to walk past him when he wobbled to the middle of the sidewalk to block our path. I guess he'd never seen anyone who looked like us. He bent his neck backwards when I walked up to him and I found myself hypnotized by dark brown eyes way too big for his little head. He said . . . *something.* When I told him I didn't understand, I realized he might be too young to know there are people who don't speak his language. He was probably wondering why a grown-up hadn't learned how to speak. We stared at each other for a good minute, trying to figure out which of us was more alien to the other. I think I won that one, but Peking *is* weird. The streets are wide in this part of town, *really* wide, but empty. Most people are driving bicycles, but strangely, there aren't that many—people, that is. There are five million in this city, but we can't see them. Wherever they are, they all left their bicycles behind. That's all there is: empty space and a quadrillion bicycles.

Xuesen asked us to meet him at this tea shop right next to Xidan Street where the "Democracy Wall" began. He didn't mention anything, but I don't think it's a coincidence. His way of letting us know where he stands. Lola and I walked the alleys looking for the place. We didn't see anyone, but the ones hiding there are all cooking something. The smells are coming from everywhere. I'm starving now. I'll eat something on the train. We're not staying in Peking.

Xuesen used his connections to get us papers for the Xinjiang autonomous region. This shouldn't take long. Some chitchat. "So good to meet you!" Then we're off. Easy. Everything is fine, but I feel like a spy entering enemy headquarters in disguise. I don't know why I'm so nervous. I'm not pretending to be someone else. I'm here as me; so is Lola. I did pretend to be my mother to get us here; maybe that's why I feel like such a fraud. That and my fake PhD in ancient wind chimes.

I'm not even sure it's the deception that bothers me. I . . . I know this man, in some strange twisted way. Mother is a part of me whether I like it or not. I spent half my life trying to be me, unique, but I see the other side now, the one where there's only been one of us this whole time. We're the Kibsu. Xuesen is a long-lost friend I've never met. I think, maybe, I'm afraid he'll realize he knows me, too.

*[Mom! That's him at the door. Sir! Over here!]*

He's coming this way, slowly. Very slowly. I don't think it's his age. He just . . . takes his time. It's rare to meet someone who's not in a hurry. He's looking everywhere, observing. I can see what Mother found so endearing about him.

—So good to finally meet you. Mother speaks of you in such glowing terms. She told us about everything you've done here, *and* in America. It's an honor, sir.

No answer. He's just standing there.

He's not moving. I feel . . . Oh. Finally.

—I fear your mother has been aggrandizing my modest achievements. Believe me, the honor is all mine.

—I'm Mia.

—It is a pleasure to meet you.

—And this is my daughter, Lola.

*[Hi!]*

He's not looking at me. In fact, I don't think he's met my gaze once since he arrived. He's been looking at Lola the whole time. I'm such a fool. I thought *I* would look like the woman he knew—I was prepared for that—but he met my mother only once when she was about thirty. He's known her for decades, but he's never seen her grow old. I'm twenty-five years too old. Lola's younger than Mother was, but maybe that's what he remembers. The youth. Whatever the reason, he can't seem to take his eyes off her.

—It looks like someone forgot to drink the tea.

*[I'm sorry, sir. What tea?]*

I was thinking about the legend of Meng Po. In Chinese mythology, Meng Po lives in Diyu, one of the many realms beneath the Earth. Diyu is the realm of the dead, and Meng Po's task is to ensure that those that are about to be reincarnated do not remember their previous lives. For that she serves a special tea to each passing soul. We call it the Five-Flavored Tea of Forgetfulness. One sip erases all memories so that the soul can be reborn without the weight of the past. You, young Lola, forgot to drink the tea.

I see your mother in you, and your grandmother. I see my dear friend. I see . . . much more than someone your age should be burdened with.

— . . .

I think I just had a heart attack.

—This is awkward. Please forgive my failed attempt at humor. Old Chinese man handing out ancient wisdom. I thought— Never mind. I am *too* old, it would seem. What I meant to say is that you seem very mature for such a young age.

[*I'm nineteen.*]

Exactly. . . . Oh, silly me. I was so eager to meet you I forgot what it is you actually came for. These are your permits for the Xinjiang region. It is very important that you keep them with you at all times. Xinjiang itself has a history of political unrest and the entire country is on edge after the ousting of Chairman Guofeng. You will likely be assigned a chaperon when you enter the region.

—A chaperon?

—A Party member whose job will be to ensure your safety, and report your every move to the government. Think of him as a very untrusting guide.

[*Lovely.*]

—I'm sure we'll have a great time. I can't tell you how grateful we are for your help.

—It is the least I could do for my old friend. Speaking of your mother, she, among her many talents, had the most beautiful understanding of flight dynamics. Would it, by any chance, be something she passed down to her daughter?

—I'm so sorry. I'm the black sheep in the family when it comes to math.

—Good for you. And shame on me for asking. This is your first visit to China. Please allow me to make amends by giving you a short tour of my city. For all its flaws, it is filled with myriad treasures if one knows where to look.

—Oh, you've done so much already, I don't want to—

[*Mom! I'd love a tour!*]

I don't want to be impolite. I also desperately want to leave. He knows I lied about the math. I might be paranoid, but I could swear that man can see right through me. With any luck, he'll spend all his time talking to Lola. It's obvious the two of them like each other. I feel awful just for being here and I don't want to have to lie to him again.

—Let us have some tea first.

[*Yes! Anything hot. China's a lot colder than I thought.*]

—We can buy you a jacket, Lola.

—You will need one in Ürümqi. It is, however, well worth a visit, and though I was unsuccessful, I do hope you get to see the bow.

—The b— Oh yes. Mother showed us a picture, but we're not here to see that.

[*We came for wind chimes!*]

—Wind chimes, yes. So your grandmother said.

We're so busted. Then again, he's not objecting to the lie. It could be he's just polite, or he's not a hundred percent sure and is giving us the benefit of the doubt. I wonder how much my mother told him. She wouldn't have told him *everything*, that's for sure, probably some half-truth about her interest in the symbols. But decades of half-truths add up to a lot of truth. Maybe he doesn't realize how much he knows about us. I don't think it was a coincidence that he and my mother hit it off right away. He must have sensed there was something unique about her, and he saw the same something in us. All the dots are there. He'll just never connect them because it defies reason and he is, above all else, a very reasonable man. Deep down he might already know what we are, or rather what we're not, but it will likely stay there, deep down, with all the other buried knowledge that we can't quite touch.

—Lola's right; I think a tour is a wonderful idea.

# 40

## *Video Killed the Radio Star*

Mom and I left Peking three days ago, on something that may have once resembled a plane. I wanted to take the train, but Xuesen actually grimaced when I suggested it. I mean, how bad could it be? Whatever, we made it. We're in Kashgar now. I love that name. Kashgar. Sounds badass. I AM KASHGAR! FEAR MY WRATH! The chaperon, the government dude following us around to make sure we're not spies or something, took us here to check out some jade stuff.

I'm glad he did. This place is one bar fight away from full-blown civil war, but I love it. We're staying in Old Town. It's surreal. Gorgeous, but mostly surreal. Everything is the same sand color. Rectangular buildings, all of them. There are no curves or diagonals here. From a rooftop it looks like someone went crazy making sandcastles with a square bucket. It's about as far as it gets from my image of China. Even the people. Kashgar is mostly Uighurs. I had no idea what a Uighur was before we came, but these people are supernice.

I met this guy, Adil. He's more or less my age and he speaks English, which is rare. Dry sense of humor. Superdark. He made torture jokes five minutes after we met. He also looks the part. There's something very . . . mischievous about him. His front teeth are shorter, or maybe he has longer canines—I don't know—but he looks like a vampire. I like him. Mom too, I guess, because she hired him right away as an interpreter. He'll come with us to Ürümqi. Government dude doesn't speak English. Also, everyone hates him, so we try to keep our distance. The Chinese government sent a whole lot of Hans to live in Ürümqi, the capital, but Kashgar is almost all Uighurs. They seem okay with us, but they make sure government dude feels properly unwelcome wherever he goes. Mom spent the last two days with him visiting museums and oases on the old silk road. Jade stuff. She says she has to, but I know she's loving every minute of it. I spend my time hanging with Adil. I'm cool with that.

He *half* kissed me. Is that a thing? Half kissing? We were laughing—I don't remember what at—and he leaned forward holding his belly like this was way funnier than it actually was. On the way down, his lips brushed against mine a little. Just on the corner. It felt, like, half-deliberate, which was sort of perfect because I only half wanted to say no. Then he pretended as if nothing had happened. I don't think I'm attracted to him. But I like . . . whatever this is. Just a dash of tension. Some acknowledgment that we're compatible and that's the end of it. Nothing ventured, nothing gained. At least this way no one gets hurt.

Sure, there was some awkwardness afterwards, but I can do awkward. I've had all kinds of practice with awkward, but I didn't know how good *he* was at it, so I turned on the radio to break the odd silence. Adil frowned, but he didn't say anything. I figured out why soon enough. The voice that came on sounded really dramatic. I asked Adil to translate and down the rabbit hole we went. I mean, holy moly! Half the stations here are batshit-crazy propaganda. There's your friendly Russian broadcast counting the many ways in which Muslims are better off on the Soviet side. Turn the dial half a notch and you get the Chinese-run horror channel. Spew-your-lunch horror stories of atrocities committed on Muslims by the Soviets. More Russian stations promoting Uighur nationalism. We even get a couple Chinese broadcasts aimed at the Kyrgyz and Kazaks on

the other side of the border. All the airwaves are about foment-
ing dissent. The Soviets hope the Uighurs will turn on China
if they invade and the Chinese hope other minorities will join
them if they decide to march into Central Asia. In the end,
it just means the Chinese trust the Uighurs even less and the
Soviets are more afraid of the Kyrgyz and Kazaks. Bad shit all
around. It's not that surprising for China to feel a bit surrounded
since the Soviets invaded Afghanistan, but this place is *intense*.
There's a Chinese camp training Mujahideen to fight less than
an hour from here.

I might have told Adil the real reason we're here—not all of it
but a little. He kept staring at me and things just came out of my
mouth. I didn't tell him the Kibsu stuff, obviously, just a tiny bit
more of it than I wanted to. I told him the bow belonged to my
family, which doesn't make one bit of sense, but he didn't seem
to mind. If I had to guess, I'd say he thinks I'm lying about the
parts I'm not lying about and telling the truth about the things
I am lying about. It's very confusing. Whatever's going through
his head, he didn't rat on me. I don't know him that well, but I
get a real sense he's a good person and I trust it runs both ways.
Mom would be pissed if she knew, but technically, there's no
rule about keeping *everything* secret.

Tomorrow we all leave for the capital. The bow isn't on display at the museum anymore, but Mom says they might let us
see it anyway once we're there. I don't see it happening. Not
unless we happen to meet the biggest bow nerd on the planet.
Like, the one guy named Bo Archer with a PhD in bows who's
been waiting for this moment his whole life. I don't think we're
that lucky. Bo will be out sick or he'll have died in a freak hunting accident. We'll ask. They'll say no. We'll try smiling, crying,
all manner of groveling, and I have the very distinct feeling I'll
be the one doing all of it. Mom is here for jade. That makes *me*
the one with the bow fetish.

# 41

## *Under Pressure*

We couldn't go into the museum vault, even with Lola on the verge of crying. She's good. I was hoping, *really* hoping, we could do this the easy way. Now I have to figure out our options. Unfortunately, there aren't that many. The facts are about as simple as they get. We need access to the bow. They won't give us access to the bow. Therefore, we have to get to the bow without being *allowed* to get to the bow, which isn't impossible, but more or less the textbook definition of a crime.

It's not all bad news. Scoping out a place is a lot easier with a guide showing you around. We found out as much as we could making small talk. Lola did. It took her a whole five seconds to immerse herself in her bank robber persona. Faye Dunaway better watch out; she was absolutely amazing. She had that poor guide wrapped around her finger so tight I thought he might give her the keys before we left. Of course, the only room we couldn't look at was the one we need to get into, but I did learn a few things. For one, the vault isn't a vault. It's basically the entire museum basement. It's a real room, though one with barred windows and a big steel door with a combination lock. Breaking in won't be a walk in the park, but it should be easier than *The Italian Job*.

I don't want us anywhere near the guards. There were three downstairs when we visited. I couldn't get a good look at the vault door behind them, but I did notice the submachine guns strapped to their shoulders. These guys aren't some low-pay rent-a-cops; they're basically soldiers. I'm not putting my daughter in that kind of danger for a poem.

Lola said we could tunnel our way in. I have to give her props for enthusiasm; she's really into this. She's a bit mad now. I snorted coffee out my nose when she said "tunnel." I apologized. I don't know why I dismissed it right away. It's not such a silly idea. A tunnel worked for plenty of heists, though I'm not sure we could dig one in a week. I suppose my real problem with tunneling is that it leaves a tunnel. I want to go in unnoticed, take pictures, and leave. If we do this right, they'll never know we were there.

The top floor of the museum is protected by infrared sensors and motion detectors. I can only assume the basement is the same. Infrared is the easiest. If we cut the power to the air conditioning but leave everything else running, no one should notice anything. The building is stone; it will have stored enough sun heat to warm up the room. With the weather we've been having, the temperature should reach thirty degrees Celsius fairly quickly, maybe a tad more. Unfortunately, our external body temperature is about thirty-four. What we need is . . . a mild case of hypothermia. If I lower my skin temperature by three or four degrees, the sensors should see no difference between me and the air around me. There are many ways to do that. Ice, for one. I can lie in an ice bath. Maybe a refrigerated truck; we could use it for transport. An hour inside the refrigerated compartment might do the trick. I'll need to test it first, but it shouldn't be that hard to do.

That leaves the ultrasonics. That will be . . . trickier. I need something that absorbs sound waves to hide behind or wear. A thick rug, a . . . wet suit. Neoprene might work if it's thick enough. I'll still need to move very slowly once I'm in. That's where it gets tricky. I won't have much time before my body temperature rises again. I'll need to be fast while being very slow. I can test that, too, I guess. I'm sure we can buy ultrasonic sensors *somewhere*. Two days to get the material, two days of testing. That gives us another three days to come up with plan B if it doesn't work. That leaves the windows. I don't know what to do about the windows. Whatever the plan is, I need to get inside. There'll be a contact sensor—that's easy to fool—but I don't know how to get through the steel bars without leaving a trace. That and I'm not entirely sure I can fit through the frame.

. . .

Theoretically . . . Lola could be the one who goes in. She's smaller than I am and, let's face it, she's in much better shape. I don't know if I'm ready to put her through this, but she always says she wants to be more involved. I did bust her out of a police station and pretend to be my dead mother for this. In context, breaking into a museum really doesn't sound so bad. Right. This is insane. It's not as insane as Mother sending me to Germany during the war to rescue a Nazi—what was she thinking?—but it's not exactly good parenting.

This is what scares me. I was convinced my mother could do no wrong when I was Lola's age. I would have followed her anywhere, even if I thought she was wrong. Who knows, maybe she found enlightenment somewhere along the way. Not me. I'm fifty-six and none the wiser. The only thing I have more of is experience, and even that doesn't mean what I thought it did. I still have no idea what the hell I'm doing. I've just gotten really used to it. I don't want my daughter to follow blindly because she thinks I know better. I should let her decide.

—Lola? Can you come here for a sec? There's something I need to ask you.

She's an adult; she can make her own choices. She's . . . nineteen. God, I just remembered what that was like. Maybe I am a bit wiser after all. Just a tad.

# 42

*Kids in America*

Paresfuckingthesia. This is ridiculous. It's three in the morning and I just stole a truck. Now's not the time for pins and needles. This is nerve-wracking enough as it is; I don't need my limbs to fall asleep. I needed *Mom* to fall asleep. She's a good sleeper. Five minutes and she's out like a light. But no, not today. I went to bed with my clothes on, ready to pounce. Two hours it took for her to doze off. I feel bad for sneaking out like this, but she didn't leave me much choice.

Seriously, a fish truck! She wanted me to freeze my butt inside a *fish truck* while drinking cold lemonade or something. "It's science, Lola!" Yeah, sure. And James Bond is a BBC documentary. I'll end up dying of hypothermia in a Chinese prison cell. In a wet suit. I almost forgot about the wet suit. Like, what the fuck is wrong with her? "Do you have a better idea?" Hell yeah! But it's not as if she'd listen to me, so I kept it to myself. I mean, she spent all day running experiments in our now thirty-degree hotel room; she wasn't going to change her mind after that. Whatever. She can sweat in slow motion to her heart's content. I've got this. Time to check in with the boys.

—Are you guys ready?

—Give us a minute. Ground Control out.

—All right. I'll wait.

I'll wait inside my big stolen truck. I'm not sure it's really stolen. It was in the museum parking lot to begin with. Keys were in it and everything. It's not refrigerated, but it does have a winch. I don't need fresh halibut; I need a winch. That and a ten-dollar set of walkie-talkies. Voilà. Adil was happy to help. He's all about "sticking it to the Man!" He even got some of his friends to tag along. I just had to agree to use code names. Boys are weird.

—Ground Control to Major Tom. Commencing countdown, engines on.

I'm Major Tom. I guess that means we go in ten seconds. I've got this, but I'm still shaking. I'm *really* shaking. Of course that fever thing never kicks in when I want it to. I need someone to make me angry. Scared shitless doesn't work, apparently. Crap, I forgot to count. Five. Six. I can do this. I'm reasonably sure I can do this. Fuck it, that's got to be ten. I'll just stick my nice big truck in reverse and hit the gas. UGH! There. It ripped those window bars right off. I knew it was a good plan. Now out of the truck and into the museum.

—This is Major Tom. I'm stepping through the window. Door, whatever.

Damn, this is tight. I won't tell Mom, but I don't think she'd have fit through here. I'm in. Adil and his friends should be throwing rocks through the front window right about now. The guards will think that's what the alarm is for and check it out. We drove a truck full of old tires in front. A gallon of gasoline and boom. Burn, baby, burn. The fire should keep the guards busy for a while. I hope everyone follows the script or this will be over quick.

Now for the hard part. I have absolutely no idea where the bow is. Big, flat crates. Those are paintings, I guess. I know a bow-shaped box would be too much to ask, but I hope to God they put it in a box that fits. Long and narrow. Long and narrow. Nope. That's a nice sword, though. More boxes. Nope. Nope. Nope. I just wish I could read the fucking labels. For all I know one of them says "the bow" in big letters. I wonder how long I've been here. Twenty seconds? Eight hours?

Ooooh. This looks promising. A nice big pile of long boxes. Jackpot! It's a bow! It's not the *right* bow, but with any luck I'm in the bow *aisle*. Unless of course they store things chronologically, geographically, or any of the other fifty ways they could make my life more difficult. Another bow . . . Something that might have once been a bow. This is . . . a real shitty bow. You knew no one in your village liked you when they gave you that bow. "Here, Steve, take this! What? No! We're not laughing at you. We're laughing *with*—"

. . .

Whoa.

This is it. I . . . I didn't think it would mean anything, the object—I only want what's on it, after all—but seeing it in the flesh . . . It's beautiful. It's seen better days, but I can still tell how much care went into making it, how much it meant to . . . us. This belonged to us. We spent countless hours carving those symbols so we could send a message . . . to ourselves, a couple thousand years into the future. This is so fucking cool, I'm . . . I think I'm crying a little.

—Can you hear me, Major Tom?

Right. Wake up, Lola. Take the goddamn pictures.

Maybe I can take it with me. I sort of want to. I mean, it's my bow, really. I *should* take it. Of course we begged everyone here to let us see it and they turned us down not two days ago. That might raise a few flags, but still. Damn, this is taking forever. Whoever invented Polaroids wasn't a cat burglar. Every. Picture. Just. Ekes. Its. Way. Out. And I never noticed how loud these things are. I should have brought a replica and replaced the bow. . . . Yeah right, I should have brought an exact replica of an ancient bow, and a wet suit, in a fish truck. One more picture and I can go.

I'll squeeze my butt out the window and . . .

—Major Tom—

Ah, to hell with this.

I hope Mom won't be *too* pissed. We can still do the wet suit thing for fun if she really wants to.

# 43

## *Private Eyes*

My angry mother impression leaves a lot to be desired. I don't have Lola's acting talents and "You went against my wishes" is really hard to say with a straight face. My mother said it; maybe that's what's bothering me. In my mind it sounds straight out of a Victorian novel. "I shall not be set at naught by my own progeny!"

—Lola, you . . . disobeyed me!

—Did I? I mean, you never told me *not* to go.

—You snuck out in the middle of the night!

—Well, you never said anything about that either. Come on, Mom! I did good, didn't I?

—You're grounded, Lola, for life. . . . But yes, you did good.

My daughter's plan was crude, but efficient. I wanted to defeat the alarm system; she just made it irrelevant. Few moving parts, easy to abort. Simpler is better; I should have learned that making rockets. More often than not, brute force does the trick and it's a lot faster than "elegant" approaches. The rocket can't reach the moon. Make it bigger. Still won't get there? Make it thirty-four stories tall. Bigger is always better when it comes to von Braun's ego. I guess I prefer brains to brawn, even if that makes me naive. Not every game is won by hitting harder. That would sound a lot smarter if I hadn't spent four days working on the most convoluted plan to do what Lola did throwing rocks at a window.

I knew the day would come when Lola would be better suited for the world than I am. I didn't know *how* it would happen. A slow, gradual process or an earth-shattering event that would make my obsolescence glaring in an instant. Now I know. It's time we add a "One" to our name.

—Are the pictures okay, Mom? I didn't have time to check.

—The flash ruined one of them, but we're good.

—Are we? There should be ten pictures. I took the whole pack.

I wonder if she knows it's coming. No, she has *no idea*. Mother ambushed me with it when we moved to Moscow. I *soo* didn't see it coming. "It's time for us to be the One Hundred." Boom. My whole world exploded. I wasted years after that. If I'd embraced it sooner, Mother would have met her granddaughter. Lola missed out on so much because I didn't feel ready. I hope she's braver than I am.

—We have what we need, Lola.

—Good. I was worried I messed it up. I don't want to go back.

—They closed the museum. Hoodlums, they said. I thought they would spin it for propaganda but no. Hoodlums.

—The youth these days. Now all we need is to translate the pictures.

—I did that already.

—You did? Like, how? When?

—It's almost four o'clock, Lola. You slept through the whole day. I saw the Polaroids on the table, so I did the translation. I also took a nice long walk. I had a box of infrared sensors to throw out.

I still think my plan had promise. I was half tempted to experiment anyway, but Lola came home so late, I didn't want her to sleep in a sauna. I was also missing a wet suit. I should have known it would be hard to come by; we're in the desert, two thousand miles from the nearest ocean.

—So? Are you going to tell me?

—Tell you what?

—What does it say?

—Oh! It says:

"I am eight. I am one and many.

Perhaps you are also me."

—Mom! We knew that already.

—I know, but that's how it begins. We didn't know that before.

—Sure. I know what comes next:

"From the underworld, she emerges in wetness.

I touch her elbow, then her mouth.

She speaks after a cold silence.

Desire awakens and I reach for her breast."

I know it by heart, Mom. What comes after that?

—There are a couple words I'm not—

—MOM!

—All right! All right!

"I taste the salt until it turns to dust.

I ask for mercy when her arrow is gone."

—God, this is weird.

—Oh, it gets weirder.

"I sleep with the lion between the dragon's ribs.

Follow his dying heart into the underworld.

I see her breast again where the dragon lays its eggs.

And hide inside her heart where death will not find

me."

The end.

—Really? It says: "The end"?

—No, that's just . . . the end.

—What does it mean?

—I'll need my books to figure that out. Hopefully, it's all based on Babylonian astronomy. We'll know soon enough once we get back to Volgograd.

—Then what?

—Then we follow the instructions.

—Together?

—Yes, Lola. We'll do it together.

I look forward to it. This is an adventure twenty-five hundred years in the making. It reminds me of the elaborate candy hunts I prepared for Lola on Mallorca. Each clue led to a piece of candy wrapped in another clue. She loved those, begged for me to make another the second one was over. I spent hours coming up with clever riddles and hiding them across town, only for Lola to solve the whole thing in forty-five minutes flat. This should take a while longer; the Eight must have spent years setting this up. I don't know what excites me the most, discovering what our ancestor wanted us to find, or that I get to embark on this quest with Lola. One last candy hunt for the two of us. The One Hundred is setting sail for its final voyage.

# 44

*Ghost Town*

Uriel is drunk again. A predictable event. These aftershocks from the quake of Raphael's death are now a weekly ritual. I am . . . disappointed in both of us. My brother is a wretched creature and I am a fool. I let the "polis" part of Persepolis trick me into thinking this would be a city. It was once the capital of the largest empire, but it seems its sole purpose was to oooh and aaah. I don't think anyone who didn't work at the palace ever lived here. Certainly, no one does now. That said, the ruins *are* impressive. The site is vast. When I saw it from a distance, my first thought was that it would take forever to explore. It did not. I found what I was looking for almost immediately.

There are three rows of reliefs at the eastern stairway of the Apadana. Most are depictions of delegates from across the world bringing tribute to the king of kings, but one relief stands out: a priestess to the water goddess Anahita holding audience. Behind her is a sphere that appears to be shining. This portion of the palace was added under Xerxes. Whatever her skills were, whatever . . . magic she claimed to perform, she must have rocketed through the ranks for her likeness to be added to the walls.

I feared the traitor would want to hide after leaving Egypt, that she, at the very least, would keep a low profile. She could easily have disappeared. All she had to do was blend in and there would be nothing for us to find. In fact, of all the positions one could occupy in the largest empire on Earth, she chose one of the handful that would draw history's attention. Uriel believes it was arrogance, that her ego got in the way, but I cannot help thinking she did it all to taunt us. She wasn't afraid of us.

We will see this through if we can. Why she sought a position of power matters little at the moment, but it got me thinking. Why haven't we? We never did, as far as I know. We have the physical strength, the intellect. We could, I assume, have risen to power at any time in history. We could have been kings, but we never were. What stopped us? It was not humility; that much is certain.

Perhaps it was a profound disdain for "them," our hatred of the other. It was *their* ladder and we never cared to climb it. Maybe we thought it would stain us, change us somehow. I think we were afraid it would make it harder to despise them all. I know now that is what our father could not stand about me. He could not bear seeing Mother through my eyes. His whole world was built on the notion that she was nothing. It would have come tumbling down if she mattered in the slightest. Whatever kept us out of the history books, it is deeply engrained. I do not aspire to rule anything, even when my basest instincts rear their heads. Conquer, perhaps—violence has its appeal—but reigning over the conquered afterwards is not the least bit attractive.

Maybe that is what separates us from the traitors. They embrace a semblance of humanity while we suppress the very idea that we could share anything with the rest of this world. Differences aside, of all the incarnations of the traitors we have encountered, this one is unique. Every traitor we came across appeared to eschew notoriety. This one sought as much of it as she could get. I do not believe she was blinded by arrogance, but she was undeniably brazen.

She visits me in my dreams. She dares me to catch her and I come *so close.* So close. We play our game almost every night and I long for the dream when we don't. Leave it to me to become infatuated with the dead. Perhaps it is only natural; I have never felt comfortable with the living. I only wish I had someone to share these thoughts with. I could never tell Uriel; he . . . He is me, but empty, broken. Like a stolen car that's been stripped for parts.

I should get back to town before he gets himself into trouble. I don't have the patience for Uriel's antics at the moment. All I can think of is the traitor. I'm eager to go to bed and see if her ghost will come to play.

# 45

*Anarchy in the UK*

—LOLA, WATCH OUT!

The car almost ran us over before it drove through the shop window. I hear screaming down the street.

—Mom?

—I don't know, Lola. I think there's a mob coming.

—Adil, what's going on?

*[I think your mom is right. We'd better not stay here.]*

Just as I thought. There must be hundreds of them coming. They're throwing bricks, rocks. They're going to ransack this whole street.

—Lead the way, Adi— OH FUCK!

Someone threw a Molotov cocktail on a parked car. It's complete mayhem out here.

*[GO BACK! GO BACK!]*

What? Oh shit. The police are here. A whole army of them. This place is going to turn into a war zone and we're smack dab in the middle of it.

\*\*Tak\*\* \*\*Tak\*\*

*[GET DOWN!]*

Shots fired. I don't know who's shooting at whom. Shit. This is not good. Where the hell is Adil?

*[Down the alley. Come! Quick!]*

—MOM! THIS WAY!

—I'm coming.

There's a little girl in the middle of the street. She's just standing there holding a worn-out doll. She's going to get herself killed. Come on, kid! Get off the street! Oh, for fuck's sake.

—MOM!

—Go ahead, Lola! I'm right behind you! I just need—

# 46

## *Crimson and Clover*

One last day in China. One day. That's all. We drove back to
Kashgar to bring Adil home and say our goodbyes. We were
barely out of the car when we saw people running in every direction. Lots of screaming I couldn't make out. A car appeared
out of nowhere and drove through the front of a luxury shop
across the street. People rushed in and started looting the place.

I asked Adil what was going on. He didn't know.

We started running. Something exploded behind me. I
turned and there was a car on fire. Mom told me to get down.
Maybe it was Adil. I don't know. I put my face to the ground. All
I could see was . . . sparkles; the sun reflecting on shiny specks in
the brown sand. There was screaming everywhere, bullets flying
over my head, but staring at the sand an inch from the ground
was—I don't know—peaceful. Everything felt muffled, slowed
down, until Adil tapped me on the calf and pointed at an alley
ten feet behind us.

I got up and ran. Adil was a couple feet in front. Mom, she—

—MOM! THIS WAY!

—I'm coming.

I ran as hard as I could. The alley wasn't that long, a hundred
feet of shade between the hell we were in and the hell on the
other street. I slowed down halfway through to let Mom catch
up to us.

—MOM!

—Go ahead, Lola! I'm right behind you! I just need—

I just need. I stood still, waiting for that sentence to end. It never did.

My mother is dead.

I saw her and my legs just gave in. Adil almost tore my shoulder off trying to drag me to safety. My knees scraped against the dirt and broken glass for twenty feet. Pain didn't register. Nothing did. Mom just lay there, a few steps away, a small red dot on her forehead. Just a dot. There wasn't any blood. She looked . . . She looked like someone had pressed pause on the VCR and stopped her midsentence. She was still talking; she . . . She didn't fucking know she was dead. I tried to pull away, but Adil held on. Two men came in to help and held me down as best they could. I kept clawing at the ground, and clawing, and clawing until my fingernails tore off. I was still painting the dirt red when the butt of a police rifle knocked me out cold.

A Han had killed a Uighur in a fight some time ago. He was acquitted in court that day and all hell broke loose. Two fucking words, or however many it takes to say not guilty in Mandarin. That's why Mom died. It was over in fifteen minutes. Six hundred arrests. Two hundred injured. Two dead. Two. They said it could have been a lot worse. Fuck them. I hate them all. The police, the rioters. The other dead. I hate the Han, the Uighurs, the whole country. I hate the world and me in it. All of it is rotten, nothing but blood, piss, and shit. Everything else is us trying to mask the stench.

I woke up in a hospital hooked to an IV. The rest is fuzzy like drunken memories. I trashed the place. That part I remember. I tore through whatever stood between me and the door. Blinding sun. I needed to go back to where she died. I must have walked there. There was a car parked over the spot. I . . . They'd cleaned it all. It hadn't been a day, but they'd swept the bullet casings, fixed the broken windows. There was nothing to go back to, nothing to cry on or scream at. She was gone.

No. Hell no. I wasn't going to let them erase her like that. They couldn't just pretend like it didn't happen, like she wasn't even here. That fucking car. It wouldn't budge. I tried pushing at one end, then the other. I found a steel bar in the alley we ran into and I fucking whaled at it. Me versus car, my butt sticking out of my hospital gown. I don't know how long it lasted. I just swung until I couldn't.

I was still panting, trying to stare that car into oblivion, when half the Chinese army showed up around a black limo. The door opened, and Xuesen stepped out. He must have been keeping tabs on us. Everyone kept their distance. I was exhausted, but I wouldn't let go of the steel bar. Xuesen gestured at the soldiers to leave me be. He walked up, slowly as ever; then he put his hand on my shoulder. I started crying for the first time. It was like he pushed a button and opened the floodgates.

Xuesen didn't speak. He listened to me cry and cry some more, then he listened to me scream, and when that ran out he just listened to me. "I won't let them forget her like that." I said the same thing a thousand times in a thousand ways hoping it would magically make sense if I said it differently. Not sure how long we were there for. The soldiers were gone when I stopped talking. It was me and him, sitting on the ground. I was shocked by the silence, like I didn't remember it existed. I looked at Xuesen, hoping for . . . fucking *anything*. He waited a few seconds to make sure I was done; then, finally, he spoke.

—Never forget, Lola. Never drink the tea.

# ENTR'ACTE

## *The Witching Hour*

### 187 BC

Why Thessaly?

She couldn't risk going to Athens again, but she could have settled anywhere. Thessaly was isolated. Vast plains, enclosed by mountains on three sides and an ocean on the other. It had been under Macedonian control for over a century and was seen as backwards by the Greeks, uncivilized. It would be hard for the Tracker to find her there, if he even thought to look. She could continue her work without drawing attention. That is what she told herself, but in truth, she had come for only one reason. Thessaly had horses, the most beautiful horses she'd ever seen.

Aglaonike, now three months pregnant, bought land in a small town west of Larissa. Someone had told her Bucephalus—Alexander the Great's legendary horse—came from there. She built an observatory on her rooftop where she could watch the stars while her sleepless mares grazed the dark pastures around her. She had studied the works of astronomers from Babylon and Uruk, works often ignored by the vainglorious Athenians. The Babylonians had studied the motions of celestial bodies for millennia. They had produced the first star catalogs and studied the phases of the moon, proposed a mathematical model of planetary motion, predicting the position of the five moving stars: Mercury, Venus, Mars, Jupiter, and Saturn. It was with that knowledge in hand that the Thirty-Two had come back to Greece, intrigued by the work of a relatively unknown mathematician, Aristarchus of Samos.

Before she could turn her attention to the heavens, Aglaonike had some earthly business to attend to. The vast swath of land she had purchased came with people, lots of people. She had ensured that the handful of slaves who worked in the house were made free as part of the transaction, but when she first stepped into her new home she found a young woman hiding in one of the rooms. Fairer-skinned than most, hair red as fire, the woman begged Aglaonike to let her stay. She claimed to be possessed by an evil spirit and feared for her life if she ever left. Aglaonike was intrigued. She had seen many women falsely accused of demonic possession, but it was the first time she had heard someone make that claim about themselves.

The people who cultivated her fields also lived on her property. The Penestae, as the Thessalians called them, were neither owned nor free. Their existence was instead tied to the land they inhabited, in this case Aglaonike's land. They were allowed to cultivate it, and as long as they paid her a share of the harvest they could keep whatever was left and sell it. Aglaonike's fields were fertile and the Penestae who inhabited it lived relatively well. While the arrangement was in theory beneficial to all parties, it involved frequent interactions and visits to the house as well as rather complex accounting, which, Aglaonike learned, had to date been performed by the one they called the "Demon Woman."

Whatever was going on with Aglaonike's redheaded guest, she was apparently good with numbers. That was reason enough for Aglaonike to let her stay, but she also wanted to know how one could become convinced they were inhabited by an evil spirit. The priest himself had apparently made the determination, but Aglaonike had her doubts and chose to spend time with her new guest. Redheaded people, especially women, were often mistrusted. The great Aristotle himself had said it plainly: "The reddish are of bad character." To Aglaonike's surprise, the woman did bark from time to time. She blinked four times as much as anyone else, often in sequences of three. She would also yell obscenities seemingly unprompted. These outbursts, Aglaonike noticed, occurred with greater frequency when the woman was under stress, but none were ever accompanied by aggressive behavior or apparent ill intent. In Aglaonike's mind, that left only two possibilities, both of which she explained in detail to the woman. The first and most probable conclusion was that there were no spirits or demons involved and she simply suffered from an unusual condition. Aglaonike had, after all, observed people whose arms and legs twitched independently of their will. The second option seemed far-fetched to Aglaonike's scientific mind, but she lacked sufficient data to completely discard it. If her guest was indeed inhabited by some vulgar supernatural entity, its control was intermittent and limited to the woman's tongue. After some consideration, Aglaonike decided either was a small price to pay for someone who was good at math. The woman seemed relieved to know that she was, at worst, 99 percent unpossessed. She asked for a new name, as the old one only brought back painful memories. Aglaonike told her she could choose for herself. She chose Pyrrha, the red-haired goddess who created women after the Great Deluge.

Aglaonike struck a deal with the Penestae. Aside from a small pasture needed to feed the horses, the Penestae would keep the entire harvest for themselves and pay her nothing. In exchange, they would send three women to work with her at the house, women who showed a natural ability for science or mathematics. The first to arrive at the door the next morning was a smaller than average twelve-year-old girl. When Aglaonike expressed doubt as to the child's abilities, she proceeded to estimate the number of barley spikelets one *stremma* of land could produce.

As if that weren't enough to convince Aglaonike, the child introduced herself as Alcmene, meaning "might of the moon." The second to show was Adrasteia—she who stands her ground—a frail woman in her late twenties who immediately told Aglaonike the rumors about her killing her husbands were entirely unfounded. The third was Althaia, the healer, an old woman who made medicine out of just about anything she could find.

Her ragtag team of would-be astronomers assembled, Aglaonike proceeded to train them in the basics, starting with the phases of the sun and moon. When they were proficient enough, they would move on to objects at greater distances. Aglaonike had followed the rules her ancestors had passed on to her in pursuit of the goal they all shared, but a lifetime spent studying the work of the most prominent scholars had left her with one unsurmountable problem: the universe was too small. Astronomers of the time could not agree on a definitive view of the cosmos. Pythagoras saw the Earth, sun, and moving stars revolving around a "Central Fire" that no one could see because a "counter-Earth" blocked the view. Most thought the Earth was the center of the universe, with everything else revolving around it: the moon, the sun, the five moving stars. *Everyone* assumed that the fixed stars were attached to the outermost layer of the universe. What they were no one knew. Prick holes showing a large fire behind them, gems glued onto a dark sphere, it did not matter. Aglaonike was to take people to the stars and these were not of the kind one could take people to. That only left the moving stars. Her whole life, she had assumed they were the destination, but surely they were not all equally suited. More important, this great evil bent on killing everyone had to come from somewhere, presumably from one of the moving stars as well. That made choosing the right one all the more important. In a universe of six worlds where one could *see* everything, moving from one world to another did not seem so salutary.

Then came Aristarchus of Samos. He hypothesized that the Earth, along with all the moving stars, revolved around the sun. Aglaonike thought it might explain why the planets did not always appear exactly where and when she thought they would. What she found even more interesting was the suggestion that the fixed stars were suns in their own right, albeit very, very distant ones. Suddenly the universe was a lot bigger, too big perhaps. If each dot in the night sky was a sun, with worlds circling around it, her mission, though all the more challenging, at least made a modicum of sense. There were, at last, places to go.

As it turned out, predicting the movement of astronomical objects was a lot easier under the assumption that the Earth circled the sun and not the other way around. Within two years, they had a near-perfect model of the moon's position and phases. By the time Aglaonike's daughter was old enough to help, Althaia had died of old age and the women were predicting the appearance of all the moving stars with relative precision. They had yet to find a way to measure the distance to any of the fixed stars, but Aglaonike held hope that they would succeed in her lifetime. Her small group of women worked well together and progress was constant. Pyrrha was taking enormous mathematical strides and Alcmene was working on a diopter at least ten times as precise as anything they had ever built.

Sixteen years after Aglaonike had settled in her new home, war returned to Thessaly. Roman troops built their encampment a mere million—about five thousand feet—away from her land. Three years later, King Perseus of Macedon was defeated and Thessaly became a part of the Roman Republic.

On a quiet spring morning, Aglaonike heard the horses pace as a new tax collector approached. She prepared the usual levy, but the man told her she had to pay five times what his predecessor had asked for. Aglaonike refused, threatened to report the man to the Council, even to Rome. Extortion, no matter how common, was still a crime. Surely the Republic would not want its new citizens to think it was corrupt. The man burst into laughter. "I know who you are," the man said. "I know what goes on within these walls." He stepped closer to Aglaonike until she felt his breath on her face, then whispered: "Heresy."

Thessaly was surrounded by myth, literally. The gods watched from Mount Olympus in the north. Kronos and the other Titans were based on Mount Othrys in the south. To the west, Mount Pelion was the home of the centaurs. Everything in between was seen as barbaric, uncivilized, heretic. The likes of Achilles and Jason, both sons of Thessaly, had been replaced in the collective mind by darker, unruly figures. While the women referred to themselves as astronomers, they were known to everyone else as the Witches of Thessaly.

Aglaonike had experienced firsthand what horrors fear and superstition could lead men to perform. She also knew how extortion worked. The moment that man believed she feared him, and she did, wholeheartedly, the abuse would begin to get worse and worse until it became untenable. Five times the tax would turn into ten, ten into twenty. Aglaonike agreed to pay but said she needed time to gather such a large sum. She told the man he should return nine days later after nightfall to collect his due.

Nine days passed and the man returned, this time with a *contubernium* of eight legionaries. Perhaps he had sensed deception on Aglaonike's part; perhaps he simply wanted to drive his point home. The men waited outside for Aglaonike, and waited, and waited. Pyrrha was first to come out, her hair glowing under intense moonlight. She walked up to the tax man, blinked three times, and told him she would pray for his soul. Three more women joined her, each holding a candle. They started chanting, softly, in words the men could not understand. The tax man protested in vain until Aglaonike stepped out of the house. She stood in front of the men and spoke loudly and surely.

—You have come to steal from me.

You have desecrated this land with your rotten souls.

You have angered your gods and mine, awakened the spirits of the underworld.

The dead shall rise as you disrupted their sleep, but you will not see them.

For you have angered ME!

The women blew out their candles and continued chanting. The legionaries stepped back.

Now bow to my power as I bring true darkness upon you!

Moments passed until the tax man broke the awkward silence.

—Arrest these witches! Burn this house of evil.

But the men stood there, frozen in time, their heads turned to the northern sky.

What are you waiting for? Arrest them!

The tax man finally looked up. Fear and awe rushed through his veins like a raging river as a third of the moon had vanished from the sky. What remained slowly withered until a slim line of light disappeared into nothingness. Armor and swords dropped to the ground. Kneeling men stood and stumbled away in the dark, leaving a shriveling tax man curled up on the ground.

# ACT V

# 47

## *How Soon Is Now?*

The unknown.

The last four and a half years had been darkness and silence. New darkness. New silence. Every day brought Lola a new breed of loneliness, despair not quite before experienced. A mind-numbing repetition of the never familiar.

Lola rose early, for once, unsure where she should look for news of the probe. It was a way to honor her mother—she knew how much Mia cared about the endeavor—but she felt a certain kinship with the contraption. It, too, traveled through uncharted space, alone in the dark. Perhaps more than anything, she envied it, for it felt none of the fear that came with her unknown, none of the pain that came with remembering.

*Voyager* remembered nothing. The robot only knew sixty-nine kilobytes at a time. Everything else it learned was stored on eight-track magnetic tapes, transmitted to Earth and erased to make room for new data. Lola wished she could forget that easily.

*Voyager* let Earth know when Uranus got closer. The radio signal, traveling at light speed, would take two and a half hours to reach Earth. A response, with any luck, would come in five. Lola stared at the coffeepot while memories of her mother poured out. Little was known about the seventh planet, but one thing had intrigued Mia for as long as she could remember. The planet was sideways. Perhaps some other celestial object had collided with it in the early days of the solar system; perhaps it was moved by other forces. Whatever the reason, its rotation axis pointed at the sun during half its orbit.

What would the planet's seasons be like? A year on Uranus lasts eighty-four of Earth's years, each season a quarter of that. This was summer/winter, when one pole faces the sun. Twenty-one years of daylight on one side of the planet, twenty-one years of darkness on the other. In the spring and fall, however, the sun would shine on the equator. Day and night would follow the planet's rotation, turning the light on and off every seventeen hours. This frantic rhythm would continue for twenty-one years until it ground to a halt and half the planet plunged into darkness again for the next two decades. Lola wondered how the phenomenon would affect the surface, then wiped her memory to make room for new thoughts.

Seven point eight million miles away, a seemingly featureless blue-green dot grew larger and larger until the robot spotted a moon, then spotted another, and another.

Humans already knew of Uranus's children. William Herschel had observed Oberon and Titania in 1787. Ariel and Umbriel were both found in 1851. It would take another hundred years for the famed Gerard Kuiper to discover a fifth moon he named Miranda. But instead of five moons, *Voyager* counted *fifteen*. It looked as if Uranus had spawned three litters of baby planets, tiny space kittens running circles in their Uranian pen. They would be named Juliet, Puck, Cordelia, Ophelia, Bianca, Desdemona, Portia, Rosalind, Cressida, and Belinda.

*Voyager* noticed something else while people on Earth christened moons with the names of Shakespearian characters. The planet had more rings than expected. We knew of nine, but *Voyager* saw two more. Dark, faint halos of water and ice circling the ghostly, elfin-looking world.

*Voyager* set its sights on the planet's atmosphere. Hydrogen and helium, like the gas giants it had encountered. Below it,

*Voyager* found ice, lots of ice. Water ice, methane ice, ammonia ice. Uranus is an *ice* giant, the coldest of them all.

During its flyby, *Voyager 2* discovered ten new moons, two new rings. It found that the planet's magnetic field is also tilted and off-center. It analyzed the planet's atmosphere and surface. It even determined the exact length of an Uranian day at seventeen hours and fourteen minutes.

The encounter had been a resounding success, but back on Earth, no one was in the mood for celebrating.

# 48

## *Red Rain*

What can you do in seventy-three seconds? Clean the bath-room mirror. Boil water in the microwave. Floss your teeth. For seventy-three seconds, they were all going to space. That's how long their dream lasted before it disintegrated over the Atlantic. Mom would say they died doing what they loved. I think they just died, but the news seems to agree with Mom.

Francis R. Scobee, Commander. Forty-six years old. He had a wife and two children. That's what the paper said about him. A wife and two children is all the humanizing he gets. He was in command of a shuttle mission. He'd been a test pilot since '72. That's how long he'd waited for this. I bet he was ecstatic.

Michael J. Smith, Pilot. As a kid, he watched airplanes take off and land on the airstrip next to the family farm. Now he was the pilot on a spaceship. A real one. That's kid's dream level, drawing buttons and levers on the closet wall, pretending you're going to the moon. Grown-ups won't dare dream that big. I wonder if he knew, if years of adulting made this feel like any other job or if he smiled for no reason in the middle of the day thinking: I'm the pilot on a fucking spaceship.

Gregory Jarvis, Payload Specialist. He met his wife, Marcia, in college and worked on communication satellites before join-ing NASA. His bio says he was "an avid squash player and bi-cycle rider. He also enjoyed cross country skiing, backpacking, racquetball . . ." Racquetball. That's what he liked. The news is talking about them only as "astronauts," as if that's really what they were. That's a career, not a person. These people were regular folks who just happened to be smarter than everyone else. They hit their toe on the table leg; they liked their eggs a certain way.

Ronald McNair. Him I'd read about before. He was the second African American to go to space. Mostly, he was cool. When he was eight years old, Ron went to the segregated library in his small South Carolina town and refused to leave when they told him to. They called the cops and his mom, but the kid wouldn't leave without his books. He got them. He played the saxophone on his first trip to space. This time, he was supposed to record a solo for Jean-Michel Jarre's next album.

Ellison Onizuka was the first Asian American in space, first astronaut of Japanese descent. How many Asian kids were watching the launch because for once the hero looked like them?

How many young girls watched Judith Resnik take off for the same reason? At thirty-six, she was the second American woman to make it to space, only the fourth on the planet. First Jewish woman. She wanted to be a pianist but turned down a spot at Juilliard to study math after she got a perfect score on her SAT. She was a pilot, an electrical engineer, a software engineer. She was a fellow in biomedical engineering at the NIH. I mean, my family's pretty badass, but Judith Resnik puts us all to shame.

Then there's Christa McAuliffe. She wasn't a pilot or a NASA engineer. She was a high school teacher from New Hampshire. She sent an application for the Teacher in Space Project and they picked her out of eleven thousand applicants to be the first civilian in space. She had two kids of her own, six and nine.

They'd set up a live feed in schools so the children could tune in, because there was a fucking teacher on board. Kids cheered during liftoff, watched the shuttle fly up straight, then roll as usual. They gasped when the external tank collapsed into a gaint

ball of fire. Most stared at the smoke snakes when the side boosters flew off in every direction. No one noticed when what remained of the shuttle hit the ocean at three hundred miles an
hour. I suppose that's a blessing.

I watched them die. Then I watched them die again and again
on the news. They must have died forty times, but by the third I
couldn't see *Challenger* anymore. All I could see was my mother's
face, a dark red dot on her forehead. I saw her dead body lying
on the street while people stole toaster ovens and portable radios.
This world is hell-bent on never making sense. That was almost
five years ago, but it might as well be yesterday. There's then and
there is now. The days in between are just filler.

Mom was right about the ozone layer. She was right about
many things, but she'd have liked to know she was right about
that, too. Scientists from Cambridge published a paper last year
about ozone losses in the atmosphere above the Antarctic. We'd
have known sooner, but the satellite they sent up there was ignoring all the data that proved it, on purpose. Figures. I wish
Mother had known. She'd have been happy. Maybe not, it's bad
news after all. She'd sure be depressed about the space race.
Reagan announced a modular international space station. It
sounded cool, but that was two years ago and not a thing has
happened since. The Russians sent one up instead. They've had
small stations in orbit since '71, but this Mir thing is a lot bigger.
It's pretty much the only good news to come out of there. They
spent all the rubles they had on a doppelgänger of the American
space shuttle.

I moved back to the US after Mom's death. Gulfport, Mis-
sissippi, 'cause why not? I still haven't unpacked. It's amazing
how little of what we own we actually use. I hooked up with the
neighbor across the corridor. I don't remember how or when,
just that one day his toothbrush was in my bathroom. He was . . .
good. He was a godsend, really. I was about as useful to the world

as a moaning old dog crippled with arthritis. I didn't dress, didn't bathe, didn't eat. I sure as shit didn't cook or clean. He took care of it, of me, until I resembled a human being again. I felt horrible for dumping him the minute I got pregnant, but I knew bad shit would come to him if he stayed.

I'm beginning to show now. I . . . I did it. Whoo. Survive at all costs, whatever. We are the Hundred and One. It doesn't feel like it, though. Not really. The One Hundred just . . . wasn't done. Mom wasn't done. I wasn't done with her. I was just beginning to *see* her, the real her. This trip we were taking, this . . . quest or whatever you want to call it, that was our time, the two of us.

It doesn't matter how much I try; I can't think of anything else. I need to see it through. I have to go back and take the journey, let the One Hundred finish what it started before I can let Mom go. Then, maybe. Not before.

# 49

## *Ship of Fools*

I can't see my own feet, or the river, or the shore, but the old man doesn't seem to mind. I don't think he ever told me his name. Maybe he doesn't have one. First name: Captain. Last name: Captain. He stares at the horizon like there is one to stare at and he fiddles with his big wheel from time to time. A bit to the left, a bit to the right, starboard, whatever. I think he does it just to look captainy while we cut through this pea soup. It's working. It doesn't help with the cold—this wet air seeps into your bones—but I don't think we'll die. Not right now anyway.

I touch her elbow, then her mouth.

She speaks after a cold silence.

She got that last part right. My teeth are chattering so much I'm speaking Morse code. Spring in Russia's not exactly balmy, but this is a special kind of biting. What are the odds it gets warmer when we hit the sea? It won't be long before we find out. Captain Captain said we're coming up on the river mouth.

I can't complain. I *chose* to freeze my butt off. Mom would have done this from our living room, drawn a line on a map and gone from there. She'd certainly have figured out the whole thing before she left. I wanted to. I also want to exercise more and eat healthier. Let's face it, patience has never been my strong suit and I think I'm pretty good at winging it. I needed to make the voyage now. I wanted to see what our ancestor saw, feel the wind on my face like she did, smell the same . . . weird fishy stink, though that might just be our boat. I wanted to figure it out as I go. Maybe I was just looking for an excuse to make this last. I get to spend a bit more time with Mom, even if she's not here. I think she'd like this. She'd make fun of me, but I think she'd like it.

This reminds me of the ferry to Algiers. Fuck, I was scared. I'd never been anywhere. I'd just watched my home burn and there was a madman trying to kill us. It was too much to take in. Mom held my hand the whole time. Almost. She let go for a minute and my little heart stopped. I didn't know she'd gone to the vending machine. She came back and handed me a Coca-Cola; I . . . I was okay. It was like magic. Right there and then I knew we'd be fine. There's nothing she could have said that would have reassured me. She knew what I needed. A little bit of normal, some sense I hadn't lost everything. It worked. It was like the world around us disappeared. It was just me, my mother, and a fizzy drink.

—I love you, Mom.

I'd give anything, literally anything, for another ten minutes with her. It's too cold for pop, but a hot chocolate . . . She liked to put marshmallows in them. I wanted mine on the side, of course. "The marshmallows aren't gone, Lola. They just melted *into* the hot chocolate." God, I miss her. I'm three months pregnant and I haven't thought about a name. I don't want to because then it'll be real and I can't do real right now. Real is: Mom's dead. Real is: we're the fucking Hundred and One and all of this is on me. The fate of the world and a child to boot. This world is in a whole lot of trouble if I'm the one who has to save it. So is this child. I thought . . . Mom said everything would change—and that scared the crap out of me—but then I got pregnant and nothing happened. That's not true; I lost my appetite. I don't know what I was expecting. I thought I'd feel . . . up to it? A tiny bit confident I wouldn't screw this up? There's still time, I guess.

Don't worry, tiny person, we'll get you a name. Just as soon as Mommy's done playing pretend, okay?

The fog is dissipating. I can see . . . a whole lot of nothing. I'm pretty sure that's the Caspian Sea.

—HEY, LADY! WE'RE FRESH OUT OF VOLGA!

—I can see that.

—SO? WHERE TO?

Desire awakens and I reach for her breast. Aim for Inanna's star, the heart of the Scorpion, when it appears in the night sky. We're right on time. Scorpius is just above the water now.

—You see that bright star southwest of here?

—Antares?

Ha! The old man knows his stars. I knew there was a reason I picked him.

—Yes. Antares. That's our heading.

—For how long?

—Until we hit land.

I taste the salt until it turns to dust.

# 50

## If You Leave

Salt turned to dust. A *little* salt turned to dust—the Caspian Sea is really more of a lake. We hit land two days ago. Lots and lots of empty barren land. That's when I realized I didn't have a truck, or a horse, or whatever for when I got on said land. I had a boat. Perhaps a *bit* more planning wouldn't hurt next time, but it all worked out in the end.

We followed the coast until we saw signs of human life and Captain Captain dropped me off. I was greeted by five overly happy Chinese men—I swear all five of them were high. I think they worked for an oil company. This is middle-of-nowhere, Kazakhstan, so I should have been surprised to meet Chinese people, but honestly, the thought didn't cross my mind until right now. Two of them drove me to the nearest town. They laughed the whole way, but they were supernice. They dropped me off in Tushi . . . Tushi something.

As it turns out, this Tushi doesn't have much to offer in the way of entertainment, but it has a shit ton of trucks and plenty of people bored out of their wits. I bought myself a guide, a nice pair of sunglasses, and one badass dune buggy that would make Mad Max proud. I saw myself sitting in it in a shop window and it. Is. Cool. I didn't know it'd be this uncomfortable, though. We've been driving for twenty minutes and my butt feels like it's being kicked by a horse. Still, I rule. And I figured out the next clue.

I ask for mercy when her arrow is gone.

It took me long enough. I thought the arrow might have something to do with the bow, the real bow. I don't have it, so that could have been a problem. But Mom said the Eight looked at the stars, so I focused on that. The arrow was a constellation. Basically Sirius—it's the one bright star in there. I assumed I had to "ask for mercy" when it disappeared from the sky. The star finder said that should happen around ten thirty these days. Then what?

Ask for mercy. I figured it meant something like fairness, which was good because there's a Babylonian god for justice and all that: Marduk. He's like the boss. There's even a "star of Marduk" called Nibiru. Oddly, I knew about it. It's on ancient tablets Mom read from when I was young because she has a weird idea of fun. *Had* a weird idea of fun. The problem is Nibiru is more of a spot in the sky than an actual star. Sometimes Mercury was there, sometimes Jupiter, but planets aren't any help. Long story short, I can't look for the "star of Marduk" because there's really no such thing.

So maybe "mercy" wasn't the right word. I busted out the dictionary. The word in Akkadian is *gimillu*. It means a bunch of things; they all do. A favor, a boon—whatever that is—mercy, kindness, compassion. That's when it hit me. It's the corn goddess. Whatever her name was, she was, well, the goddess of corn, and good harvest was seen as kindness from the gods. I found her in Mom's big book. Shala, that's the corn lady, holding an ear of grain. Her constellation is part of Virgo now. Ask for mercy when her arrow is gone. Head for Virgo when Sirius disappears from the sky. Boom. Take that, Indiana Jones.

Okay, Dr. Jones might still have an edge. We're heading in the right direction, but I have no idea when to stop. I need to find a sleepy lion, or a dragon. Whatever, we're driving. With any luck, we'll hit an ancient zoo along the way, or a fire-spitting . . .

something. I'm betting on whatever it is being big. The Eight wouldn't have sent us after something we had no chance of find— We're slowing down, for whatever reason.

—Hey,

Crap, I forgot his name.

Why are we stopping?

There's nothing here. Like, nothing nothing. I don't think I've ever been anywhere with less of something. It's just sand and a few plants wishing they were dead. Maybe my guide needs to p— HOLY SHIT! He busted out a gun!

—Get out!

—What? No! You can't leave me here. There's nothing here—

—I SAID GET OUT!

Whoa. He put the tip of his gun on my forehead. I peed myself.

—All right. All right. I'm out. Just don't sh—

He's gone. . . .

What the *fuck* just happened? He hit the gas and left me standing in a big cloud of dust like a disgraced mobster in some bad Vegas flick. He *marooned* me! The son of a bitch marooned me! I didn't know that was a thing, people getting marooned.

Fuck!

I'm totally marooned.

# 51

## *Don't You (Forget About Me)*

The traitor led me to Pakistan. She was a wearing a white dress, her ghostly shape floating above my bed. She reached down with a gentle hand and touched my face. I felt myself weigh less and less until I stopped feeling the mattress on my back. I was . . . overwhelmed with joyful emotions and I started laughing. I laughed so hard, I flew across the room. My weightless body bounced on walls and ceiling. I could no longer tell which way was up until she caught me with both arms. Our embrace lasted for hours and mere moments at once. I tried to hold her gaze, but I felt . . . intimidated. She put a finger under my chin and raised my head proud; then she grabbed my hand and we flew out the third-floor window.

It was so . . . real. Disturbingly intimate. I felt freer than I've ever felt. I miss that feeling, about as much as I hate the headache I now struggle with. A small lapse in judgment on my part. There were riots in the city when we landed in Islamabad. They said the leader of the Peoples Party was arrested. People took to the streets. Uriel and I took a cab for Rawalpindi but found ourselves stuck in traffic between protests. The heat was unbearable inside the car. After twenty minutes spent motionless on some busy street we decided to get out and explore. We explored for about twenty meters until we found a hotel bar with air conditioning. I was in a drinking mood. It was good news that brought us here, but this thirst was born of self-pity and not the celebration kind.

The traitor died. Uriel found some sort of eulogy at the Central Library of Astan Quds Razavi in Iran. She . . . died. She lived twenty-five hundred years ago, so that should not have come as a surprise, but I was still profoundly saddened to read of her demise. King Xerxes, it would seem, held her in high esteem. His successor, Artaxerxes, preferred to surround himself with familiar faces and brought his entourage to the palace. The priestess—we never learn of her name—traveled to the eastern end of the empire to teach astrology at "a great school in the Hinduš" and died shortly thereafter. How news of her death traveled back to Persepolis I do not know. It was, presumably, of little importance to Artaxerxes or to the empire. Nonetheless, here we are. As always, this particular traitor had an uncanny tendency to leave an indelible mark on history, much as she did on my mind.

I was still mourning when we found that hotel bar. Uriel was his usual giddy self and very pleased with me despite my irritable state, as I did not protest when the bellboy suggested we "go out back and try something different." After a bottle of something called *desi sharab*, it became clear that Uriel would ride my sudden openness to vice as far as it would take us. I don't remember where we went to eat opium, but I have a vivid recollection of the camel milk cheese they served us. Sweet and salty, obsessively springy. I vomited all of it, then ate some more. More cheese. More opium. Then, the dream, though I evidently made it to our hotel at some point in between.

I feel surprisingly good despite the insistent hangover. No bruised knuckles. Minimal self-loathing. I found traces of semi-digested cheese on my shirt but none of the telltale reddish brown that so often follows a night on the town. I was, it would seem, still in control during this depravity, and while morning comes with a migraine and severe dehydration, I feel a certain sense of pride at my restraint.

Today we should find the traitor's grave. There are several tombs near the ruins of the university at Taxila where she taught until her death. With any luck, one of them belongs to her. We are closer than ever. The drugs certainly helped, but I cannot stop thinking that the intensity of my dream had as much to do with proximity as poppy plants. She lies nearby in a bed of stone, waiting for me. Today the wait ends.

Later today. We had agreed to leave at first light, but our departure will have to wait. I seem to have lost Uriel.

# 52

## *Running Up That Hill*

My blood is boiling. The fever is spiking, fast. My honed Kibsu instincts are in high gear, but they are saying bupkes. I usually see the outcome, know what to do, but this . . . I don't fucking know how to fight a wolf.

He's *big*. A wisdom-gray giant flecked in black and cinnamon. Long legs, wide paws. His lines are so perfect he doesn't look real. Not a real wolf, but someone's idea of a wolf, or maybe a god taking animal form. The fur of his mane stands on end to make him look bigger. Not that he needs to; he's fucking *magnificent*.

His snarling is the only sound around. Lips curled, incisors on full display. The white rings around his eyes make them stand out even more. What do his eyes say? They say kill; that's what they say. Just death, spelled out in pale yellow. There's no curiosity here, no apprehension. He's all business. He must be sick or starving to have ventured this far into the open. Let's see if I can put some fear into him.

—AAAAAAARRRRGGGGGHHHHHHH!!!!!

So much for that. He didn't even flinch. His ears are straight. He's not the least bit afraid of me. I don't know what I can do. Forget running. There's nowhere to run to, nothing to put my back against. My asshole guide left me to die in the middle of the . . . semidesert.

The wolf is crouching, ready to pounce. My fear is turning into rage now. The animal in me wants to go down fighting. Come at me, motherfucker. I'll take your head right off! Except I won't. That wolf is faster and stronger than I am. I need brains right now, not guts. Mom kept saying everything is science. Right. . . .

My head feels like it's about to explode. Think. I have to think. He's my size. I won't overpower him. I guess it comes down to weapons. He has teeth and claws. What do I have? I have more useful limbs, opposable thumbs. His jaw is stronger than anything I've got, but if I remove it from the equation I might have a shot. FUCK! FUCK! FUCK! I know what to do. I just . . . I have to sacrifice a limb.

I'd better do this now while I'm burning up or I won't have the nerve. Grab a rock. One foot forward. Oh shit, he's coming. Deep breath. He should go for my forearm if I put it in front of h— AAAAAAGHHH! His canines sank two inches into my flesh, but his mouth just keeps on closing. My hand went limp. I felt one bone snap. Ugh. The other. I need to stay conscious.

If I let myself fall, I can wrap my legs around his body, wrestle him to his back. Agh! I can't get a grip on his face to gouge his eyes out. Fuck me! I hit him on the head, twice, but he didn't care. I have to find more pain receptors. . . .

—THAT'S RIGHT, ASSHOLE! I'LL RIP YOUR FUCK-ING BALLS OUT!

I squeezed and yanked as hard as I could. I don't know what's still there, but he let go of my arm. He squealed like a puppy and jumped out from under me. It won't last, though. He backed off, but he didn't run away. I need a bigger rock, any weapon, but there's *nothing* in this wasteland.

He's coming again. I have to give him my limp arm, again. I'm not sure I can do it without passing out. AARRRGGGH-HHH! FUCK! There's nothing left to break. He's grinding bits of bone now, turning my hand into pulp. I think I'm done. I can't reach his balls. I have nothing to hit him with and I'm not strong enough to strangle him. I'm . . .

I don't need to strangle him to make him choke. My dead arm is propping his mouth open. I can just . . . shove my good hand in there HARD, deep into his throat. Oh no, asshole, you're not leaving my grip this time. He's gasping for air. It's working. He's scared now, panicking, but he's exhausted. He's not nearly as strong as he was a minute ago.

He stopped struggling. He's just staring at me. I don't know what I'm looking at. It's not anger, nor fear. I think he just wants to know. He doesn't understand what I am or what's happening to him. I wish he didn't have to die. He'd rip me to shreds the moment I let him go, but I'd kill him even if he didn't. We're both animals right now. Rage is the only thing keeping me alive.

One last struggle, a final attempt at living. This is nature talking; I know the wolf has given up. He's not moving. His chest is slowing down. He's not dead yet, but he's waiting for it.

. . .

. . .

You can rest now.

It feels wrong to leave his body like that, but I can't feel my arm anymore. I'll wrap what's left of it in my shirt if I manage—

—AAAGH! COME OFF ALREADY!

. . . but the crimson beast next to me says I've lost too much blood already. I need to find help before the shock wears off. I was walking south before the world spun a thousand times. I don't know where that is anymore. Footsteps. I see my footsteps. Over there. I remember now. I was heading for that small mountain.

I'm on another planet. Castle-shaped rocks. Colors the likes of which nature doesn't make. And a mountain that looks like a cake. Lemon, with meringue on top, but the sunset is slowly changing the flavor. Lemon to orange, orange to chocolate. I think I can smell it. Sweet, warm cake. The temperature dropped, or *my* temperature dropped. Either way I'm cold, tired. I need to rest for a minute. Just . . . one . . . minute . . .

WAKE UP, LOLA! I'm not dying and neither is my daughter. Not today. Not here, next to fucking cake mountain. I need to keep my legs moving. I need to stay awake.

I sleep with the lion between the dragon's ribs.

That's not a star—stars are headings, not destinations—it's a place. I just haven't found it. The dragon's ribs could be anything. The whole Babylonian creation myth is crawling with dragons. The big one is called Tiamat. Tiamat wasn't always a dragon; she was . . . seawater, I guess, and then she hooked up with freshwater and they created the gods and cosmos. Bad shit happened, of course, and Tiamat went berserk. She created all kinds of monsters and turned herself into a giant dragon. She wreaked havoc until Marduk showed up. Before Marduk was the king of the gods, he specialized in thunderstorms. He stopped Tiamat with some kick-ass wind and killed her. Then he chopped her up. He took half her body to make the heavens, half to make the Earth. Hello, body part metaphors. He makes mountains from her breasts, rivers from her eyes. I think morning mist is the dragon's spit. It's gross and awkward, but in the end everything is dead dragon.

I needed a lion. I got a wolf instead. I'll get the next part right, I guess—follow his dying heart into the underworld—but I fucking failed at everything else. I didn't have to come here. I'm pregnant, for Chrissake. Preserve the knowledge. Survive at all costs. I knew better, but I did it any—

Lights. I see lights ahead. There's a Jeep! There's people!

—HELP!

I hope they can see me.

—HEEEEELP!

Oh my god. She's coming. They saw me.

—*Oh, mon dieu!* Here. Let me help you. *Laurent! Elle est couverte du sang! Va chercher la trousse de secours dans la voiture!*

French. That was French.

*Tout va bien aller, mademoiselle.*
What are these people doing here?
—Who are you?
—*Je m'appelle Marie-Thérèse.*
—Why are you here? *Pourquoi . . . êtes—*
—We were on a tour. We came to see the mountain.
—What?
—*La montagne.* Sherkala, the lion's fortress.

# 53

*Live to Tell*

I jumped when I saw my reflection in the hospital window. My hand looked like I'd put it through a meat grinder, but I hadn't seen the rest of me. Carrie on prom night, with bonus claw marks all over. My hand hurt so much I barely noticed the wolf had plowed my chest and back. I must have scared the crap out of Marie-Thérèse. They drove me all the way to Aktau. The clinic in Shetpe couldn't handle it and their one ambulance had a broken transmission. Thank god for French tourists. Nine hours I spent in surgery. They put me back together as best they could. Screws and bolts, and a whole spool of suture. It's not pretty. There's half a pound of metal in my forearm, but my baby's fine and I won't lose my hand. That's good enough for me. And they didn't draw blood, so I won't have to burn down half of Kazakhstan.

It's my fault—I know that—but it's not as if that was a good thing. I really wish there were someone else I could blame it on. I wanted an adventure with my mother. Well, I guess that was an adventure, and I sure feel Mom's judgment right about now. It's not all bad. I found the sleeping lion thing. I almost died right in front of it, but I found it. What comes next should be easier.

Follow his dying heart into the underworld.

The star of the Lion's breast. That's what's the Babylonians called Regulus. It's in the constellation Leo, a lion to this day.

I'm supposed to follow it when it sets, but I don't need to. We drove by what I was looking for on the way to the hospital.

"I see her breast again where the dragon lays its eggs."

I saw the dragon's eggs. They're hard to miss. Large spherical rocks as far as the eye can see. They call it Torysh, or the Valley of Balls. It's a good name. Not the most poetic thing, but it *is* a valley with balls. It looks like a man-made set for a cheesy sci-fi show. Spectacular in a trippy sort of way. It's not just the balls. Sherkala, the ridges, everything. This whole region is one big Dalí painting. It's also intact. In any other place, I would have to use my imagination to picture what it was like three thousand years ago. Not here. Except for a small road here and there—and Marie-Thérèse—I don't think the Eight could tell the difference.

There's only one line left on the bow.

"And hide inside her heart where death will not find me."

This is the end, Kibsu for "X marks the spot." I have a pretty good idea who Death is. I watched my home burn because of him. I just need to find her heart. *Her* heart. That's Inanna again. Mother and I found her heart already. I reach for her breast. It's Antares, the heart of the scorpion goddess Ishara. Of course, the Eight didn't hide anything in the sky; she hid it in the Valley of Balls. All I need is to find the right ball. How hard could that be? My first instinct was fuck it, I'll just go there and figure it out, but noooo. I learned my lesson. I got aerial photos of the place and spent three days staring at them. It felt very adult. I looked for any set of balls that resembled the constellation of the Scorpion. I ignored the smaller ones—they might have moved over time—only looked at balls big enough to stand the test of time. And I found it, I think. It's . . . Well, it's a ball, where Antares would be if it were a constellation of big rocks. With any luck, whatever I fought a wolf for is buried under there. I just have to dig it out.

That's what we're here for. Me and a couple of guys with

shovels and pickaxes because my arm is in a cast. Shady characters, both of them, but I told them they'd only get paid when we
were done. Besides, I kind of need shady for this. I'm not sure
who owns the land, but I'm fairly certain digging through here
is not the most legal thing I've ever done.

# 54

## *The NeverEnding Story*

The traitor earned herself a mausoleum. It is rather small but evidence she did not die unremembered. I am thankful for that. It feels wrong to catch up to her here, to disturb whatever peace she found. I tell myself she brought this sacrilege on herself. One could say she asked for it, leaving her mark everywhere she went. According to the tablet we found, she took her orb with her into the underworld. If any of us has a soul, I wish hers had a safe voyage, but I hope she traveled light. The sphere belongs to me.

—GOOD GOD! It stinks in here!

—Don't be so loud, Uriel. Show some respect.

—Like you did to those cops outside?

That was different. Their arrival was untimely, their deaths unfortunate. I took no pleasure in it. Uriel can't understand that. He revels in violence like our father did. I am ashamed of my brother, embarrassed I brought him here, because my prey might think less of me. The dead don't care, but I no longer pretend to be rational when it comes to her. I am beguiled, and I hope that besting her and finding the sphere will not put an end to the spell. It is only when dreaming of her that I feel truly awake.

Here she is. Her stone tomb appears intact. The etchings on its sides are remarkably well preserved. I wish I could spend the time and decipher them. Perhaps they tell a different part of her story, perhaps all of it. Unless she gave instruction to the artisan herself, these words are testimony from people who knew her, as a teacher, a priestess, a friend. I wish I knew what they had to say, but we'd better not linger. I left two eviscerated bodies by the entrance.

—A little help, Uriel? We can push the cover to this side.

—Say when.

—I will not. Just push.

Uggghhhh.

—What the actual fuck, Sam?

Well said. She is . . . gone. There are no remains in her tomb, but the sphere is here. I suppose it does not matter; we did not come for a body. I am, nonetheless, quite impressed. This is certainly one trick I did not see coming. She is not here. She has risen.

She left me my prize. I find it difficult to grasp the full significance of this discovery. Three thousand years of effort are finally coming to fruition. Every minute of every life we have lived has led to *this*, this very moment. I always imagined that finding the sphere, if I were the one to find it, would fill me with immeasurable pride. This is an oddly humbling experience.

It looks like copper. One-half is covered in patina. I see no button, no mechanism, nothing to break the smooth surface except for a seam in the middle. Perhaps there is something on the other side. It feels so strange to touch it, to hold it in my— This is odd. It weighs almost nothing. Something's not right.

I wonder if I can separate—

Oh.

My.

It's empty, except for some straw and a small . . . wooden figure at the bottom. There's nothing here, just two copper bowls squeezed together to form a ball. A wooden doll with a large smile carved onto it.

She is laughing at us.

—AAAAAAARRGGGHHHHHHHH!!

—Are you okay, Sam?

—No, Uriel. I am most definitely not okay.

Thirteen years! We spent thirteen years of our lives playing her game. We did not find the clues that led us here because we were clever; she wanted us to find them. Three generations, one name. She wanted us to find *her*. She made sure the right people knew where she was going. She left bread crumbs everywhere she went. She sent us on a wild-goose chase halfway across the globe. She . . .

She was smarter than us.

# 55

*We Belong*

We did it, Mom.

We found a buried treasure. It looks like gold. Maybe it is. It's . . . perfect. Perfectly round, perfectly smooth. It's spellbinding. I can't stop looking at it and my warped reflection can't stop looking back.

Unfortunately, I know what it is I'm staring at. Some sort of beacon that will lure countless more like the Tracker to this world. I know the one who tortured Grandma could have lied about it, but I don't see the point. This thing exists. They're willing to kill for it, and we're willing to die to keep it from them. I think I'll take the devil at his word on this one. What do you think, Mom?

I'd give anything for you to be here right now. I don't know what to do, not that I ever did. We climbed the mountain together because it was there to climb. Now you're gone and I'm stuck on the summit, too fucking scared to get down. Everyone's gone. I'm alone. I remember when you told me to picture the Eight. I couldn't, but I can see her now. I see her leathery skin, her scarred body. She stops right in front of me, reins in her horse, and gives me the most gentle, heartfelt smile. And just like that, she's gone. I don't bother running after her. I watch her fade into the sun again and I know that she is relieved. It was on her before, unrelenting, weighing her down like lead running through her veins. Now, for the first time, she's free. It's not on her anymore. It's on me.

She left us a note. Three words on a piece of leather. I wonder what she did to preserve it. "Useless without . . . *naptû.*" My dictionary says the word is "opener." Maybe the sphere opens, but I think it means key, something to activate it. I was . . . disappointed. I don't know why—well, I do know. I'm a child who got a broken toy for Christmas, but I also know I could never use it. You're making fun of me now, aren't you, Mom? Yes, I'm mildly disappointed. I'm also fucking grateful it doesn't work. If I had found this thing thirty years ago, I wouldn't even know what I was looking at. I would probably try to turn it on. Tinker tinker, then beep beep or whatever. I'd have undone everything without— I need to think about something else. I'm giving myself an anxiety attack. Then again, it might not matter. Even if everything the Tracker said was true, this is three-thousand-year-old news. A lot could have happened since then. They could all be dead. They could be sipping space margaritas on a blue sand beach and not give a damn about this planet.

There were teeth—at least I think they were teeth—next to the sphere. Someone was buried with it. The Eight obviously did it. I wonder who the body belonged to. An enemy, a friend. A child. That's my guess. Someone she cared deeply for, someone whose final sleep she did not want disturbed. Maybe that person was meant to watch over the sphere, like that old knight guarding the Holy Grail from Nazis. We'll never know because I didn't touch the teeth. Like, eeew.

What would you do, Mom? Would you put this thing back in the ground, let someone else find it three thousand years from now? Would you destroy it right here? I thought *I* would, but the Eight could have done the same thing. Maybe there's a reason she didn't. What would you do, Mom?! I need your help. . . . I know you'd have picked up those teeth.

Right. So this is it. This was our time. One last Coca-Cola together before you leave me for good. I don't know that I'm ready, Mom. I don't know if I can do this without you.

# ENTR'ACTE

## *Let Not the Sun Go Down on Your Wrath*

### 1888

—Stop staring at the sun, Annie! You'll go blind!

Emily had spent her life looking at the night sky. Her daughter, Annie, also looked at the stars, but she preferred them closer.

Annie wondered how, in a world filled with such technological wonders as the gramophone and moving pictures, we had yet to understand what made the day bright. The sun had been right here, forever, and no one knew exactly what it was or how it worked. Progress had been made during Annie's lifetime. When she was one year old, the spectroscope was invented. It allowed one to split light into different wavelengths, like a rainbow, and identify the chemical elements present based on the wavelengths at which light was absorbed. A year later, an Italian astronomer had the idea to combine a spectroscope and a telescope. One could now look at the stars and know what their surface was made of. As it turns out, the same chemical elements found here on Earth.

But how did the sun keep on burning? Thanks to brilliant work by the likes of Joule and Lord Kelvin, the world now had principles of a new discipline called thermodynamics. With these understood, it became clear that chemical combustion was an insufficient explanation and that the sun did not simply burn coal, as had previously been thought. The theory by which the sun was fed energy by a constant influx of meteors was also losing favor. The prevalent explanation now was that gravity was causing the sun to shrink, creating pressure and heat. Annie had her doubts.

Annie was one of the first students to study mathematics at Girton, the first ever women's college at Cambridge. That made Emily both extremely proud and somewhat jealous of her daughter. Girton or not, Cambridge did not grant women degrees, but it was a step in the right direction, and something Emily had often dreamed of when she walked the campus grounds in her youth.

Upon graduation, Annie moved to London and found a job at the Royal Observatory in Greenwich as a "lady computer" in the solar department. The job only paid four pounds a month, but she got to spend her days photographing the sun. Working there meant delaying marriage—married women could not hold a public service job—but neither Annie nor her mother seemed to mind. Though she died before seeing her granddaughter, Emily lived to be sixty-one years old. She was killed while visiting her daughter in London.

It was a brutal murder. Emily was stabbed thirty-nine times with no apparent motive. She was neither robbed nor raped. There were no signs of a struggle, which meant she was caught by surprise. The police attributed her death to one of the gangs operating in the East End.

It wasn't until another woman was murdered on the same streets that Annie began to suspect something more sinister was at work. The killing was even more horrid. The victim's throat was slit, her abdomen cut completely open. Parts of her insides were removed and her small intestines were placed next to her head. This was no ordinary cruelty. Annie began to consider the possibility that the unruly beasts she was raised to fear were responsible for her mother's death.

The Whitechapel murders continued, each more grisly than the last. Kidneys and uterus removed, noses cut off. Intestines again placed next to the victim's head. One victim almost completely emptied. Annie was convinced: this was the work of the Tracker. She also felt something new, something more raw and powerful than anything she had ever experienced. Wrath.

Annie was consumed by anger and a burning lust for revenge. She was also a woman of science but reasoned that these two things were, in this instance, quite compatible. Despite the uncertainties about the sun, what everyone agreed on was that it was doomed to die and everyone with it, which, in Annie's mind, made understanding how it worked a moral imperative. It also cast doubt on the pertinence of the rules she was raised to follow since our sun's looming death had not factored in their creation. There would be no one to take to the stars if ours stopped burning, and running from the Tracker now would undoubtedly slow progress. Removing the smaller threat was the best way to mitigate the larger one.

Annie went to the post office and spent ten shillings on a gun license before purchasing what the salesperson described as a proper, ladylike pistol. For two months, she worked at the observatory during the day and roamed the inauspicious streets of Whitechapel when the object of her study disappeared. She posed as a prostitute and hung by the brothels and common-lodging houses where some of the victims were found.

The nights were now cold and crisp. Annie did not mind; it made her work that much easier. November rid the streets of anything lawful. Whoever braved the outside past midnight had something ugly to hide.

Annie was about to call it a night when she heard a struggle in a nearby alley. She saw a man slashing at a woman's corpse with a penknife.

The man turned as Annie approached, but she didn't react.

—You're quite bricky, standing here like this. You should turn around before you end up like Biddie here. Are you Irish?

Maybe I should cut you up, too. Bogtrotter whores spreading disease all over town. It's not enough you steal our jobs and our food; you got to make us *sick*. I've had enough of your bloody—

Annie shot him twice in the head. She dropped her pistol down the nearest sewer, put the dead man in a wheelbarrow, and threw her coat over it before walking up the block to the Pavilion Theatre. She went in through the service entrance, shoved the body inside the theater furnace, and walked home feeling nothing but disillusion. These murders weren't the work of the Tracker. It wasn't some mythical evil that robbed her of her mother. It was just another weak man blaming others for the rot inside him.

Annie never gave the Tracker another thought. She quit her position at the observatory and married her supervisor, a man she loved deeply. A year later, her daughter was born. Annie spent the rest of her joyful life traveling the world and studying her favorite star. "Whatever comes of us," she said, "at least my daughter will know what makes the day bright."

# ACT VI

# 56

*Under the Milky Way*

> Nothing can be sadder or more profound than to see a
> thousand things for the first and last time.
>
> **Victor Hugo**

The last twelve years and seven billion kilometers had brought
many firsts. Now came the lasts. Last planet. Last moon. Last
everything.

The gas giant was getting bigger, but *Voyager* could barely
see it. Neptune lives in the dark. Thirty times farther from the
sun than Earth, it receives only one-thousandth of the light.
Taking pictures of it would require a long exposure, which
might prove difficult when whatever is in front of the camera
zips by at ninety thousand kph.

Fortunately, NASA had a plan for the planet to hold still. As
*Voyager* flew five thousand kilometers from the cloud top—the
closest it had ever come to a planet—it gently fired its thrusters
to rotate. Like a race car driver doing a hand-brake turn, the
robot kept its eye on Neptune as it spun around it. The probe's
driving was sharp, and the pictures in focus.

The signal from home was faint, and there was doubt *Voyager*'s 13-watt transmitter would be up to the task when the
time came to transmit its findings. Four hours after *Voyager*'s
message was sent, humans huddled around a JPL computer as

images of Neptune appeared on-screen. The probe had been gone long enough for NASA to modernize the network of radio antennae it used to listen. Earth would be able to hear *Voyager* and its twin for decades.

Neptune was blue. Blue meant there was methane in the atmosphere, an atmosphere thought to be too cold to have disturbances. *Voyager* found a giant storm pattern, clouds swept around by near-supersonic gusts of wind, the fastest in the solar system. It discovered four faint rings, and half a dozen new moons around the eighth planet.

A quick thruster burst sent the robot towards Triton, the planet's largest moon. What looked like a big ball of ice, with the coldest surface temperature of anything *Voyager* encountered, turned out to be active, spewing giant geysers of whatever magic lay below its surface.

Accomplished. That's what the mission was. The word implies success, but it also means over, done. Finished. There were no more planets to explore, no more moons to discover.

The camera turned to Neptune one last time. Everyone in the control room stared as the planet got smaller, willing the giant closer, hoping to slow its ebb. Inexorably, the planet shrank until all that remained was a dot and, for all of its very brief existence, that dot was the most precious thing in the universe.

# 57

## *Everybody Knows*

I wanted answers. I wanted them so bad I was willing to die for them. Mom *did* die for them. Be careful what you wish for, I guess. I was lost before, but now . . .

"You'll know the minute you see your daughter born." That's what she said.

One look, and I'll know who I was this whole time. Every fear, every doubt, gone. Poof. Magic. I'll feel this overwhelming, unconditional love. I'll know when my child needs me, when to hold her, when to feed her. I will protect her, always, because every fiber in my being tells me to do so. A mother's instincts are strong. Mine, especially. *This* is what I was born for. It's in my genes, all of them. We, my daughter and I, are the Hundred and One. We are the Kibsu.

Except I didn't fucking know. I'm just as full of doubt now as I was then and I'm no closer to figuring out who I am. I look at my daughter and I'm just . . . terrified. That's the one constant emotion. Unshakable fear. I don't know what I'm supposed to do or when to do it, or how. Catherine's almost three and . . . we're *slowly* getting to know each other. She was a complete stranger. We built what relationship we have one giggle, one burp, at a time. It didn't fall from the sky like everyone says. It's a slow process. She barely speaks, to me or anyone else. I know she can. I can see her little brain working overtime. She keeps it all to herself as if I'm not worth her trust. She's right—I wouldn't want me as a mother either. Whatever light childbirth was supposed to turn on is either burnt out or broken.

I'm doing my best, and I try to convince myself that's enough. I keep her alive. Then I remember the metal sphere I buried under the garage floor. I brought this curse into her *home*. That ball may be utterly useless without the key, but it's still a death sentence. The Eight knew that.

It's not just the sphere. I can get rid of the sphere, but they'll hunt us down regardless. They'll hunt *me* down. I'm painting a giant bull's-eye on her tiny back. Only I can't just drop myself at the bottom of a lake. Or can I? It never bothered me when I was the child. It sure as hell bothers me now. We make our children prey. That's . . . messed up. I suppose the Eight knew that, too.

That's what I keep coming back to. She knew *everything*. Why did she want me, one of us, to find the sphere? What could we use it for but to undo everything she bled and died for? I'm sure it's not indestructible. Hit it hard with a rock. Throw that shit down the fires of Mount Doom if you have to. Then you *know* those assholes won't get their hands on it. But she didn't. What stopped her? Fear? Guilt? Doubt?

If "our people" are out there, somewhere, if they'll all perish without a new home, as the Tracker said, she must have known about it. It wouldn't be so easy to live with that, knowing you might be the bad guy in the story. She also knew she'd spend her life running, that her child would be prey. *All she had to do* was hand that thing over. She might have wanted to keep that option open for her daughter, or her daughter's daughter, or me. Of course, back then we hadn't died one after the other for three thousand years. Seven people. That's who she had to betray to save her child. Seven *dead* people.

The cost went up a lot since then. A *hundred* lifetimes is the going rate. At this point, it might as well be a thousand, because the only one that truly matters is the one that came just before.

Screwing over the Thirty-One is a very abstract thing. The real question is: Could I do that to Mom? *That's* the price to pay for my daughter's life. To throw Mom's down the drain. To make it . . . not matter.

I sent my plans for an ion drive to JPL. Maybe someone there can find a use for it. I don't have it in me anymore. It's funny, somehow. Mom wanted so much to learn about the Eight. She thought it would change things. And it did, just not in the way Mom thought it would. I understand her now. I know her doubt, her fears. The Eight is me. The only difference between us is how much we're willing to pay.

The doorbell is ringing. It must be Child Services.

—Come in. I was expecting you.

—Is the child ready?

—Almost . . . Catherine, come here. Let Mommy hold you for a minute.

Her little heart is drumming against mine. I think, for the first time, we truly understand each other. I hope I get to come back to her. I hope I get to feel this again. If I don't, at least this way she has a chance. My life and a hundred more for the promise of one. It's not such a bad deal if you ask me.

# 58

## *About a Girl*

I thought it was just Uriel and me, but there are more of us, apparently. Our uncle Charles's widow inherited a sizable sum of money upon his death, enough for a young man to come forward and claim the money should be his. Uncle Charlie, everyone knew, was quite the busy bee, but it now seems he left one of his many conquests with more than a few bruises and some bad memories. I doubt he ever knew—no woman in their right mind would have wanted Charles to raise their children—which means *the child,* whoever he is, does not know either. How different it must feel going through life without the burden of our past. I do not know if it is the fascination with the idea, or my being too exhausted to care, but I have not made the effort to hunt him down, nor have I told Uriel about him.

—Samael?

— . . .

He must be like us, identical in every measurable way. Yet I am willing to bet he would see us as strangers. What we really are doesn't matter as much as how we perceive ourselves. What would I be without my father's influence? I can imagine, but I know my vision is severely myopic. I struggle to be different, which only means different from him. *He* is my one point of reference, the box I so desperately try to escape.

—Samael!

—What?

—What was it the traitors called themselves?

—The ones our uncles found in California were called Sarah and Mia.

—No, not their names. The— The ancient shit?!

—Kibsu. They called themselves the Kibsu. Why?

—They're in the newspaper.

—Have you been drinking again, Uriel?

—Here! Have a look at the personals.

—The p—

**I AM THE KIBSU. CALL ME AND WE CAN HAVE A BALL.**
1-800- . . .

I will be damned. Twenty-five hundred years later, she is not done toying with me.

—It's her, right? It has to be. How does she know we're in London?

—I don't think she does. She must have placed that ad everywhere.

—Everywhere like the whole world?

—If it were me, I would start with major cities. Unlike them, we have no reason to hide. One of us is bound to read the papers. Can you hand me the phone?

—Why?

—Because I cannot dial the number without it.

—You're gonna call? It sounds like a trap, Sam.

—Of course it is.

—Then what do we do?

—It would seem that is no longer up to us, my brother. She is hunting *us*.

# 59

## *One*

The rain keeps on raining. It's harmless at first, but give it enough time and it bends everything to its will. People give up first, then grass, trees, roads, mountains. This rain is committed. It's fucking cold, relentless. I feel right at home in it. I'd never seen New York and now it's all mine. I have its streets to myself. I don't care about the cold, or the rain. Nothing matters anymore. I *have* nothing.

I have no honor. I broke a promise we've kept for three thousand years. I spit on the graves of every one of my ancestors. They gave everything to keep that promise. They gave their lives for it and I betrayed them all. Mom too. She was everything to me. She held my hand when I was scared; she . . . I lost so much when she died, there's no putting it into words. All I had left was her memory. I cherished it, more than anything. And then I threw it away. I'm sorry, Mom. I know it doesn't mean anything, but I am.

I have no soul. If I ever had one, I sold it when I left my daughter behind. I abandoned my child. I robbed her of her past, her family. She'll have no one to turn to when things get rough, no one to explain why she's the way she is. She'll be alive, but there's no redemption for me. I never cared for God, but I deserve every bit of my daughter's judgment. I know how much I failed her.

I have no family. The first hundred Kibsu are dead and no

one will know they ever existed. I'll be the last to remember them.

I have no pride left, no desires. I have no hope. Every reason I had to live is gone, because I got *rid* of it. I made a list of things that mattered and I burned them all in a giant bonfire. There's nothing they can take from me now, nothing left to hold me back, to rein me in. There. Are. No. Rules.

I'm about to draw a shit ton of attention.

I couldn't care less if I survive or not.

And I'm done running. I'm so fucking done running.

I have one thing left and that's rage.

I'm going to end this.

# 60

*Devil Inside*

I wonder why she chose this place. Grand Central Terminal is like a French palace. It's majestic, monumental. Globe-shaped chandeliers lighting the room like small suns. I see a handful of people looking down from the balconies. Down here, it's elbow to elbow in every direction. There are more people here than I can count, more smells that I can distinguish. Pastries, sweat, unfortunate cologne choices.

I see her now. It's exhilarating beyond words. Her hair, her skin, both are darker than ours. I don't know why it surprises me, only that it does. I had no reason to, but I imagined a feminine version of us, what my sister would look like. She is not like me. I have dreamed of this woman a thousand times, but I have never *seen* her. What I imagined, what face came to me at night, was devoid of concrete features. She had eye-colored eyes, skin-colored skin. This one is real. Every bone in her body, every inch of her, real. She has brown eyes.

—Is it just the two of you, or are we expecting someone else?

She speaks. I can tell that she is . . . different from the one we chased. I dare not imagine the planning and patience it took her ancestor to set a trap over three generations, the required foresight and meticulousness to leave the exact dosage of information to seep through the ages. This one is younger, unhindered by such things as wisdom or prudence. I see the same commitment in her, the same fire, but it burns harder, faster.

—We are the only two left. What about you?

—It's just me.

—And you are?

—Lola.

What's in a name? We have never met, never touched, and yet . . . In another lifetime she spun her web for me. She did it slowly for a person who did not yet exist and I have shared my dreams with her long after she died. We have known each other longer than either of us has lived. This is . . . destiny. Our lives, both our lives, led to this. This is our moment. Montagues and Capulets sent on a collision course by forces beyond control. She was but a ghost, a figment, a character on film. Now she steps through the screen and into my world. I wish for her with every breath.

—Did you bring the sphere with you?

—Uh-huh. You said you wouldn't come otherwise.

She taps her duffel bag.

—Can I ask you a question, Lola?

—Go ahead.

—Did you come here to fight?

—Yes.

At last. Let our hearts beat loudly as a summons to war. As Uriel would say, shit is about to get real.

# 61

*Two Tribes*

Breathe.

Breathe.

Breathe.

—Can I ask you a question, Lola?

—Go ahead.

—Did you come here to fight?

—Yes.

—And yet you brought the sphere.

—Got to make sure you don't run. I know you won't leave without it.

—I won't. We could talk if you want. There is no reason for anyone to get hurt. I for one would rather not die here today.

—What's your name?

—Samael.

—Can I be honest with you, Samael?

—By all means.

—I don't give a fuck.

—Then why the train station?

—Because I didn't think you'd bring a gun to a crowded place.

—A sensible precaution.

—I know. But *I* did.

I squeeze the trigger with all I've got. The shot echoes into the vault ceiling, a hundred of me firing at once. I see mouths open in the crowd, but all I hear is the gun. I pump bullet after bullet at one of the Trackers. Gotcha. That one went through his gut. He falls. Now I know they bleed like everyone else. I squeeze and squeeze. The gun's empty, but I keep pulling the trigger. I'd shoot my fucking heart at him if I could.

Reload. I hear the empty magazine ping on the marble floor. I have one more of them to kill. This one has better instincts. He ducked as soon as I started firing. Soda cans burst in slow motion as he runs behind the shop counter. Fireworks of food dye and artificial flavor. I'll kill this fucker with flying colors. Root beer. I missed his head by an inch. Orange. Grape. You can run, but you can't hide from me. Cherry. I put another six rounds through the glass display before my pistol slide locks back. He's not dead. I should have brought more bullets.

I drop the gun. Now I can hear the screams. This place is madness. A thousand terror-struck people run in every direction. One crashes into my shoulder. I fight my way through the stampede. One step back, two steps forward. I'll get to you, mother-fucker. I push one man to the floor. Another. A young girl falls down by the main staircase. She puts her hands over her head, afraid people will step on her. They do. This is what Mom saw in Kashgar, a little girl who needed help. She didn't think twice. I won't either. I'm sorry, kid. You're going to have to fend for your-self. I'm not my mom and I have a demon to kill.

Knives out. I see him now, crouched behind the counter.

—I don't want to fight you, Lola! We can end this. We can end it together. No more dying.

That would mean a lot more if I didn't see the meat cleaver behind his back.

—Fuck you. But you're right; this ends now.

These monsters hunt us for sport. We die and die and die and they keep on coming. There'll be no more dying once I've killed every last one of them. Close the distance. I swing right to left at his throat. I miss. If at first you don't succeed, just keep fucking swinging. Mom said the trick when wielding a knife is not to leave yourself open. I say fuck it. Slash hard with both hands. He's fast, but I can be faster. He's on defense. I can fail a hundred times. He only has to fail once.

And there. I cut his arm.

—You fucking b—

—You got *that* right.

—Don't make me do this, Lola. I don't want to kill you!

—Tell that to every one of us you murdered and tortured. Tell that to my grandmother, you piece of shit.

—That wasn't me! I've never met any of— URIEL, DON'T!

Pain. Behind me. A blade, I think. It went in near my kidney. His brother's not dead. He's—

—AAAAAAAAAAGH!!!!

He's pulling up, plowing through my insides. He took the knife out. More pain, I . . .

Silence. The pain's gone, all of it. I turn to face him, but nothing moves. Not my arms, not my legs. I can't feel anything anymore. I can't breathe. He must have severed my vertebrae. *Human Anatomy*, Volume 1. Immediate loss of motor functions. My lungs won't work on their own anymore. My legs are buckling. I'll piss and shit myself first, but I *will* die. There's no stopping it.

Mom said panic is knowing there is a way out but not knowing what it is. Calm is the absolute certainty there is not. It doesn't get any calmer than this. At least it's painless. It's everything-less, really. I can't feel the air on my skin, the cold marble floor on my back. I can't feel my own weight. This is not how I imagined it would end. It's oddly . . . serene. I was prepared to die. I came ready. I just wish I'd been facing him. I guess this'll have to do. Here he comes to finish the job. Or maybe that's the other one.

—Lola! I didn't mean . . . It wasn't supposed to end like this. All I wanted was the sphere.

—It doesn't matter. . . . You'll never get it working without the key.

— . . .

—You'll never—

—Shhh. Don't speak. You're right. I'll never get it working.

—You lost.

—I did. You beat me in the end, Lola. You won.

—I . . . w . . .

# 62

## *Hazy Shade of Winter*

She's not gone, not yet, but her eyes say she isn't with me anymore. I don't know where her mind took her, only that it's a
private place. I'm not welcome there. It didn't have to be this
way. She didn't have to die. So much is lost, so many things left
unsaid. I lost her. Someone took her from me.

—Samael, help.

Uriel is alive. . . . *He* took her from me.

—Why did you do that, Uriel?

—Sam, I'm bleeding bad here. I need a doctor.

—You didn't have to kill her.

—Sam, I saved you! Now help me up, please!

—You are badly hurt, Uriel. . . .

—That's what I said. I'll be okay. I just need to get to a hospital. The doctor will fix me up; then you and I can look for that
key together.

—Oh, we have the key.

—We do?

—I didn't have the heart to tell her, but she is wearing it
around her neck.

—Her necklace?

—Yes. . . . So you see, we don't need to find it together.

—Sam? What are you saying?

—I'm saying you should have treated her better.

—What? Who are you talking about? The traitor?

— . . .

—Wait! Samael, stop!

—I would have preferred it ended differently, but you forced my hand. You killed someone I care deeply for, because you can't understand or even fathom having a meaningful connection, to anyone. You robbed me of her as if she was ever yours to take. She was MINE, Uriel! You always took what did not belong to you. No more. You will NEVER take from ME again!

—Sam . . .

—This was . . . inevitable. If not today, tomorrow, or a year from now, but you know it had to happen. You would have hurt her, Uriel. You would have hurt her like you did before. This way you won't hurt *anyone*. You won't call our mother names. You won't throw things at her face because you didn't like your BLOODY BREAKFAST. You never deserved her. None of you ever did. It took me a long time to understand it, but there should have been only one. Can't you see? How this was *preordained*? What must seem to you like a terrible injustice is just nature restoring itself

Goodbye, Brother.

# 63

## *This Woman's Work*

I'm cold. I'm scared. Not of dying, that's more or less done now. I'm scared for my daughter. I couldn't save everyone else, but I hope I did enough to save her. I have no regrets if I did. She won't forgive me, but I don't need her forgiveness. I only need her to live.

I wish I knew what her life will be like. Then again, not knowing was sort of the point. *She* gets to decide, to make it up as she goes. All I can do is imagine. I do. She's all grown up, sitting alone on a near-empty beach. A couple kids run past. She makes a funny face and growls at them. She keeps looking around. I think she's waiting for someone. A new someone, maybe. The kind of someone who makes your heart pump faster just thinking about them. The kind of someone you never see coming. A hand lands on her shoulder. She doesn't look, just puts hers on top and squeezes slightly. She's— That's not a smile, not really. Just her face shifting a little, unable to hide the warmth inside her.

I was cold a second ago. I feel warmer now, like I, too, am lying on hot sand. Maybe I am. Maybe I've been somewhere else this whole time. Alone in a barren land. The heat is soothing like a hot blanket. I look around. I know what I'm looking for. I can't see her yet, but I know she's coming. I hear a horse stomping the ground in the distance. Here she comes. She's close now; I can hear her horse panting. I try to look, but the light is blinding me. She nudges her horse forward to block the light and I see.

She's younger. None of it has happened yet. She hasn't felt the pain, the sorrow. I can tell she's happy. I am, too. No reason. It's just contagious, I guess. There's so much I want to ask her even if I know she won't stay. I brace myself for the void she'll leave behind, but she doesn't ride away. Not this time. She pats her restless horse on its side; then she gives me her hand. She helps me up and I sit behind her, my arms wrapped around her waist. I don't know where she'll take me. All I know is I want to be there.

There's someone ahead of us, a silhouette standing tall atop a sand dune. I want to see who it is, but we're slowing down. Our horse stopped now. I think she wants me to get off. Whatever this is, it's for me alone.

I head towards the sand dune. It's farther than I thought. The hot sand singes my feet as I inch closer to the silhouette ahead. I can almost make out who it is. Almost . . . Almost . . .

—Mom?

What happened? We're not outside anymore. This is our home on Mallorca. I must be five or six and Mom's tucking me in for the night.

—And he said: "Monsieur, the planet of which you indicated the position really exists."

—He said "Monsieur"?

—He said "Monsieur." He was very polite.

I know what this is! I asked for that same story every night. I knew it by heart, but I was always trying to change the ending.

—We found a planet, Mom! Emily did the math and Neptune was exactly where she said it would be!

—No, Lola. John Couch Adams and the Ninety-Six *almost*

discovered the planet Neptune. They came *this close*, but they weren't the ones to find it.

—But *we* should have found the planet!

—We weren't alive back then, Lola.

—Grandma should have found it!

—Emily wasn't your grandmother; she was your *great-great-*grandmother, your grandmother's grandmother. And we got the knowledge; it's all that matters in the end. Besides, no one ever really *found* Neptune, you know. It wasn't lost or anything. Close your eyes now, Lola. Time to sleep.

—It's not fair.

—You know who else came close to finding Neptune? Galileo Galilei, over *two hundred years* before Emily.

He was the first to use a telescope to look at the night sky, so he was the very first person in all the history of the world who could have seen Neptune. And he did! He saw it twice, but it wasn't moving fast enough and he didn't realize he was looking at a planet. He—

—Mom, wait. His name was Galileo Galilei?

—Yes.

—That was his real name?

—A hundred percent real.

—Like . . .

—Like William Williams.

—Haha! Steven Stevens.

—David Davis. Alan Allen.

—Lola . . . Lola.

—Yes, Lola Lola. Now go to sleep.

She'll turn the light off now. I don't want her to go; I—

—Mom?

—What, honey?

— . . . I need you to say it. I need to hear the words.

. . .

—I forgive you.

— . . . I love you, Mom.

—I love you, too. Good night, Lola.

# 64

*Let the River Run*

## DECEMBER 5, 1989

Cameras off.

The darkness of space makes way for something darker. This time, *Voyager*'s eyes will not open again. Its camera software will be erased to make room for something new, something useful. *Voyager* will never come close enough, to anything, to take pictures again. Ever.

It will never see another hurricane larger than our world, or cracks on an icy moon above an endless ocean. It will never again show us halos of moon dust, volcanoes erupting sixty times higher than Everest. It will never watch another world spin to count the minutes in an alien day.

The probe will never be first to see anything again, or second, or last, but it doesn't need to see because it already has. The *Voyager*s triumphed, and neither time nor space can stop their eternal wander.

This isn't the end, far from it. Where one mission ends in darkness, another comes to light. The probe still has most of its heart. As long as we listen, it will continue to share the wonders it perceives. Million-mile-per-hour solar winds. The ringing of interstellar space. One day, its heart will stop, but it will continue to carry its message across the Milky Way, until something, or someone, stops it and listens to our words.

This is a present from a small distant world, a token of our sounds, our science, our images, our music, our thoughts, and our feelings. We are attempting to survive our time so we may live into yours. We hope someday, having solved the problems we face, to join a community of galactic civilizations. This record represents our hope and our determination, and our goodwill in a vast and awesome universe.

**President Jimmy Carter on the Golden Record**

# CONCLUSION

# It's a Sin

I closed her eyes before I took the necklace off her neck. Even in death, I didn't want her to know. She looked at peace, something I never truly felt. I did not want the stench of failure to disturb her rest. There are many things I want and will never get, but one of the things that saddens me most is never understanding what her true motives were. One does not simply condemn their kind to die out of spite. She was obviously driven by a larger purpose, one at least *she* understood as noble. Whatever cause these women ascribed to mattered more than their lives. I wish I knew what . . . Lola died for. I wish I knew her.

I took the bag off her shoulder and opened it halfway. I stared for a moment, hypnotized by the gold shine of the sphere, then laid the necklace against it. I felt it. A subtle hum, almost imperceptible. The roots of my hair tingling ever so slightly. I zipped the bag closed and left.

Five seconds was all it took. Five unceremonious seconds spent crouching on the floor next to a pair of corpses. It was, perhaps, a defining event for two civilizations, or perhaps my hair tingling was the end of it. However history judges what happened here today is beside the point. This was life altering for Lola and me. It ended her life, and it changed mine irreversibly.

I have sent the signal. Whether anyone hears it I may never know, nor do I really care. I have lifted the curse. We are free now—I am—no longer subject to an age-old covenant, a slave to someone else's sense of duty. Our lives could very well have been a colossal waste of time, but it matters little if we are fools or heroes. It's over. I can have what none of us ever had. I, for the first time, get to live *my* life. I get to live. So does my mother.

I have waited so long for this, rehearsed this moment more times than I can count. And yet I stand by the door as nervous as I was when I left her eighteen years ago, terrified of three innocuous sounds: knock, knock, knock.

—Hello, Mother.

It takes me a second to read her. She is as beautiful as ever, but the years have added traits that blur her expression. I cannot tell if she is happy or sad. Perhaps she cannot tell either. I don't think she knows which one I am.

— . . . Samael, is that you?

— . . .

—Samael! You look . . .

She is happy, I can tell, but there is still sadness. I forgot I, too, was not the same. As much as I tried to be different from him, I must look exactly like Father when they met. I remind her of *him*.

—Mother, I—

—You look good. Where are my manners? Come in! Come in! I'm . . . surprised. I expected it. For a long time, I expected it. I knew, someday, there'd be a knock at the door. I didn't think . . .

—You didn't think it'd be me.

—I didn't think it would take this long. But I hoped it would be you. Come here, Samael. Let me look at your face. My little boy.

—I have missed you, Mother.

—Why did you wait so long?

—I had to. But I am here now. You're free, Mother.

—Free? Was I not free before?

—You can do what you want, go wherever you want to go! You are safe now.

—This is where I want to be, Samael. Why— Why would things be different now? What changed?

—It doesn't matter. Do you still garden?

—Don't change the subject, Samael. Why am I safe? What happened?

—They won't hurt you anymore, Mother. No one will.

—What are you saying, Samael? What did you do?

— . . .

I saved her is what I did. I saved her and a whole species. I saved everyone.

—Sam? Where are your brothers?

— . . .

I know this is not the denouement she was hoping for. She would not wish ill on anyone. That's why she needed me. *I* saved her because she could not do it herself. It might take some time, but she will get over her disappointment. They were going to kill her. Now she gets to live. I—

—Answer me, Sam! What did you do?

I saved her. I—

This I recognize. I have seen this countenance many times, but never from her. I don't know if I can take it from her. It's not disappointment she feels; it's—

—Please, Mother!

—DON'T TOUCH ME!

She is afraid of me.

—Mother, you don't understand. They would have come for you; I—

—You need to get out now, Samael.

—No, I—

—GET OUT!

— . . .

I see fear, disgust. She thinks *I'm* the monster. She doesn't understand. I did it for *her*. It was always about her.

I— I killed them all. I killed my father. I killed Raphael, and Uriel. I killed my entire family FOR HER. SHOW ME SOME GRATITUDE, YOU INGRATE LITTLE B—

. . .

*Snap her neck!*

NO! Not her. I won't hurt her. I am stronger than the urge. It does not control me.

*Kill the bitch!*

NOOOOO! I AM STRONGER THAN THE URGE! IT DOES NOT CONTROL ME!

—Sam . . . stop. . . .

Stop wh— My hands. She's on the floor. My hands are wrapped around her throat. I don't understand. I never— I need to leave.

—I'm sorry, Mother.

—Sam . . .

Run. Run as far as I can, away from her.

. . .

. . .

This street. This is where they came from, the people I paid. Mother didn't know. I thought she did. She would have seen him, the police. Raphael lay right on her doorstep. I got her son killed in front of her home.

Raphael never saw it coming. He didn't think I'd hurt him, not after all the punches he took for me. He watched the world change color as he waited for the end. First his shirt, then the sidewalk beside him. I remember the smile on his face when he realized it was me. A strange mixture of pride and betrayal. No anger. I think he forgave because it was me. I doubt he ever cared for Mother, but he did love me.

. . .

Uriel begged while I slit his throat. I know he never had any love for Mother. She— Come to think of it, she was the only person I ever saw Uriel get truly angry with. I wonder what that means. I don't think I ever truly noticed Uriel. He was always there, but I didn't care, not in the way one does for a person. Uriel was more like the family pet. I never gave much thought about how he felt about me; I thought— It was only in the end, while I pushed the blade deeper into his neck, that I realized I mattered to him. "You and I can look for that key together." Together, he said. He wanted us to go on another adventure.

. . .

They were going to kill Mother. They were going to kill her before they killed Dad, because I made them do it. I made them both kill their father because I wanted him dead. I can still see Dad's face when it all dawned on him. His pride. Dad was mean, cruel, vicious, and when he died he was proud of his son. Not because I was different, he was proud because I was all these things. He was proud because I was better at it.

I thought *they* were the monster. I thought all of them were.

I am the evil I ran from.

My father knew. My brothers did in the end. Perhaps the traitor knew. I could see fear in her eyes when I held her head. I thought . . . I thought she shrank from death as all living things do from eternal loneliness. But hers weren't the eyes of a spineless funk. She came ready to die, so what did she dread so much, if not death?

It was me. I am the monster in their dreams.

She wasn't afraid of dying; she was afraid of me living. Now I know what got them up in a sweat at night, why they were so willing to die. They feared they were like me. They feared our entire species was. This was never about hurting our kind. They were trying to save everyone else, from me. An army of me.

I slaughtered my kin. I didn't do it in a fit of rage. I planned it, meticulously, because . . . I am the scorpion in the fable. It is in my nature. This is what I saw in Lola's eyes. She feared what legions of us would do to this world. *She* and everyone like her were saving my mother from me. They knew that if one of us succeeded and sent a message home, it would mean the end of all.

And now, I have.

# FURTHER READING

Hello again! I hope you enjoyed Mia and Lola's story. As with *A History of What Comes Next*, I learned a bunch of things writing this book, and I thought I'd share some of it with you. I've added links to online articles whenever possible. You can also Wikipedia most things in this story.

So many new technologies entered our homes during the timeline of this book: pocket calculators, computers, microwave ovens, et cetera. It's also filled with countless memorable events: the Vietnam War, the oil crisis, the Yom Kippur War, the National Archives fire, Nixon to China, the *Challenger* accident, and, of course, the moon landing. Many of these made their way into the story in one way or another.

So, in no particular order, here are some interesting facts about things and events that came up in these pages.

## THE PLANETS

The exploration of the planets is a recurring theme in the book, but before we could *explore* the planets we first had to discover them. The first five, Mercury, Venus, Mars, Jupiter, and Saturn, are all visible to the naked eye, so humans have been looking at them for as long as there have been humans to look at them. How much they understood about them is another story, but the Babylonians knew they weren't like the other points of light over three thousand years ago. Earth, well, we also knew, so that only left Uranus, Neptune, and Pluto to be "discovered."

## Uranus

This one is kind of boring. Sir William Herschel found it in 1781. It was a complete accident. He was looking at faint stars and noticed one passing in front of another. He realized he was looking at a planet and calculated its orbit. He wanted to name it Georgium Sidus, after George III, which sounds like the name of a pretentious Sith Lord. It's not the most interesting story now, but it must have been awesome for young William. It's not every day you find a planet, especially as an amateur astronomer. Herschel is one of the most well-known astronomers of his time, but he was a musician before discovering Uranus. The king was so impressed with the planet-finding thing, he made Herschel "official" Court Astronomer. I'll come back to him later to talk about his sister.

## Neptune

Remove Emily, the Ninety-Six, from the second Entr'acte and you more or less have the real history of how Neptune was found. John Couch Adams, an undergraduate at Cambridge, noticed that the tables predicting the position of planets erred ever so slightly when it came to Uranus, which he thought had to be caused by another planet's gravity. Up until then, Newton's laws of gravitation had been used to describe the effect planets have on one another based on their mass and position. Adams turned the formulas on their head, attempting to predict a planet's mass and location based on the effect it had on another. It's supercool. He wasn't the one to discover Neptune in the end, but the math itself is worth a place in history. Discovering a planet with a telescope is cool, as in "Ooh, look, a planet! Cool!" Discovering a planet with math is really badass.

## Pluto

Okay, so it's not a "real" planet anymore, but it was when it was discovered, and I really like the story. As I just mentioned, the planet Neptune was discovered because of irregularities in the orbit of Uranus. The mass and location of the presumed planet were predicted and Neptune was found in 1846. About half a century later, a man by the name of Percival Lowell discovered "wobbles" in the orbits of Uranus and the new planet, Neptune. Lowell did the math, predicted the location and mass of a new Planet X, and he looked for it. He looked for it for a decade without success. A young astronomer named Clyde Tombaugh was later hired to search for it at the Lowell Observatory using some new techniques and, in 1930, he found Pluto. Bravo. The only problem is, Pluto is way too small, and distant, and on a different orbit, so it couldn't have that kind of effect on the orbit of a distant planet as massive as Neptune. As it turns out, the "wobbles" in question were just an error in estimating the mass of Neptune, something *Voyager 2* helped remedy when it flew past it in 1989. So Pluto was discovered using mathematical predictions that turned out to be completely baseless, but they found it anyway, which is kind of cool. The guy supervising Clyde Tombaugh at the observatory was W. H. Pickering. I have absolutely nothing to say about him, but I'll talk about his brother later on.

The notion of "discovering" something is interesting in and of itself. People had been observing Uranus since 1650. Galileo Galilei, inventor of the telescope, was observing Jupiter moons in 1612 when he made note of a star that did not appear on any chart at the time. On January 28, 1613, he even noted that the unknown star appeared to have shifted its position in relation to another star. Galileo observed Neptune 233 years before Galle discovered it. Both men did the very same thing.

They looked through the eye of a telescope and observed light reflecting on the same celestial body. Their state of mind is the only thing distinguishing them. One knew he was looking at a planet and the other did not (or he suspected, surmised, supposed).

## THE MOON

I barely mention the moon landing in the book even if it was, by far, the biggest event in the space race, because it was, by far, the biggest event in the space race. Half a billion people watched all over the world. In the US, all three networks had over thirty straight hours of programming built around it. Armstrong took his small step at 10:56 P.M. EDT, but the walk was originally scheduled a little after 2:00 A.M. Thirty hours is a lot of TV time to fill and tons of guests were brought in, including a handful of people from the book world.

CBS had Arthur C. Clarke. (*2001: A Space Odyssey* was released in '68), along with Orson Welles narrating a sci-fi movie live from London. Isaac Asimov was on ABC. NBC's guest list included a dramatic reading by James Earl Jones (no Star Wars yet, but he'd been in Stanley Kubrick's *Dr. Strangelove*) and Michael Crichton, whose first book under his own name (and one of my favorite books), *The Andromeda Strain*, had come out two months earlier.

The landing happened during the Pan-African Cultural Festival of Algiers. While the Western world watched people set foot on a black-and-white world, Africa celebrated the birth of a postimperial world in the wildest way. In contrast to the previous festival held in Senegal three years earlier, this one included representatives from just about every rebellious group fighting against racist colonial regimes, from Africa, of course, but also from America. Several Black Panthers attended the festival, including early leader Eldridge Cleaver, who was wanted in the US following an altercation with Oakland police. What he tells Mia in Algiers is an actual quote from him at the festival. If you can find it, there is a documentary directed by William Klein, aptly called *The Pan-African Festival of Algiers 1969.*

The moon landing was the high point of the space race, but it also signaled the beginning of the end. The Americans had won, end of story. Ironically, all of the other firsts involving the moon were Russian firsts. *Luna 9* was the first probe to make a soft landing and transmit from the moon. The first living beings to orbit the moon and come back safely were tortoises on a Russian spacecraft. First soil samples automatically extracted on the moon, first robotic moon rover. The Russians were first to Venus, first to Mars. They sent up the first space station in '71, then the first permanently crewed space station in '86. First man in space, first woman in space, first Hispanic and black person in space, first rendezvous in space, et cetera, et cetera. Despite all that, the race ground to a halt after the moon landing. It had such an effect on the collective mind that people lost interest. Not sure that's true? Who was on the second team to walk on the moon? The answer is Pete Conrad and Alan Bean in November 1969 and, yes, I had to look it up.

This is probably the main reason I wanted the Kibsu to be less involved in space exploration this book. Fewer things were happening; budgets were shrinking. Yes, there was the Space Shuttle, but we weren't going farther. We'd gone to the moon. Mars should have been the next step. Instead, we went back to Low Earth Orbit. Reagan announced an international space station in 1984 and it took over a decade for anything to materialize. Japan, Canada, and the EU expressed interest, but it wasn't until the Russians joined the program in 1993 that things really started moving. There was a lot of brilliant work being done, the shuttle main tank is a wonder of engineering by itself, yet there wasn't anything I found truly inspiring, except for one thing: space probes.

Venus came first. The Soviets launched *Venera 1* in 1961, *before* the Gagarin flight. It flew by the planet, but we'd lost radio contact, so it really just "flew by." *Venera 3* reportedly hit Venus in 1965, but contact with the probe was also lost before it reached the second planet. In 1970, *Venera 7* performed a soft landing on Venus and transmitted data from the surface. *Venera 9* and *10* would be the first to send back pictures of the surface in 1975.

Mars was more complicated. *Mars 1*, a Soviet probe, was first to launch for the red planet in 1962 but failed. The Americans got a couple wins when *Mariner 4* flew by Mars in '65 and *Mariner 9* first orbited the planet in '71. Two weeks later, though, *two* Soviet probes made it to the surface. *Mars 2* made it "abruptly," i.e., it crashed, but the *Mars 3* lander made a soft landing, with a tiny rover on skis called PROP-M on board. The probe transmitted for only a few seconds and the rover never did anything, but it's still on the surface and it got there first.

By 1971, we'd landed probes on the surface of Mars and Venus, and *Mariner 10* launched for Mercury in 1973. The first planet is too close to the sun, so the American probe went into orbit around our star to observe it. That left only the outer planets to explore. We had the technology to reach Jupiter, but it was doubtful we could reach Saturn, Uranus, or Neptune with the rockets we had.

## THE GRAND TOUR

Mia discovers a unique planetary alignment that occurs once every 175 years and makes an Earth-Jupiter-Saturn-Uranus-Neptune trajectory possible. In real life, that discovery belongs to JPL employee Gary Arnold Flandro. You can read the paper he wrote online.[1] Skip the math if you want: it's an interesting read even without.

Mia provides a brief explanation of how you can use a planet's gravity to change the speed (and direction) of a rocket or probe. I found an awesome explanation[2] online at planetary.org. It's superclear and it includes little diagrams for every maneuver *Voyager 2* did around the planets. You can also see the 1977 planetary "alignment" or where all the planets were relative to one another on any date at heavens-above.com.[3]

I thought I'd have a hard time finding the distance of each planet to Earth over forty years ago, but it turns out the nice folks at Casio Computer Co (Yes, CASIO! I had a red cassette player from them, and an alarm clock!) put a bunch of calculators online, including the aptly named "Distance of planets from Earth Calculator."[4] Thanks, Casio!

The Voyager mission is such an amazing feat, I could spend a whole book just talking about it. Imagine launching something the size of a Mini Cooper and hitting a planet at just the right distance and angle over four hundred million miles away, about eighteen hundred times farther than the moon. That's just the first planet. When it reached Neptune, *Voyager 2* had traveled 4.3 *billion* miles.

They did this with the most basic tools. The probes launched in 1977, but you don't use any new, untested technology in a project like this, so whatever was on board had to exist around 1972. The computers on board were about eight thousand times

1. G. A. Flandro, "Fast Reconnaissance Missions to the Outer Solar System Utilizing Energy Derived from the Gravitational Field of Jupiter," *Astronautica Acta* 12 (1966): 329–337, available online at http://www.gravityassist.com/IAF2/Ref.%202-123.pdf.
2. David Short, "Gravity Assist," The Planetary Society, http://www.planetary.org/blogs/guest-blogs/2013/20130926-gravity-assist.html.
3. https://www.heavens-above.com/planets.aspx.
4. https://keisan.casio.com/exec/system/1224746378.

slower than your iPhone, the transmitters a hundred times slower than your old dial-up connection. The probes recorded their data on eight-track tape recorders before transmitting to Earth and recording over the old data.

The two probes are more or less identical. I have a soft spot for *Voyager 2* because it visited all the planets. On November 5, 2018, *Voyager 2* entered interstellar space, six years after its twin. It's still transmitting useful data, but it will never come close to anything ever again. In about forty thousand years, it will pass about ten trillion miles from the star Ross 248. In another quarter million years, it should come within twenty-five trillion miles of Sirius, the brightest star in the night sky.

The batteries in both *Voyager* probes are running out of juice, but this book will have been out for a couple years before they stop working. In January 2020, *Voyager 2* shut down its science instruments after failing to perform a spin maneuver, but scientists at JPL were able to fix it. You can follow the probes in real time at https://voyager.jpl.nasa.gov/.

Fun fact. The Voyager mission skipped Pluto in favor of the Saturn moon Titan, so it wasn't until 2006, when the International Astronomical Union demoted Pluto, that humans had "officially" sent a probe to every planet in the solar system. That was achieved retroactively in 1989 when *Voyager 2* flew by Neptune.

I could go on and on about the Grand Tour. You HAVE to watch the documentary *The Farthest* about the Voyager mission. It was on Netflix when I wrote this. It's worth watching even if it's just to see how emotional the people involved get talking about it.

On February 14, 1990, at the request of Carl Sagan, *Voyager 1* turned around and took a picture of home before turning its camera off. The picture, which became known as the *Pale Blue Dot*, shows Earth as a tiny speck, one-twelfth of a pixel in size.

Here's an excerpt from Sagan's book *Pale Blue Dot*, inspired by that picture:

> Look again at that dot. That's here. That's home. That's us. On it everyone you love, everyone you know, everyone you ever heard of, every human being who ever was, lived out their lives . . . Think of the rivers of blood spilled by all those generals and emperors so that, in glory and triumph, they could become the momentary masters of a fraction of a dot. . . . In our obscurity, in all this vastness, there is no hint that help will come from elsewhere to save us from ourselves.[5]

## THE BOW AND THE PRIESTESS

The bow in this book is inspired by a real Scythian bow discovered in the Xinjiang region near Ürümqi.[6] No alien symbols, but it's a very nice artifact.

While the Kibsu search for their ancestor's bow, the Tracker follows bread crumbs left behind by an Egyptian priestess named Mer-Neith-it-es. You can see her remains in the Nicholson Collection at the Chau Chak Wing Museum in Sydney, Australia. The museum acquired her sarcophagus, along with three others. The coffin was, at the time, believed to be empty. They only just found out there was someone inside. Mer-Neith-it-es died when she was about thirty, around 600 BC. They poured some resin into her skull to preserve it after her brain was removed. Her remains don't tell us much about her day

5. Carl Sagan, *Pale Blue Dot: A Vision of the Human Future in Space*, Random House, 1994.
6. Bede Dwyer, "Scythian-Style Bows Discovered in Xinjiang: From the Photographs and Drawings of Stephen Selby," http://www.atarn.org/chinese/scythian _bows.htm.

job, but fortunately, they wrote a bunch of stuff in hieroglyphs on her sarcophagus. She was a high priestess at the Temple of Sekhmet, the lion-headed goddess, in Thebes. You can see pictures and read more about the discovery online.[7]

## THE HOLE

The ozone layer, or more accurately the gaping hole in it, was the big thing in the latter part of the eighties. No one really cared about the environment; this was about everyone getting skin cancer. Remember the ad for blue sunblock in *Robocop*? "They say twenty seconds in the California sunshine is too much these days, ever since we lost the ozone layer. But that was before Sunblock 5000." It all started in 1974 with this paper by Mario J. Molina and F. S. Rowland that Mia keeps talking about. The government did its own research and came to the same conclusion. In 1978, following Sweden's lead, the US, Canada, and Norway banned the use of CFCs as propellant in aerosol cans. Hairspray would never be the same, but unfortunately, that didn't amount to much. Four countries aren't enough obviously, but the regulation left out the other bazillion uses for CFCs. Aerosols only accounted for about 30 percent of emissions. This is when things get really weird. In October of '78, *Nimbus 7* launched on top of a Delta rocket from Vandenberg Air Force Base. One of the things this satellite was meant to do was monitor the ozone layer. Everyone waited for the data to come in expecting confirmation of the scientists' findings. Nope. The satellite kept showing no drop, no hole. Everyone went back to the drawing board. Researchers were reluctant to publish because satellite data said they were out to lunch.

---

7. Laura Geggel, "Archaeologists Were Surprised to Find the Mummy of an Egyptian Priestess in This 'Empty' Coffin," *Live Science*, https://www.livescience.com/62142-mummy-unexpectedly-found-in-sarcophagus.html.

It turns out the satellite was ignoring the relevant data on purpose. No, it's not a conspiracy and it's not as crazy as it sounds. If you leave some machine to measure, say, the temperature outside your house, it will read things like 65, 71, 64, 900, 64. Now, yes, it could mean your street was covered in lava on Thursday, but it's more likely your thermometer is broken or there was a guy soldering right next to it. The solution to this is to ignore data points above or below a certain threshold. No one, anywhere, had ever detected ozone levels below a certain point, so the satellite software was flagging and ignoring readings that seemed too out of whack. There were a lot of those at the South Pole in October 1983. Scientists at Goddard Space Flight Center noticed, and while they first suspected a faulty sensor, they submitted a paper to a conference in Prague, one that included a map of the South Pole with a gaping hole in the ozone layer above it. Their paper was not presented anywhere before Farman et al published an article in *Nature* in 1985 using new data. It wasn't until 1986 that the proper analysis of the satellite data was made public. By then, the *New York Times* had talked about the dangers of ozone depletion and the public had started using the word "hole."

## THE ENTR'ACTES

I love doing research on historical figures to find candidates for earlier iterations of the Kibsu. You've probably recognized a few names in the Entr'actes and I'm sure many of you have guessed that the women portrayed in these chapters are actual people. Some are among the earliest known astronomers; others have made some of the most significant discoveries in their field.

It should come as no surprise that there have been women astronomers for as long as there have been astronomers. I will also not shock anyone when I say there have been fewer than men because doors were systematically closed to them, and they were closed early. As a result, many of the names you find are immediately followed by "wife of X, sister of X, daughter of X," not because their contributions were not equal but because they would never have had the opportunity to make them without the connection. Take for example Theano, wife of Pythagoras, one of the first women astronomers from antiquity whose name we know. Pythagoras's school included many women and it is very likely that many of the discoveries and inventions we ascribe to him (the identity of the morning and evening stars as the planet Venus, the triangle thing, et cetera) were the product of his school and not just him. Plato's school also allowed women. Aristotle, on the other hand, thought women were inferior and cold (literally, one of the reasons he found women inferior is because their bodies were too cold to produce semen), and the Christian Church went the Aristotle way. The Church did a number on science as a whole during the Middle Ages and women scientists got it even worse.

Here's a bit of what I learned about the people in this book's Entr'actes.

## Aglaonike (a.k.a. Aglaonice, a.k.a. Aganice) of Thessaly

No one really knows when she lived, nor do we have undeniable proof of her existence.

In the first century AD, Plutarch wrote[8] that "Aglaonice the daughter of Hegetor being thoroughly conversant with the periods of the Full Moon when it is subject to eclipse, and knowing beforehand when the Moon was due to be overtaken by the Earth's shadow, imposed upon audiences of women and made them all believe that she drew down the Moon." She obviously

8. P. Bicknell, "The Witch Aglaonice and Dark Lunar Eclipses in the Second and First Centuries BC," *Journal of the British Astronomical Association* 93, no. 4 (June 1983).

had to live before Plutarch could write about her, but she could have been one of his contemporaries, and it was around the third century BC that the Babylonians were first able to predict lunar eclipses. That leaves her a window of a few hundred years to do her thing.

It's interesting to note that while many myths survived the test of time, serious efforts were put into debunking Aglaonike's powers very early on. Her story is used in Greek comedic texts and even gave rise to a Greek proverb, "Yes, as the moon obeys Aglaonice," used, presumably sarcastically, to say that something is certain to happen. It seems fairly obvious that the idea of a woman astronomer, who by virtue of being a woman could not have received "proper" training, was unpalatable to the men of the era. She had to be a witch or, worse, pretending to be a witch.

I don't particularly care about her motives, but what should be obvious to everyone is that two thousand years ago, they weren't filling coliseums with people "thoroughly conversant with the periods of the Full Moon when it is subject to eclipse, and knowing beforehand when the Moon was due to be overtaken by the Earth's shadow." You had to be a genius.

### Hypatia

One of the most brilliant minds of her time, she is unfortunately better known for her death than for what she did. Granted, it was quite the death, but I like to imagine how much she had to piss off the Church for them to want to kill her, kill her again, cut her to pieces, and kill the pieces. I would like to have known her. There's a good article from University at Albany[9] on what

---

9. Michael A. B. Deakin, "Hypatia and Her Mathematics," *The American Mathematical Monthly* 101, no. 3 (March 1994): 234–243, https://www.albany.edu/~reinhold/m552/hypatia-Deakin.pdf.

little we know about her science. One thing we do know is that she built astrolabes. Many of the ancient women astronomers we know of did. From Zulema la Astróloga, the Moorish astronomer, to Mariam al-Asturlabi of Syria who inspired Nnedi Okorafor's *Binti*.

Interestingly, we don't always know what it is people were making when we read about astrolabes. The word was used for two very different things, both of which are awesome. First, there is the armillary sphere, sometimes called spherical astrolabe, which is a three-dimensional model of the heavens. A bunch of rings, usually metal spinning around a model of the Earth or sun. It looks ridiculously cool, but it's normally big. This is the kind of thing you put in your office, but you would hurt yourself if you tried to carry it around and use it in the field. Then there's the more practical instrument that Ptolemy theorized and called "little astrolabe." It's a two-dimensional model of the heavens, so it's made of discs spinning inside a flat casing. This one you can carry around. It was used to identify celestial bodies, calculate altitude, all sorts of things. It looks incredibly complex. It's also one of the most beautiful instruments ever created.

At the time of Hypatia, models of the heavens were pretty much all spherical, with the fixed stars attached inside the outermost sphere. The idea that people thought all the stars were glued to a giant sphere seems ludicrous in our times, but that belief did not simply arise from ignorance. There was actually some science behind it. Let's do a little experiment. Grab two objects, could be anything, and place one at eye level a couple feet in front of you. Take the other one and put it far behind at the same height. Now go back to where you were. Unless you miraculously placed these two things exactly behind each other, you should see some space between them. Move a little to the right, now a little to the left. The space between your two things should get bigger or smaller as you move, as if the closer thing were moving. Right? That whole phenomenon is called parallax. That's how we're able to estimate the distance between us and things in space, by measuring their apparent movement against things that are farther away as the Earth rotates around the sun. People have understood the phenomenon for a long time, but because stars are really, really, really really far away, and because telescopes wouldn't be invented for another fifteen hundred years, people like Ptolemy were unable to measure any parallax effect between stars. They concluded that all the stars had to be at the same distance from Earth, forming a giant sphere around it. The observation was flawed because they lacked the technology to measure the effect at such distances, but if we assume the observation is correct, there is no other logical conclusion. No matter how silly something may look now, always remember that smart people were always smart people.

### Blue Teeth Lady

I called her Agnes, but she is inspired by a woman named Ende from the tenth century. She wasn't an astronomer but what was called an illuminator. The difference between artist and artisan was blurred during the Middle Ages. Art often served a practical purpose, including teaching. Books were made by hand, written by scribes, then embellished with gold leaf, paintings, and/or fancy colored letters. Red was originally the main color added and the pigment used was called minium. The people adding the minium were called *miniators*, which became "illuminator."

Before I go on, I hope you noticed this is linguistic gold, no pun intended. You'd think "illuminator" had something to do with light, but the word comes from the name of a red pigment. Even cooler, the word "miniature" is derived from that because the *miniators* were making tiny tiny paintings.

Back to Ende. Making books was doing God's work (books were mostly about God) and it was normally work reserved for men—monks. Ende was a nun, and she is the first European woman whose art was identified by an inscription. She was good enough she got to sign her work. *"Ende pintrix et Dei adiutrix, frater Emeterius et presbiter* (Ende, painter and God's helper, Emeterius, brother and presbyter)."

Ende was thought to be the exception. Women, it was believed, rarely took part in this kind of work until much later. Enter SCIENCE! The third entr'acte is based on a real science paper titled: "Medieval Women's Early Involvement in Manuscript Production Suggested by Lapis Lazuli Identification in Dental Calculus."

Yes! They looked at gunk on thousand-year-old teeth and found blue pigment, which suggests not only that women were commonly involved in manuscript production earlier than thought but also that lapis lazuli was more widely available in Europe at the time. I LOVE SCIENCE!

You can read the paper online at *Science* magazine.[10]

## Annie

I made her the daughter of Emily from the second Entr'acte, but in real life Annie—born Annie Scott Dill—was one of six children born in Ireland to devout Christian parents, neither of whom was murdered by Jack the Ripper. All of the children went into academia. Annie went to Girton College and finished at the top of her class. She received the second-highest honor bestowed to math undergraduates at Cambridge. She went on to work as a computer at the Royal Observatory in Greenwich under Walter Maunder, whom she later married. She studied

---

10. A. Radini, M. Tromp, A. Beach, E. Tong, C. Speller, M. McCormick, J. V. Dudgeon, M. J. Collins, F. Rühli, R. Kröger, and C. Warinner, "Medieval Women's Early Involvement in Manuscript Production Suggested by Lapis Lazuli Identification in Dental Calculus," *Science Advances* 5, no. 1 (January 9, 2019), https://advances.sciencemag.org/content/5/1/eaau7126.

sunspots and produced groundbreaking work on the subject. She left the observatory to marry Walter (married women were indeed banned from public service jobs), but the two continued to collaborate. They went on eclipse expeditions together to photograph and study solar eclipses. Norway, India, Mauritius, they traveled the world and produced amazing photographs of the sun. She's the one who coined the term "plume" to describe long, feathery jets she observed during these expeditions.

When the Royal Astronomical Society finally allowed women fellows in 1916, Annie Maunder was one of four women to receive the honor, along with Margaret Theodora Meyer, Mary Proctor, and Francisca Herschel, the great-niece of Caroline Herschel, who had been named an "Honorary Member" by the RAS in 1835. More recently, the Royal Observatory in Greenwich named their new telescope after Annie.

Though she was near London during the infamous murder spree, I have no reason to believe she hunted serial killers at night. The Whitechapel Murderer, a.k.a. Leather Apron, a.k.a. Jack the Ripper, was never caught.

It's interesting to note that it wasn't until very recently (my dad was alive) that we figured out what powered the sun. If you're interested, there is a fun paper[11] from 2016 on all the theories that were being thrown around in the late nineteenth century.

There are tons of women astronomers you can read about, amazing people I often wish I could include as characters in this series but can't for all sorts of reasons. You can start with Enheduanna. She was a Sumerian high priestess in the city-state of Ur in the twenty-third century BC (long before the

---

11. Helge Kragh, "The Source of Solar Energy, ca. 1840–1910: From Meteoric Hypothesis to Radioactive Speculations," *EPJH* 41, 365–394 (2016), https://arxiv .org/pdf/1609.02834.pdf.

Kibsu arrived). She was also a poet and an astronomer. She was so cool they made her an EN-priestess. You had to be royalty to be an EN, but not her. She wrote several prayers to the goddess Inanna (remember her?). Enheduanna is—get this—the first named author in the history of the world. This is an excerpt from one of her poems in which she describes her work.[12]

> The true woman who possesses exceeding wisdom,
> She consults a tablet of lapis lazuli
> She gives advice to all lands . . .
> She measures off the heavens,
> She places the measuring-cords on the earth.

She was a scientist.

Let's move forward a bit to the 1700s. I already talked about William Herschel, the musician, who discovered Uranus and quit his day job to become Court Astronomer. Well, William had a sister, Caroline. Caroline got typhus as a child and her growth slowed. Her parents didn't think she could find a husband and kept her home as a house servant. That is, until William took her in. He gave her music lessons and she became a professional singer. She also helped her brother make telescopes. When William got his new gig as Court Astronomer, he hired Caroline as an assistant. She was the first woman to actually get paid as a scientist and the first British woman to hold a government position. She discovered a bunch of nebulae and comets and cataloged thousands upon thousands of stars, comets, and nebulae. In 1828, she got a Gold Medal from the Royal Astronomical Society for her work. It would take over a century for another woman to receive the honor. Go, Caroline!

12. http://womeninastronomy.blogspot.com/2013/05/enheduanna-our-first-great -scientist.html.

If you make a list of known women astronomers and organize it chronologically, you'll hit a cluster of Americans in the late 1800s, early 1900s. Many of them belonged to a group known as Pickering's Harem. The name is horrible, I know, but a good reminder of the challenges these people faced, and their story is amazing. The Pickering in question is Edward Charles Pickering, director of the Harvard College Observatory and brother to W. H. Pickering, who supervised the guy who found Pluto.

In 1881, Edward Charles Pickering fired his assistant, who apparently sucked at cataloging stars. To replace him, he hired his maid, Williamina Fleming, and this is how the story begins. More than half a century before the human computer of *Hidden Figures*, there were the Harvard Observatory computers. During Pickering's tenure, over eighty women were hired to analyze stellar spectra (light split into a rainbow with gaps that tells you what stars are made of) and to compute and catalog astronomical data. Several of them made significant contributions of their own, starting with Williamina Fleming. She devised what was called the Pickering-Fleming system for classifying stars. In 1890, she and her team produced a catalog of more than ten thousand stars classified according to spectrum. During her thirty-four years at Harvard, she discovered dozens of nebulae, over three hundred stars, and ten novae. She was also the very first person to observe a white dwarf. I encourage you to read about Annie Jump Cannon, Antonia Maury, Florence Cushman, and Henrietta Swan Leavitt—scientists who, despite performing groundbreaking work, rarely or never received individual honors or recognition.

That's it for this book. More coming in the last one, I promise. Oh, almost forgot. Someone did steal Led Zeppelin's money from a safe-deposit box at the Drake Hotel.

# PLAYLIST

24. "Sound and Vision," David Bowie (1977)
25. "(Don't Fear) The Reaper," Blue Öyster Cult (1976)
26. "Marquee Moon," Television (1977)
27. "White Rabbit," Jefferson Airplane (1967)
28. "Lola," The Kinks (1970)
29. "Psycho Killer," Talking Heads (1977)
30. "Let's Go," The Cars (1979)
31. "Sara," Fleetwood Mac (1979)
32. "Take Me to the River," Syl Johnson (1974)
33. "The Logical Song," Supertramp (1979)
34. "Walking on the Moon," The Police (1979)
35. "Boys Don't Cry," The Cure (1979)
36. "Mother," Pink Floyd (1979)
37. "Brass in Pocket," The Pretenders (1979)
38. "Don't Stop Believin'," Journey (1981)
39. "Rapture," Blondie (1980)
40. "Video Killed the Radio Star," The Buggles (1979)
41. "Under Pressure," Queen and David Bowie (1981)
42. "Kids in America," Kim Wilde (1981)
43. "Private Eyes," Hall & Oates (1981)
44. "Ghost Town," The Specials (1981)
45. "Anarchy in the UK," Sex Pistols (1976)
46. "Crimson and Clover," Joan Jett (1981)
47. "How Soon Is Now?," The Smiths (1984)
48. "Red Rain," Peter Gabriel (1986)
49. "Ship of Fools," World Party (1986)
50. "If You Leave," Orchestral Manoeuvres in the Dark (1986)
51. "Don't You (Forget About Me)," Simple Minds (1985)
52. "Running Up That Hill," Kate Bush (1985)
53. "Live to Tell," Madonna (1986)
54. "The NeverEnding Story," Limahl (1984)

# ACKNOWLEDGMENTS

There was a two-year gap between the release of *A History of What Comes Next* and that of my last book, *The Test*. That meant a good year with nothing to promote, few if any conventions to attend. My family and I took the opportunity to travel and we spent a little over five months in Indonesia before the pandemic brought us home. I wrote a good portion of this book at the Wasabi Hotel in Pererenan, Bali, so if any of the staff ever reads this, *terima kasih* for making us feel like home. Thank you again to everyone at Tordotcom: Lee, Irene, Sanaa, Alexis, Amanda, Lauren, Mordicai. Thanks to Jillian, Sriya, Zana, and Lucy at Michael Joseph. A gigantic belated thank-you to the amazing audio team for *A History of What Comes Next*. What you did with my story is nothing short of spectacular. A big thank-you hug to my family. As always, thanks to my agent, Seth, and to Will, Rebecca, Jack, and Ellen at the Gernert Company. Thank you, wonderful readers. I've always been extremely grateful, but hearing from you during these hellish times has truly meant the world to me. I hope (knock on wood) I get a chance to meet some of you this time around.